"Run like crazy!" the Highbulp roared, heading for parts unknown. "Got big sal'mander!"

Never slow to take flight, gully dwarves ran in all directions, some heading for hidey-holes, some running in circles, some bumping into one another.

Abruptly, just beyond them, the big tunnel was filled with a monstrous salamander.

Lidda, high on the cavern wall, reached down as far as she could, toward the circular brass shield below. She got her hand under its catch and lifted. The plaque banged open and something long, dark and deadly shot from the hole behind it, whistling.

In an instant, the missile flashed across the room and into the gaping mouth of the salamander, deflecting upward from the thing's lower jaw to erupt from the top of its flat, ugly head.

An angry hiss filled the cavern as the salamander twitched and lay still.

But the hiss went on. Wide, terrified eyes staring at the dead monster turned slowly, looking for the source of the sound, growing even wider when they found it.

From the Creators of the DRAGONLANCE® Saga

THE LOST HISTORIES

The Kagonesti
Douglas Niles

The Irda
Linda P. Baker

The Dargonesti
Paul B. Thompson and Tonya Cook

Land of the Minotaurs
Richard A. Knaak

The Gully Dwarves
Dan Parkinson

The Dragons
Douglas Niles
Available September 1996

DragonLance® Saga

The Lost Histories
Volume V

The Gully
Dwarves

Dan Parkinson

DRAGONLANCE® Saga
The Lost Histories
Volume V

THE GULLY DWARVES

Random House and its affiliate companies have worldwide distribution rights in the book trade for English language products of TSR, Inc.

Distributed to the book and hobby trade in the United Kingdom by TSR Ltd.

Distributed to the toy and hobby trade by regional distributors.

Cover art by Larry Elmore. Interior art by Karolyn Guldan.

DRAGONLANCE is a registered trademark owned by TSR, Inc. The TSR logo is a trademark owned by TSR, Inc.

All TSR characters, character names, and the distinctive likenesses thereof are trademarks owned by TSR, Inc.

First Printing: June 1996
Printed in the United States of America.
Library of Congress Catalog Card Number: 95-62209

9 8 7 6 5 4 3 2 1

8373XXX1501

ISBN: 0-7869-0497-6

TSR, Inc.   TSR Ltd.
201 Sheridan Springs Rd.   120 Church End, Cherry Hinton
Lake Geneva WI 53147   Cambridge CB1 3LB
U.S.A.   United Kingdom

Introduction

It has been said of the Aghar that no such race could exist in a practical world. It has been said that the gods of creation must have been terribly distracted when the Aghar were created . . . either distracted or crazy. The scholars insist such a race of creatures as the Aghar—commonly referred to as gully dwarves— could not possibly survive for generations among the harsh realities of life. The pathetic little things have nothing on their side.

In a world of strong races, the gully dwarves of Krynn are surprisingly weak. They are neither fierce nor menacing, neither bold nor especially lucky, neither strong of limb nor fleet of foot. Their only natural defense against enemies is a tendency to inhabit those places no one else wants, thereby going unnoticed most of the time. They lack the stubborn strength of true dwarves, the unpredictability of humans, and the inherent skills and longevity of elves. Compared to any of these races, gully dwarves are hardly more than vermin. They have no defenses, no skills beyond a certain clumsy furtiveness, and certainly no command of magic.

As for intelligence, the gully dwarves—while more or less human or dwarven in appearance—are barely smart enough to come in out of the rain.

The continued existence of gully dwarves on Krynn is a puzzle to those who consider such matters. But then, those same scholars might insist that neither bumblebees nor dragons can fly. Yet no matter how avidly the scholars pursue their logic, bumblebees and dragons go right on flying . . . And gully dwarves continue to survive.

The little creatures have not only existence, but also a history. Indeed, there are odd legends among various cultures about gully dwarves. Some believe that a gully dwarf clan, long ago, may have had something to do with the destruction of mighty Istar—might have figured somehow in the Cataclysm itself. Odd tales sometimes circulate across the ale boards, linking gully dwarves to unlikely enterprises including a mine that produced wine, claiming they were involved in the ogre massacre of the slavers of Doon, even hinting that gully dwarves may have been the first occupants of ancient Thorbardin, where their descendants are more or less tolerated to this day.

The most improbable of these tales, yet one of the most persistent, has to do with an unlikely alliance between a gully dwarf tribe and a dragon during the War of the Lance. Among humans, elves and even true dwarves there are those who swear that they actually witnessed the phenomenon—a group of gully dwarves traveling with a green dragon.

Such accounts suggest a truly notable history. Still, these tales cannot be proven or even verified by the gully dwarves themselves. The people called Aghar have few great skills, but one of them is the ability to promptly forget anything beyond their understanding, and that covers almost everything in the world.

Thus it is a rare gully dwarf who can clearly recall any event prior to yesterday. Such individuals are as rare as a gully dwarf who can count past two.

In the befogged history of these bumbling little people, though, there have been a few such rare gully dwarves. The first Grand Notioner of the Tribe of Bulp—an intuitive individual named Hunch who may well have done most of the group's serious thinking during the long and eventful reign of the Highbulp Gorge III—was one of them. Hunch was burdened with an awareness that there were times further back than yesterday. He was bright enough to deduce from this fact that there might be times beyond tomorrow.

Another uncommon gully dwarf was old Gandy, Hunch's successor and heir to the mop handle staff of office. Gandy knew that there were quite a few people in his clan, and that the number—while it varied from day to day—was almost certainly more than two. Lacking either the words or the theory to express such ideas, he usually kept them to himself.

But his intuition told him that if he perceived something so arcane there might be others capable of perceiving it, too. He suspected one of them might be a young gully dwarf—a mere child at the time of the finding of the Promised Place—whose name was Scrib and who sometimes tried to draw pictures of the world around him.

prologue
Verden's Egg

Above a world in shambles, where low, smoke-darkened skies reflected the somber glow of fires burning out of control amidst the darkness of charred battle-fields, Verden Leafglow beat upward on mighty wings. Higher and higher she flew, talons cradled close against her scaled body. Her great tail a graceful rudder beneath her, her long neck stretched upward as she reached for altitudes beyond the madness that reigned below.

It was all over. A mighty war had been fought—a game of gods in which good and evil had met head-on, regardless of the carnage on the field of play. Takhisis the Dark Queen, goddess of all that was evil, had played her game for control of the world Krynn, but in the final hours she had lost.

To Verden Leafglow, it was inconceivable that Takhisis could have failed. Intent upon rule or ruin, the dark goddess had unleashed her mightiest forces upon the world, uncaring of the chaos in her wake, aloof to the suffering of mortal beings caught up in the maelstrom. Darkest of the gods, lover of dominance and mistress of betrayal, Takhisis had thrown her dice with the certainty of victory . . . and then had lost!

Now, like a vengeful child, Takhisis the spiteful goddess turned her back on the agonies created in her name and left the world of Krynn to recover as it could—or to rot if it would. Now madness ran rampant beneath the triad moons.

Yet, even in turning away, the Dark Queen was vengeful. To those who had defeated her ambitions, she bequeathed her legacy of ruin. For those of her followers who had failed her—in any slightest manner—far worse was in store. The dark goddess was venomous in her spite, and she demanded satisfaction even in defeat.

On emerald wings, Verden Leafglow sought the sky and soared high above the madness below. Beneath her, the plains of death fell away to remote distance as she beat upward, escaping the carnage far below.

She had seen much in these past days. In fields of havoc she had seen draconian footmen, those darkling spawn of the betrayal of the mighty by the mighty, dying by the thousands at the hands of their own kind and of those who had been their allies.

She had seen fabrics of black sorcery collapse upon themselves, and upon the dark-robed ones who were their weavers. And the worst of the manic fury was among the dragons—those who had been Takhisis's mightiest allies. In a matter of days, Verden had seen dragon turn from foe and attack ally, and even her own keen instinct for betrayal had barely saved her.

She had seen the mightiest of all the dragons of evil—the magnificent and deadly Venge Scarlet—pluck his rider from his back, tear his head from his shoulders and cast the pieces earthward like so much debris. She had seen the cunning, malicious Ebon Nightshadow turn on a goblin force that had come to aid him in defense of the Token Portal. He drenched them with acid breath, and watched with contempt as they writhed and screamed, melting to sludge.

These were things that Verden Leafglow herself might have done, had she had a human rider or a goblin troop. But she had been afield when the end came with nothing more than some puny human mages working their spells to create a secret way into the remote Dominion Garrison of Sablethwon.

In her mind the knowledge had come—it was over, the Dark Queen had turned away. With a disdainful blast, Verden had parted company with her allied mages. Two of them, two who had angered her especially, she left sundered, literally torn to shreds. Their companions choked about them, strangling on their own tongues, blind and dying from her parting gift—a cloud of thick chlorine vapor. A few of them had escaped her fury, but only a few. Among them was a cowering little magic-thief with an ivory fang totem, the two had become so interlinked by their magic that neither could function without the other. There were maybe one or two more survivors. But they did not matter.

She had gone then, heading for the mountains to the west. It was the last place she had known Flame Searclaw to be. If the Dark Queen's business was at an end, then Verden Leafglow had business of her own, unfinished business that she had not forgotten. She had a revenge of her own to be taken now, and she spread great emerald wings and went hunting.

Flame Searclaw! Verden spread her keen senses, searching. Great eyes glittered with hatred as she remembered the day she had paved the way for the destruction of the human city of Chaldis. She remembered the injury she had sustained there and the cold humor in the voice of Flame Searclaw when he sensed her there, sorely wounded and buried beneath the rubble of a ravaged city. He had known that she was there, had told her so. He had known she needed help, but her plight amused him. He passed her by.

Verden Leafglow had not forgotten. She had been betrayed and abandoned. There was a score to settle.

With all of her senses at peak pitch, she climbed the sky and beat westward, where the mighty peaks of the Kharolis Mountains etched the horizon. Flame Searclaw was out there, somewhere.

Would mindcall still function, now that the war of conquest was ended? Verden didn't know. The distance-calling was a magical power, granted by the Dark Queen to some of her agents, to serve her purposes. Pitching her mind as she had learned, she pulsed a message into the distance. "Flame Searclaw! I know you are there! Once I needed your aid and you deserted me! Once I called out to you, and you responded with torment! You even taunted me, commanded me to come to you when you knew I could not. Well, I am coming now, Flame Searclaw! I am coming for you, and I will find you!"

Moments passed, and then an answer grew in her mind, tiny with distance, but clear. He had perceived the challenge. Cruel laughter echoed in the soundless response. *Green snake! It is you! I am here, green snake. You dare to challenge me, pathetic thing? How wonderful! I am ready for you! Don't worry about finding me, green snake, I will make it easy for you. I will find you! And when I do, I will—*

Abruptly the voice in her mind was stilled, along with all other perceptions. As though a cold, impenetrable curtain were drawn around her, Verden Leafglow's world went silent, and into the silence came a vision—an image clear and brilliant, shutting everything else out of her mind. In eerie silence she saw a small green globe, and knew what it was.

Her egg! Her own, single egg, hidden away long ago in a place only she knew . . . Yet now she saw it in her mind, and it was not where it should be. Something was very wrong.

She concentrated on her egg, turned toward its distant hiding place, and wavered in confusion. Always, wherever she was, she could sense her egg. But now she could find no sense of it. The curtain of mind silence parted slightly, and she could see—with distant vision—the place where it should be. But there was no sense of her egg in that place. It was not there.

And now, deep in her mind, a different voice grew, an immense, resonating, vengeful voice. It was a voice that was far more than a voice, and echoed in every fiber of her.

Your egg? The voice seemed to sneer. *You want your egg?*

"Goddess queen," Verden responded, shaken. "You speak to me."

You failed me, Verden Leafglow. The huge, quiet voice rippled and pulsed within her, dominating her. *There was a moment when I needed you, and you were not there. When you should have been within the mountains, you were elsewhere. You were dawdling, Verden Leafglow. Dawdling with the least of the least. You failed me.*

Verden remembered, the memory brilliant and tormenting in her mind. There had been a time—only once—when she was distracted. Because of Flame Searclaw's betrayal, she had found herself hostage to those despicable little creatures, the Aghar. Wounded and weak, and with her self-stone lodged within the body of one of the creatures, she had been forced to guide them to Xak Tsaroth—to their Promised Place.

Aghar. Gully dwarves! The least of the least. The humiliating memory burned within her, haunting her.

"Goddess, I had no choice," she protested. "I was saving myself from death."

Your loyalties belonged to me, the voice of Takhisis thundered within.

"I would have died without my self-stone," she tried to explain.

You were answerable to me, Verden Leafglow. Not to them, to me!

"I could not help—"

You failed me, the voice rasped. *Now you must pay for your failure.*

In her mind again came a vision of her egg, her own single egg, deep within some shadowy, cavernous place where small things moved in the shadows.

Your egg, the voice said. *You want your egg, Verden Leafglow? So it shall be, though not in this life. Your life—this life—is forfeit. But you shall live again. See your egg, Verden Leafglow. This egg's hatchling will be you. You shall die and be reborn through your own egg.*

"Reborn . . ."

Reborn. You shall be your own hatchling, Verden Leafglow. It will be a new life for you, but not a free life. You shall serve those who bring you forth from your egg. You shall be their chattel. Serve them, Verden Leafglow, and be powerless against them. Be completely at their mercy! This geas I give to you, Verden Leafglow.

This is your damnation! Once you kept your word to gully dwarves. To them, but not to me! Therefore I reject you. You are no longer mine. You will be theirs, Verden Leafglow. Let them do with you as they will.

"Them?" in her mind she screamed it. "Them? They are nothing. Only gully dwarves. Detestable, unspeakable beings."

Theirs, Verden Leafglow. And at their mercy, for as long as they want you.

"No! Dark Queen, oh mightiest, I plead—"

Theirs, the voice said, as though relishing the word.

Horror grew in Verden's mind. "Goddess, have mercy! I beg—"

You are mine no longer. The voice seemed to turn away, cold and indifferent. *If you want mercy, ask it of them. Die, Verden Leafglow. Die now, and seek mercy in rebirth from the gully dwarves who will own you.*

The voice faded and only the vision was left in her mind: the egg. Her own egg was deep within a dark place, unguarded and vulnerable. Beating powerful wings, Verden Leafglow turned in the direction of the vision and sped toward it . . . .

Sped toward it, and began to die.

Ahead, mountains rose to meet her, and beyond the mountains was a dimness that grew by the moment. There—just beyond there, yet so far away—was the place. She knew it then. She recognized the place, knew where it was, and fresh horror rose in her dimming mind. Xak Tsaroth. The Pitt.

Aghar and vermin. Gully dwarves and rats.

The mountains rose before her, and her sight dimmed to darkness. Her wings faltered, flapped erratically and failed. The mountains were below her now and they rose to meet her, great jagged peaks reaching for her as she spiraled downward, unseeing. In her last moment of life only one thing remained for her to see—a vision of her egg, lost in a place of shadows where small things moved.

PART 1

Legacy of the Least

Chapter 1
A Throne For Glitch

A great many things had happened in the seasons since the wandering tribe of Bulp came to This Place. There were a great many things that no one really understood, things that were mostly unpleasant and invariably confusing.

Other Aghar had been in this place then, but as slaves, tormented and abused by horrible creatures beyond anyone's understanding. Misery and death had lurked everywhere in the Promised Place, and the newly-arrived followers of the Highbulp Glitch I, Lord Protector of Anyplace He Happened to Be, had spent a long and miserable time hiding in holes and cracks that even the other gully dwarves of This Place had not found.

It was a time of torment, and of fear, and some had been lost. Then other kinds of people had come and gone. There had been several kinds of humans, whom the Aghar thought of as "Talls," and various other large animals, creatures and unthinkables. The stink of magic and the clamor of battle had filled This Place and always there were the ugly things that had lizard faces, dry, crackly voices and seemed determined to do harm to every creature they encountered.

People and things had come to the place some called Xak Tsaroth. They had come, they had fought, and then they had gone away, and the Aghar—the wandering tribe of Bulp and many others who had happened to join them—had suffered through it all the only way they knew how. They hid, cringed and lurked in the darkest places. They fled in panic when they could, and groveled when all else failed, and waited for the turmoil of war to recede from This Place.

Some other clans—those that had already been there when the Highbulp Glitch I led his people in tumultuous descent into the place long seasons before—had fled the Pitt entirely. Many of those who fled eventually returned, though fewer in number and more confused by what was going on outside of Xak Tsaroth than by what was going on inside.

Things happened everywhere that defied Aghar understanding.

Whatever it had all been about, though, it seemed to be over now. Some parts of the Pitt were still littered with fallen weapons, mummifying corpses of various kinds and the odd heaps of dust that had once been the ugly lizard-things. With the return of some normalcy, Glitch I had taken it upon himself—since nobody else seemed to care one way or another—to declare himself Highbulp of all survivors, ruler and lord protector of all the miscellaneous clans.

It didn't matter much to anyone else. Any High-whatsit was of little practical use to the Aghar—whom others called gully dwarves—and was generally a nuisance. But somebody had to be the High-whatever, and as long as *somebody* was willing to be it, everybody else was satisfied.

How long had it been since the invasions and the fighting had ended? No one knew for sure, except that it was before yesterday, which put it into the distant past along with other things not worth remembering. So most of them had put it out of their minds and gone back to the pressing tasks of today—foraging, scrounging, keeping the stew pot going and now and then considering ways to keep the Highbulp from becoming grumpy.

At the moment, that involved coming up with a throne for him to sit on.

Somewhere along the way, Glitch had gotten the idea that he was a great and majestic personage. He had once had a personal dragon—according to him—and had led his people to the Promised Place, which was now This Place. He was therefore a legend, at least in his own mind, and was becoming a real nuisance about it.

He had already changed his regal designation from "Glitch the First" to "Glitch the Most, High-bulp by Persuasion and Lord Protector of This Place and Everyplace Else that Mattered." And that was only the beginning.

He had demanded attention, which he sometimes received if he shouted loud enough. He had demanded a crown, to the point that some of them finally made one for him. He had demanded a personal flag, which he didn't yet have, and now he was demanding a soft chair. Great rulers of mighty nations sat on soft chairs, he reasoned. Therefore he should sit on a soft chair.

Now that things were quiet again, and he had nothing else to think about, Glitch had become obsessed with the idea of a special place to sit. He complained constantly, every time he decided to sit down.

"Rocks!" he would grumble. "Alla time sit on rocks. *Anybody* can sit on rocks. Glitch th' Most is Highbulp. Highbulp oughtta have sof' chair. Other kings an' stuff got sof' chairs. Why not Highbulp?"

He had become such a nuisance about it that even the Grand Notioner, old Gandy with his mop handle staff, had lost patience. "Why don't Highbulp go find sand dump an' sit on it?" he confronted his liege. "Ever'body tired of hearin' you gripe."

"Highbulp need th . . . thro . . . sof' chair!" Glitch snapped at his chief counselor, his eyes slitted and his crown of rat's teeth aslant. "Kings got thro . . . thr . . . those things. Highbulp good as kings. Who else ever had personal dragon? Highbulp want a whatsit . . . a *throne!*"

"Highbulp wouldn' know throne if he saw one," Gandy pointed out.

The Lord High Protector of Everybody in This Place glared at him. "Would, too. Throne sof' chair. Highbulp need sof' chair."

"Rats," Gandy muttered, turning away.

"What?"

"Rats. Stew pot runnin' low. Need rats an' stuff. Got no time for Highbulp now. Everybody busy with own rat killin'." Gandy turned and stomped away, muttering to himself. "One thing then 'nother. Want new name. Got new name. Want crown. Got crown. Now want throne. Highbulp a real nuisance."

A hunting expedition had just returned from somewhere. A dozen or so Gully Dwarves carried bundles of whitish roots, some unidentifiable greens, a clutch of freshly-bashed subterranean snails and other odds and ends they had found. All the edible forage was dumped into stew pots, the rest tossed aside for later inspection. At one of the stew pots, Gandy noticed, the Lady Bruze was examining the contents with a frown. "Too much snail," she muttered. "Need more rat. An' mushroom. Need mushroom."

She searched about for her husband, a sturdy gully dwarf called Clout who was considered Chief Basher for the clan. Finally she found him, sound asleep in the shadows, cradling his bashing tool in his arms.

She went to him, stood over him for a moment, frowning, then kicked him in the ribs. "Clout wake up," she demanded.

Abruptly awake and confused, Clout sat up, flailing about him with his bashing tool. Bruze dodged the swinging stick, got behind him and kicked him again. "Clout!" she snapped. "Wake up! Clout a sleepy lout. Wake up! Go find fresh rats for stew."

Clout rubbed his eyes, yawned and got to his feet. "Yes, dear," he said. With a longing glance at his sleeping place, he padded off toward the dark caverns where the best rats were usually found.

Gandy had watched with interest. Now he leaned thoughtfully on his mop handle and muttered, "Sof' chair not what Highbulp need. Wife what Highbulp need. Somebody keep him in line."

However, he did spread the word again. "Anybody find sof' chair, bring it back for Highbulp. Might shut him up for a while."

And those who heard told others. "Some clown gripin' 'bout need sof' chair. Anybody see a sof' chair anyplace?"

"Nope," most said. "For who?" some asked.

"For what's-'is-name. Th' Highbulp. He want sof' chair."

"Why?"

"Dunno."

Most of them promptly forgot all about it. The whims and notions of High-whatevers were rarely worth remembering. But the idea did persist, vaguely, as they went their various ways.

*　*　*　*　*　*

It was some of the ladies who found it, though they didn't realize right away what they had found.

The Lady Bruze—wife of the Chief Basher, Clout— and some of the younger females had organized a forage into lower levels of the Pitt in search of mushrooms, fat crawlies and anything else that might be useful for stew. They were creeping furtively through the echoing shadows of what might once have been a vast dungeon, when one of them stopped, squinted and pointed. "What that?"

Several of them coming up behind her collided

with one another, and some fell down. "Sh!" the Lady Bruze hissed. "Wha' happen?"

"Somebody see somethin'," someone said. "Then somebody fall down."

"Oh." The Lady Bruze looked back. "Who see somethin'?"

"Me," one said.

"Lidda? What Lidda see?"

"Somethin' there," Lidda pointed again. "Wasn' there minute ago."

They all squinted in the gloom. There was something there. Just to the left of the path they were following, something vaguely ovoid lay in shadows among fallen stones. Cautiously, they crept closer for a better look.

"What that thing?" someone whispered.

"Kinda green," another observed.

They gathered around it, looking at it first one way and then another. It was about waist-high to most of them, a dull, featureless thing like a squat globe, resting in the shadows. As they approached, it seemed to radiate softly—a dim, greenish glow coming from within it, barely visible even in the murk of the cavernous ancient place.

"Big mushroom, maybe?" someone suggested.

"Looks pretty solid," another said.

Lidda crept closer and reached a hand toward the thing. When nothing happened, she prodded it quickly with a curious finger, then ducked back. Again it seemed as though the thing had glowed slightly, dim and greenish.

"Kinda sof'," Lidda told them. "Not like mushroom, though. Like, uh, like leather."

"Leather mushroom?" the Lady Bruze wondered. "Maybe good for stew?"

Lidda squatted, peered beneath the thing and shook her head. "No stem." She leaned close to it, sniffing. "Don' smell like mushroom, either."

They looked at the thing curiously for a minute or two, then began wandering away. Having no idea what it was, and seeing no practical purpose for it, they lost interest in it.

The Lady Bruze looked around and saw her expedition scattering. "Come on. This not good for anything."

Lidda lingered, though, fascinated by the way the thing seemed to glow dimly now and then.

"Lidda come on!" the Lady Bruze called, sounding angry. "I say come on, you s'pose to come on!"

Lidda waved absently, ignoring the command. The Lady Bruze could be a real pain sometimes. She repeated her inspection of the green thing. When she looked up, she was alone with it. The others had gone somewhere else. "Lady Bruze prob'ly right," she told herself. "Thing not good for anything. Not up to her, though. I decide."

On impulse, she hoisted herself atop the thing and sat, bouncing a bit to test it. It was soft and springy, and glowed happily as she sat there. "Make nice chair for sit," she told herself, then recalled something she had heard. Somebody had been looking for a soft chair.

She looked around again in the eerie gloom of the ancient place. The other ladies were long gone, off on their foraging. She was alone, and not sure where they had gone. She shrugged, got down and took a deep breath. See if thing will move, she decided.

The thing was heavy, but Lidda was strong. Although she was barely three feet tall, she was sturdy and determined, and after the first hard shove, the thing rolled along handily. She kept pushing and it kept rolling, like a big, squashy ball. Driven by the guiding forces of all gully dwarves—inertia and inadvertence—and keeping a wary eye out for salamanders and other nasties, Lidda rolled her leathery green "chair" back the way the ladies had come, heading for This Place.

The journey took hours, and Lidda was nearly exhausted when she came into the firelight and clamor of the gully dwarves' primary caverns. Crowds of the curious gathered around her, wondering what she had, but she fended them off and kept going. "Hands off," she ordered. "This for What's-'is-name."

"Who?"

"Th' Highbulp."

"Oh, ol' Glitch."

"Yeah, him. Get outta way."

She found the Highbulp where he usually was—in the center of things, demanding attention—and rolled the thing over to him. "Here," she said. "For you."

He stood, pushed his crown of rat's teeth back from his eyes and squinted at what she had brought. "What this?"

"Chair," she explained. "Sof' chair, for Highbulp."

"Chair?" He looked more closely. "This a roun' thing. What kin' chair roun'?"

"This kin'," she said, irritated at the great leader's attitude toward her gift.

Gandy, the Grand Notioner, came shuffling from somewhere, and squinted at the round thing. "What that?" he asked.

"Chair," Lidda repeated. "Sof' chair for Highbulp."

Glitch gazed at the thing, beginning to sneer. "What kin' chair look like that?" he pointed at it, turning to Gandy.

With the inspiration of his office, Gandy poked at the thing with his mop handle and nodded, looking wise. "Throne," he declared. "Throne look like that."

"Throne?" Glitch's eyes widened. "This thing a throne? What I do with it?"

"Sit on it, Highbulp," Gandy suggested.

Uncertainly, Glitch climbed atop the "throne" and sat. It felt soft and comfortable, and the fact that it glowed with greenish light as his backside began to warm it only added to the regal picture of himself that came to his mind. "Throne," he pronounced, feeling very pleased with himself. "Highbulp's throne."

If Lidda had expected even a word of thanks, it was not forthcoming. Gratitude was not generally a primary quality of the Highbulp. Tired, irritated and a bit confused about why she had gone to so much trouble, she turned and wandered away, then paused when someone spoke to her. It was Gandy, leaning on his mop handle. "Who you?" he asked.

"Lidda," she reminded him.

"Sure. Lidda. I 'member. That pretty good thing you bring, Lidda. Oughtta keep Highbulp quiet for day or so."

"Fine," she snapped, starting to turn away.

"Day or so," Gandy repeated. "Then he think of somethin' else, start all over again."

"Highbulp a nuisance," Lidda pointed out.

"Sure," he agreed. "Goes with bein' Highbulp. Be better if he had a wife. Keep him in line."

"Him?" Lidda stared back at the preening, self-important little figure sitting on the green thing. The green was brighter now, glowing with a contented, pulsing light. "Who be dumb 'nough to marry *him?*"

"Dunno," said Gandy, shrugging. "How 'bout Lidda?"

"*Me?*" She stared at him, then her eyes brightened with indignation. "No way! You want him married, marry him yourself!"

With that she stomped away, angry and insulted.

Gandy watched her go, nodding his approval. "Pretty good choice," he told himself. There was something about that particular female—something he had forgotten, but that now came back, dimly. She was stubborn, he recalled.

Chapter 2
Faces on the Wall

Though Lidda was young, there were many who had noticed her from time to time. Lidda had a definite stubborn streak. And, such as it was, she tended to have a mind of her own. This in itself was a bit mystifying to most of the gully dwarves. As a rule, the Aghar generally had better things to do than think. But there were occasions, now and then, when thoughts could come in handy.

There had been a time, in the still-recent torment times, when a group of the lizard-things had almost found the clan. A whole line of the ugly creatures had passed a crack that was the opening to the hiding place, and one had stepped aside and paused, as though to look inside. He had not looked, though. From somewhere above, a fist-sized rock had fallen, striking him on his helmet. It distracted him, and one of the others barked at him, and they had all gone on.

The Grand Notioner, Gandy, had noticed that incident, and had puzzled over it. The rock had been no accident. He remembered that it had been dropped intentionally, from a high shelf. And the person who dropped it was Lidda.

It was all very confusing, but somehow, it seemed, little Lidda had kept that bunch of uglies in line.

"Lidda might keep Highbulp in line, too," Gandy told himself now. "Keep lizard-things in line, keep anybody in line. Real good choice."

Thoughtfully, he looked back at the Highbulp, who was reveling in being the center of attention. Glitch sat straight and proud atop his brand-new throne, his crown slightly askew, the expression on his homely face a study in self-importance. He grandly permitted those who cared to, a chance to come close and admire him.

Beneath him, warmed by the regal bottom as well as by the radiance of nearby stew fires, the throne seemed to be just as happy as he was. It glowed cheerily with a radiant, greenish light.

* * * * *

Lidda found something else with which to occupy herself. High on one wall of the ancient chamber the combined clans had claimed as their home, was a mosaic of carvings surrounded by a framework of dark marble shelving set into gray stone. In some forgotten time, artisans had worked the stone within that frame, shaping forms and sculptures—a grand, intertwined mosaic of figures of all kinds, people, animals, vines and flowers interwoven with strange symbols, all sculpted in the stone.

In the very center of it all was a circle of faces. Had Lidda—or anyone else around—been able to count past two, they would have known that there were nine visages staring from the cold stone of the wall there. Each stood out in stark relief from the surface of an oval plaque. The nine "faces" were not really faces, exactly—certainly they were like no faces any gully dwarf had ever seen—but seemed images of things far beyond understanding.

Everybody knew the stone mosaic was there. It was in plain sight, and everyone had glanced at it from time to time, but it had no more meaning to most of them than any other unexplainable thing in their world. They didn't know what it was, or why it was there any more than they knew why some areas of the ancient ruin to which they had come were full of water, or why the largest of the covered corridors leading away and upward from their living area sometimes whined and wept with distant winds that drifted through the halls of the Pitt and made stew fires flicker.

Lidda had been noticing the mosaic on the wall a lot lately. Somehow, it seemed to her, it looked different than when she first saw it, and it puzzled her why it should.

Now, with nothing better to do, she went to look at it again, squinting upward in puzzlement as she walked back and forth beneath the sculpture. Then she saw it. One of the faces was tilted slightly outward, as though the plaque on which it rested had partially separated from the stone of the surrounding mosaic.

Curious, Lidda found handholds and toeholds in the surface of the wall and began to climb.

It took some time and effort to get there. The entire mosaic extended from just above the floor—eye-level to Lidda—into the shadows high in the great chamber. And even though the circle of faces was only halfway up, that still was more than twenty feet above the floor. But once set on a course, she tended to follow it, and eventually she was high on the wall, clinging to chiseled stone vines with the tilted oval plaque just above her.

It was larger than she had guessed—as wide as she was tall. The face on it seemed to be a representation of a bearded man with a string of beads across his forehead and jutting mustaches that came to sharp points at each side. Then again, it might have been a sculpture of one of the lizard-like creatures who had occupied the Pitt until recently or something else, entirely. It was hard to tell.

It wasn't the art, though, that held Lidda's attention.

It was the crack behind the plaque. The oval, seen closely, turned out to be old, tarnished metal rather than stone, and she stuck out her tongue to taste it. It was iron. Each of the plaques in the circle was made of metal of a different sort, and each had a hinge at the bottom and a catch at the top. The one she was exploring was separated from the wall because its catch had rusted.

Leaning close to peer into the crack, she saw that there was a hole in the stone behind it.

"What this?" Lidda muttered to herself. "Maybe somethin' good inside?"

With visions of treasure—nests full of forgotten eggs, piles of pretty rocks hidden away, maybe shoe buckles—dancing in her mind, Lidda grasped her handhold, braced herself against the sculpted stone, wrapped strong little fingers around the nearest edge of the loosened oval, and pulled.

For a moment, the rusted catch held. Then it gave way and the entire plaque swung downward, shaking Lidda loose from her precarious perch. She clung to the falling edge of the oval and glanced upward as something shot from the exposed hole over her head—something long, dark and very fast that whistled in the air as it shot past her.

The plaque clanged against stone and quivered. Lidda hung from its lower edge with one hand, high above the floor of the great chamber, shouting for help. And somewhere across the chamber, in shadows at the far side, something big crashed against stone, throwing sparks and skittering off into the main corridor.

Below was a babble of surprised voices: "Here, now! What goin' on?" "What that flew past?" "Somethin' noisy in tunnel." "Look! Somebody up on wall!"

Clinging desperately to the now-inverted oval shield, high above the floor of This Place, Lidda chirped and chattered in panic, trying not to fall.

"Who that up there?" someone below asked.

"Lidda? That you?" someone else wanted to know.

"Me!" she shouted. "Somebody help!"

"What goin' on?" The Highbulp's voice sounded irritated. "Who that up there?"

"Lidda," someone said.

"Lidda come down!" the Highbulp demanded.

31

A female voice echoed him. The Lady Bruze put her hands on her hips and stamped a foot. "Lidda! Get down from there!"

"Can't!" she shrieked. "Barely holdin' on!"

"Then turn loose!" the Lady Bruze insisted.

Directly below her, old Gandy's voice called, "No, don' turn loose! Swing feet!"

Since that sounded like a better idea than the one immediately prior, Lidda kept her grip on the metal rim and swung her feet. Her toe touched the carved wall, slipped away, and she swung again, this time finding a toehold in the mosaic surface. She clung for a moment, getting her breath, then eased herself beneath the hanging shield and found a handhold. Within seconds she was scurrying down the sheer wall, sighing with relief.

A few gathered to watch her descent, but with the crisis past, most of the gully dwarves had turned their attentions to the far side of the great chamber where something had entered the main corridor at great speed, thrown a mighty shower of sparks, and disappeared up the tunnel.

When Lidda reached the floor again, only the Lady Bruze was there to face her. Hands on hips, she leaned toward the younger female and snapped, "Lidda stay off wall! Got no business climb wall!"

"Checkin' out hole . . ." Lidda pointed upward, trying to explain.

"Bad Lidda!" Bruze's words bored in. "Why you always do dumb stuff? Like bring us back green thing 'stead of hunt mushroom an' . . . like . . . like . . . dumb stuff!"

The lady's tone was so severe that Lidda backed away a step.

"Now mess up wall stuff!" Bruze chided, glancing

upward. "Prob'ly broke somethin'. Dumb Lidda!"

Lidda had taken all she was going to. With her own hands on her own hips, she stomped her foot and thrust a pugnacious face forward, nose-to-nose with Bruze. "Shut up, Lady Bruze! Got no right talk on me that way!"

Bruze recoiled for an instant, surprised, then straightened her back, stuck her nose in the air and turned away. "Dumb Lidda," she snorted. "An' sassy, too." With a sniff of disdain, she stalked off, leaving Lidda to fume and sputter.

Old Candy appeared beside her, leaning on his mop handle and peering upward. "What Lidda fin' up there?"

"Nothin' much," she answered, still smarting. "How come Lady Bruze can throw big weight aroun' alla time?"

Gandy frowned thoughtfully, then shrugged. "Lady Bruze got Clout," he said. "Gives her stat . . . rank . . . priv . . . uh, she get by with a lot."

"Not fair," Lidda decided.

"Way it is, though." The Grand Notioner shrugged again. His eyes narrowed thoughtfully. "Lidda want clout, too?"

"Clout already married," she pointed out. "To Lady Bruze."

"Then get somebody else," the Grand Notioner suggested. "Maybe somebody better. You want marry Highbulp?"

"Stop that again! No!"

"Why not?"

"'Cause Highbulp a lazy, worthless twit, is why not. Highbulp never think 'bout anybody 'cept own self."

"Yep," Gandy agreed. "That him, alright. So why

33

not marry him?"

Lidda stared at the oldster. "Can't stand him, is why. Why else?"

"So what? Nobody can stand Highbulp. Marry him anyway. Do him good, have somebody keep him in line."

Across the chamber, an excited crowd had gathered. Several gully dwarves had crept into the corridor there, looking for whatever had gone that way. Now they were returning, and they had the thing with them. It looked like a huge spear, and it took several of them to carry it.

"Whoever marry Highbulp be consort," Gandy persisted.

Lidda turned to him again. "Be what?"

"Consort."

"What consort?"

"Highbulp's wife. Got more clout than Chief Basher's wife."

"Consort have to put up with Highbulp, though," said Lidda. She shook her head back and forth. "Forget it."

She walked away without looking back, and Gandy leaned on his mop handle. "Good choice," he muttered to himself. "That'n might shape up Highbulp. That'n fulla vinegar."

Chapter 3
Perils of the Pitt

The Aghar scouts recovered the missile — a twelve-foot-long spear of iron with a steel point as wide as a shovel—from far up the "big tunnel" where it had lodged itself in a stone wall after skipping and caroming for several hundred yards. It weighed at least fifty pounds and required four sturdy gully dwarves to carry it back to This Place.

"That thing dangerous," the Highbulp declared, studying it from his perch atop his glowing green throne. "Where come from?"

"Murder hole up there," someone pointed toward

the far wall with its stone mosaic. They had built up the fires, and the hole behind the iron face up there was visible.

"Somebody throw that thing through that hole?" someone asked.

"Throw itself, prob'ly," Gandy said, his mop handle staff thudding against the floor as he stepped past the fire, gazing at the hole high in the wall. "Ol' trap somebody set, for guard big tunnel. Lidda open hole, trap sprung."

Faces peered with renewed interest at the decorated wall. There were still eight more undisturbed faces.

"More of these up there?" the Highbulp asked.

Gandy squinted at the remaining eight plaques. "Yep," he decided, "two more."

They buzzed and hovered around the spear for a time, but could think of no use for it. It was inedible, and far too big for even Clout to use as a tool. Finally, with no better idea in mind, Gandy tied a scrap of stained cloth to the point of it and supervised as a dozen of them hoisted it upright and thrust the butt end of it into a hole in the paving, a few feet from the throne.

"There," he said, when at last it stood tall and secure.

"'There,' what?" somebody asked. "What that supposed to be?"

"Flag," Gandy explained. "Highbulp's new flag." He turned. "See, Highbulp? Got new . . ." He stopped, and sighed. Glitch the Most wasn't listening. The Highbulp was all tuckered. He lay curled atop his "throne," asleep and beginning to snore.

"Lidda right," Gandy growled. "Highbulp a twit."

The throne seemed happy, though. Beneath the

Highbulp it glowed a steady green light, and seemed to pulse a bit, as though it were matching the Highbulp's breathing.

Gandy frowned, tilting his head as he looked at the throne. He was almost sure that it was growing. It was noticeably larger now than when Lidda had first brought it.

*   *   *   *   *

Out of nothingness, she swam slowly into a kind of awareness. Vague, slow dreams drifted around her and she was part of them. More feelings than images, they drifted, curling and coalescing in first one way and then another—feelings of comfort and discomfort, of longing for . . . something long since gone, and of anticipation of something yet to come.

She floated among the dream-streams, knowing nothing except what they told her. The odd longings were less than memory, but more than dream. They were longings for things past and gone—feelings of freedom and power, of exhilaration and cruel joy, of confrontation and combat, of flying on great wings that ruled the skies above a vast and servile world. The feelings were bittersweet, clouded by a certainty that all of that was gone now, gone forever.

And yet, the other feelings—the anticipations— were warm with promise, as though what had ended forever might still, somehow, begin anew.

Timeless time passed, and the images became more clearly defined. She became aware of herself as a presence and dimly sensed other presences around her, presences beyond the limits of the green universe that was herself, but not far away.

The presences were not like herself. They were

lesser things, yet presences. A vague instinct said, these are food, and abruptly she recoiled as though huge, unseen claws had raked her, punishing her for the thought. It was a lesson. Not food, then. Lesser beings, nearby, but not food.

Then why did they matter? The glowing greenness swam and coalesced and within it a darkness spoke to her. *They own you*, it said. *You are theirs.* Cold certainty flowed about her. *You cannot harm them*, the darkness declared. *You can only serve them. You are theirs. Soon you will know.*

Cruel, cold humor flowed from the darkness. *Grow quickly now*, it commanded her. *Grow and awaken to your destiny. Awaken to your fate. Soon*, the essences told her, *you will understand. Soon you will know, just as you knew before. And that is when your punishment begins.*

* * * * * *

As the days passed, what was obvious to Gandy became apparent to everyone else in This Place. The Highbulp's throne was growing. For a time, this greatly pleased Glitch the Most. With each day, it seemed, his loftiness above his subjects became greater, reinforcing his importance.

The problem was, the Highbulp kept falling off, and the fall was greater each time he did. Sometimes he fell off by his own doing—rolling over in his sleep and winding up in a heap on the hard, cold floor. But now and then the throne trembled and squirmed, and sometimes its violent spasms were enough to throw him from his perch.

It had grown big enough that it was increasingly difficult to get back on top of it when he fell off.

"Highbulp need ladder," he grumped to all those around him after a particularly forceful expulsion from his throne.

Nobody had the slightest idea how to make a ladder, but Glitch the Most was becoming grumpier by the hour, and an inspiration occurred finally, out of sheer aggravation.

It was a gully dwarf named Tunk who came up with it. While he and others were exploring far regions of the Pitt, where inexplicable wonders had been left by the lizard-things and others from the past, they bumped into a giant salamander who had been trying to get some sleep.

Instantly they fled in gibbering panic along a dark tunnel, just steps ahead of the huge, slithering thing with a mouth bigger than they were and teeth as sharp as needles. Giant salamanders were one of the hazards of life in the Pitt. Although the Talls and the lizard-men had gone, there were many other large, unpleasant things living here and there in the rubble of the Promised Place.

Tunk could feel the thing's hideous breath on his back by the time someone in the lead found a crevice to dart into, and he left a shoe dangling in the thing's snapping teeth as he scurried into safety. They could hear the salamander scrabbling behind them, but it was too big to follow, and could not break through the stone that barred its way.

The exploring party had scurried through the crevice, tumbling out the other side into a great, cavernous space that none of them had seen before, a place where balconies lined stone walls beneath an immense, vaulted roof high above, and the central arena had a floor of packed sand.

"Whew!" Tunk declared, looking back at the crevice

that had stopped the salamander. "That way too close!"

The danger behind them then, they wandered out into the enclosed arena, gawking at the enormity of it.

"What kin' place this?" one of them wondered aloud.

"Dunno," another said. "Big, though. Maybe got good stuff to find?"

Then Tunk saw it, and his eyes widened. "Lookee there!" he pointed. In the center of the arena was a flagstaff with a lanyard, and something came together in Tunk's simple mind. "That what Highbulp need," he said. "That shut him up from gripin' so much."

When they eventually returned to This Place—by other routes, to avoid the ravenous salamander that had chased them—they were laden with equipment. Among other things, they brought a coil of rope and a pulley with ring clamps. Without ceremony, they marched to the center of This Place—casting worried glances at the throne, which was more than five feet high now and had an alarming tendency to twitch—and dumped their treasures on the floor beside Glitch the Most, who had just landed there himself.

"Here, Highbulp," Tunk said.

He glared at the pile of things. "What all this?"

"Hoist," Tunk explained. "For get back on throne."

Within an hour, the Highbulp's "flagpole," which was now within inches of the growing throne, was rigged with a serviceable lanyard, very much like the flagstaff in the arena. A curious crowd gathered as Tunk proudly tied the Highbulp's rag flag to the pulleyed line, and hoisted it to the top.

"There," he said, grinning happily.

Beside him, Glitch frowned at the flag atop the great spear. "What good that do?" he snapped. "Take down flag, put up rope, haul flag back up. For what?"

Tunk cast him a baleful glance. "Trial run," he said. Quickly he lowered the flag, untied it from the lanyard and, before Glitch the Most could object, looped the lanyard around the Highbulp's chubby middle. "Lend hand here," he beckoned several of the others. "Haul 'im up!"

Sputtering, cursing and struggling, Glitch the Most found himself rising from the floor, alongside his spear, then dangling above his throne. "Cut that out!" he shrieked.

Gandy had shown up from somewhere, and he studied the situation and nodded. "Pretty good," he approved. "Now swing him 'round that way."

Overhead, the Highbulp found himself arcing through the air, out from the pole, then directly over the throne and in free fall as Gandy gave the order to curtail the hoist. Glitch thumped down atop the twitching, glowing throne, and it responded so violently that he almost fell off again. He clung, though, swearing every oath that occurred to him as the throne twitched busily and those below congratulated one another on a job well done.

"Pretty good," Gandy assured the hoisters. "What about the flag?"

Tunk scratched his head, frowning. "Might haul 'im down again, tie flag to him," he suggested.

Gandy thought it over, glancing up at the livid face of his Lord Protector. He shook his head. "Better let well enough alone," he decided.

Chapter 4
The Awakening

Vague awareness became tumultuous dreams, disturbing the liquid green comfort of her deep sleep. Then the dreams gave way to annoyance as irritating little presences, presences just beyond awareness, repeatedly jostled and abused the greenness where she slept.

She didn't want to awaken. Something—some knowledge just beyond the grasp of dreams—told her that she would regret awakening. Still, the presences were there, all around her, and they bumped, jostled and poked at her comforting limbo. They babbled and tumbled, shouted and shoved, drawing her toward angry response. Kill them, she thought and felt again the punishing agony of great, invisible talons raking her mind.

No, something dark said. *You will not kill them. You will not injure them. You are powerless against them. It is your fate.* Somewhere far off, somewhere not of this world, she sensed cruel, mocking laughter.

She railed against the vicious, ironic cruelty being inflicted on her, railed against the awful feeling of being absolutely powerless, but in the dream-knowledge there was not the slightest lenience. A decree had been issued, and there was no appeal. Once, it seemed, she had dedicated herself to a god. Now that god had renounced her and left her to an eternal punishment. *You are theirs*, the darkness said. *Awaken, sleeping one. Awaken and face the fate you have earned.*

The green comforts began to diminish, and awareness grew of the world outside. It was a world where pathetic little creatures waited to torment her, a world where she, to whom power was all, would lack the power to strike back even at them.

Awaken, the dream voice commanded, and gave purpose to the twitching of her body. She turned, rolled over, extended her needle-tipped talons, and raked at the leathery shell beyond the liquid where she grew.

* * * * *

Clout and the dozen or so other rat hunters with him were puzzled. They had hunted for hours in the maze of cells that covered a vast area up the "big tunnel" from This Place, and had not found a single rat. It was unheard of. Ever since any gully dwarf could remember, the Pitt had abounded in vermin. It had always been full of rats. Usually they were everywhere, and the maze of old cells—interconnected cubicles that might once have been sleeping quarters for Talls or lizard-things—was prime rat hunting territory.

Yet today, no matter how they searched, there was not a sign of stew meat anywhere. It was as though every rat in the area had gone into hiding.

"This whole place fulla empty rats." The chunky, bearded Tote shook his head in disgust. "Where they all go?"

"Dunno why no rats." Clout muttered. "'No' one thing. Lady Bruze not gonna like us come back 'thout rats."

"Plenny sign," young Blip pointed out, squatting to study the floor. "Rat drops all over. Tracks, too."

"No rats, though." Peady gazed around. "Maybe somethin' eat 'em?"

"What eat rats?" Clout scoffed. "Who hunt rats, 'cept us?"

"Somethin' scare 'em off, then. All go hide, maybe?"

"What scare rats?" Clout glanced around as a gasp sounded behind him. Tote was staring into the shadows of a tunnel a dozen yards away, his eyes huge, his mouth hanging open. He closed it with a snap and pointed. "That," he quavered, then spun on his heel and ran.

The rest peered into the shadows, and gaped as something huge moved into view. They had seen giant salamanders before, but the one emerging now from the tunnel was monstrous. It seemed to fill the entire tunnel, and as they saw it, it sensed them, and charged.

"Run like crazy!" Clout shrilled, and pounded

away after Tote, the others right behind him. Behind them, they heard the squishy padding of the salamander's webbed feet, the slithering of its huge, gleaming body, as it pursued.

Though nearly brainless and almost blind, the salamander had a keen sense of smell, and was startlingly fast on its feet. The gully dwarves darted through portal after portal, trying to lose it, but each time they glanced back it was still coming, and coming closer at every turn. As they neared the big tunnel leading downward toward This Place, the thing was virtually on their heels. Its wide, flat mouth gaped like a cave full of short, sharp teeth.

"Don' lead it home!" Blip panted, seeing the familiar turn just ahead. "Go other way!"

But it was too late. In panic, Tote had turned and the rest pounded after him.

Blip would have followed them, except that the idea of turning left had become lodged in his head. By the time he got around to reversing the notion, he was already headed upward, alone in the main corridor. When the idea of changing his mind and turning right translated itself into action, he veered right and bounced off a stone wall. He stumbled backward and fell, the wind knocked out of him. "Rats," he muttered, trying to scramble to his feet.

He noticed then that he was alone. The salamander, huge and swift for all its bulk, had gone the other way, following Clout and the rest. Confused, Blip sat down and considered what to do.

Going on up the tunnel wouldn't do any good, but going down-tunnel where the beast had gone didn't appeal to him at all. If the thing caught the others before they got to This Place, it would eat them. And if he came along behind it, it would eat him, too. On the other hand, if the hunting party managed to stay ahead of the salamander long enough, they would lead it right into This Place, and in that case This Place would be no place to be.

That left him only one remaining option. The Lady Bruze had sent them out to hunt rats for stew. Maybe, now that the big salamander was gone from the rat place, the rats would come out where they could be hunted.

Comfortable with his keen logic, Blip headed back to the cells where the chase had begun. The only sensible course of action now, it seemed to him, was to hunt rats.

* * * * *

When the Highbulp's throne attacked him, Lidda was up on the sculptured wall again.

Since the episode of the big spear and the murder hole, she had avoided climbing the carvings, until the idea occurred to her that the hinged iron plaque, still hanging up there where she had left it, might be useful for something if she could somehow get it loose from its hinge.

That, and the fact that the Lady Bruze had forbidden her to ever climb the wall again, were reasons enough to climb the wall. Sometimes Lidda felt that Lady Bruze herself was all the reason anyone needed. Tracing the route she had followed before, she began climbing and soon was clinging to vines beside the dark, open hole from which the deadly spear, which now served as the Highbulp's "flagstaff," had come.

Cautiously, she peeked into the hole, and saw nothing but darkness. Then, her eyes adjusting, she could make out details within. The hole was deep—

deeper than the length of the missile that had come from it, and in the depths rested a spiral of metal—the spring that had propelled the shaft. The spiral was too deep for her to reach, and the hole was a little tight for her to crawl into, so she turned her attention to the inverted iron shield that hung from its hinge below.

The hinge was fairly simple—a short series of interlocked rings with a metal pin through them. She grasped the pin and began to work it this way and that, pulling as she twisted. It gave a bit, then a little more, and she kept at it. Grudgingly, the pin slid from its rings, an inch at a time.

Below, a voice called, "Lidda? What you up to?"

She glanced down. Gandy, the Grand Notioner, stood directly below. He was looking up at her. "'Up to 'bout here," she advised him. "Better stan' back, 'fore this fall."

The Grand Notioner shuffled away a few steps, and another voice, high and cranky, came from below. "That Lidda up there again? Lidda! Come down right now!"

"Go sit on a tack, Lady Bruze!" Lidda suggested, not bothering to look down at the Chief Basher's wife. "Be up here if I want to!"

The pin gave another inch, then another, and the heavy iron shield shifted, grating against the stone beneath. "Better get outta way!" Lidda snapped, and gave the pin a sharp tug. It came loose in her hand, the shield's hinge parted, and thirty pounds of rusty iron hurtled floorward.

The clatter when it hit was deafening, and was echoed by the sounds of Lady Bruze tripping over the Grand Notioner, by a howl from the Highbulp as he suddenly stood bolt upright atop his throne, then tumbled off of it to land in a heap on the stone floor, and by the scramble of startled gully dwarves heading for cover.

Confused by all the commotion, Lidda swung around to look out over the great chamber of This Place. "Wha' happen?" she called.

"Somethin' fall down," several voices responded.

"Highbulp fall down, too," several others chimed in, but their voices were overpowered by an angry roar from Glitch the Most, getting to his feet. "Somethin' stab me!" he shouted. Rubbing his bottom, frowning furiously, he stood on tiptoe, trying to see the top of his throne.

From where she was, high on the wall, Lidda could see everything clearly. The Highbulp's throne wasn't glowing anymore. Instead, it was writhing violently, greenish fluids flowing from long rips in its fabric, and there were things like busy daggers thrusting from its top.

Lidda gaped at the amazing sight, almost losing her hold on the wall. Then, from somewhere beyond the cavern, other sounds grew—shouts, shrieks and the sounds of pounding feet, coming from the mouth of the big tunnel across the wide hall.

"Run!" a voice shouted from somewhere. "All run like crazy! Got sal'mander!"

Never slow to take flight, gully dwarves ran in all directions, some heading for hidey-holes, some running in circles, some bumping into one another. From the big tunnel spewed more of them, led by Tote, who galloped into the open just in time to collide with several citizens going the other way.

They all went down, and the ones behind Tote piled up on them. Clout was on top of the heap. He started to rise and run again, then realized he had lost his rat-hunting stick in the melee. Forgetting why he had been running, he set to work methodically tossing gully dwarves this way and that, searching for his bashing tool.

Abruptly, just beyond him, the big tunnel was full of monstrous salamander. This Place resounded with shrieks of panic, and Lidda found herself peering out of the murder hole high in the wall. Instinctively, she had backed into it to hide.

"Run like crazy!" the Highbulp roared, heading for parts unknown.

"Clout!" Lady Bruze shouted. "Stop foolin' aroun'! Bash sal'mander!"

"Somebody do somethin'!" Gandy quavered.

When he reached the pile of people, Clout had recovered his bashing tool, and heard his wife's orders. "Yes, dear," he called, and turned, raising the two-foot stick in both hands.

The salamander's mouth opened wide, and Lidda—high on the opposite wall, decided the Grand Notioner was right. Somebody really should do something. She still had the hinge-pin in her hand, and on impulse she leaned out of the murder hole, reaching down as far as she could, toward the brass shield below—the next plaque down, in the circle. She could barely reach the top of it, but she got her hinge-pin under its catch and twisted.

The plaque banged open and something long, dark and deadly shot from the hole behind it, whistling.

In an instant, the missile had crossed the hall of This Place. It flashed past Clout, missing him by an inch, and into the gaping mouth of the salamander, deflecting upward from the thing's lower jaw to erupt from the top of its flat, ugly head. Clout's determined swing of his bashing tool missed its mark as the salamander was thrown backward, away from him.

An angry hiss filled the cavern as the salamander twitched and lay still.

But the hiss went on. Wide, terrified eyes staring at the dead monster turned slowly, looking for the source of the sound, growing even wider when they found it.

The Highbulp's throne was no longer a throne. Instead, it was a sagging, shredded thing, partially collapsed amid pools and runnels of green liquid. And something was emerging from it, hissing with an anger that became a shrill howl.

A few among them had seen a dragon. Some remembered the green dragon that had carried Glitch the Most and led the rest of his tribe to This Place. This dragon, freshly-hatched, was not nearly as big as that one had been, but it was definitely a dragon. Within seconds, there wasn't a gully dwarf in sight anywhere in This Place, except the chubby Tote. He had been at the bottom of the gully dwarf pileup, and was just getting to his feet, gaping around in total confusion.

He stood, blinked at the dead salamander in the big tunnel, brushed himself down, turned . . . and froze in place. Directly over him, towering more than twice his height, cruel, intelligent eyes opened in a scaled, crested green face, and looked down at him.

A taloned "hand" reached for him, then suddenly recoiled as though it had been swatted away. The crested head descended toward him, dripping fangs agleam, and stopped inches from his face. The hiss that came from that dragon's mouth almost stopped his heart, and the breath of it whipped his beard and smelled of chlorine. The thing stared at him, hating him, then turned away.

The dreams had been right, and now they had come true. Aching with frustrated anger, Verden Leafglow turned from the pathetic creature, unable to harm it even though that was what she craved to do. It was as though a wall stood between her and the little creature, a wall that she could not penetrate, and that punished her when she tried.

Licking and cleaning herself, she looked around slowly as the knowledge of hatching wove itself together in her mind. She knew who she was now. She knew where she was, and knew the awful reality that had befallen her. There was no recourse from the will of a vengeful god. Her fate had been promised, and now it was real.

The Aghar before her hadn't moved, hadn't so much as blinked since he first saw her. He stood as though frozen, his mouth agape and his eyes bulging, not even seeming to breathe. And there were others, as well, all around her, peering from cracks and holes, their fear a tangible thing in the still air of the cavernous chamber. Did they think she couldn't see them? Did they think she couldn't sense exactly where they hid? There were dozens of them in this chamber, and dozens more not far away, running and hiding from her.

And there wasn't a thing that she could do about them. The Dark Queen had made her powerless against them. The keening roar of her anger and anguish echoed from the stone walls of the place, making things rattle and grate, causing little showers of ancient dust to fall from above.

Powerless!

But only against *them*. She spotted the huge, dead salamander in the mouth of the corridor, and her tail twitched. With a hiss of rage she threw herself upon the giant corpse and began tearing it apart.

Chapter 5
Dragon Bound

Freshly-hatched and ravenous, the dragon ripped and tore at the salamander's flesh. Her frenzy filled the great chamber with the hideous slashing and slathering sounds of a dragon feeding.

The cold flesh of the cave beast was revolting to her, especially with so much warm meat so near at hand, but each time she thought of scooping up a handful of gully dwarves and munching on them the way a human might munch on roast chestnuts, the geas in her mind sent spasms of pain through her. She could almost hear the goddess laughing.

She willed herself not to think of the Aghar. What was done was done, for now. She needed food, and she needed sleep, and she could think about what to do next when her immediate needs were met.

She paused and raised her dripping face. A sound had interrupted her. Somewhere behind her, metal rasped on metal. She turned barely in time to dodge a spring-thrown iron skewer that was longer than she was. The big spear thudded into the mangled corpse of the salamander, and Verden looked across the chamber for its source. There, high on the far wall, a tiny, ashen-faced female gully dwarf clung to stone carvings beside a rebounding hinged portal of tarnished silver.

Annoyed, Verden pointed a taloned finger at the little figure. "Stop that! Don't do that again!" she hissed.

For a moment there was total, stunned silence in the great chamber. Then dozens of muted, whispering voices began to babble: "Thing talk!" "Hear that? Thing tell Lidda cut it out." "What kin' thing look like that, an' talk?" "That a dragon, Dink! Hush!" "Dragon? Real dragon? Like Highbulp's dragon?" "No, that was big dragon. This jus' a little dragon." "Look pretty big to me!" "Somebody gonna make dragon go 'way? This no fun at all."

The voices were an irritant to Verden Leafglow, a din to her ears. "All of you shut up!" she demanded. "Quiet!"

In the ensuing silence, she ate some more salamander, then curled up beside the still-immobile Tote and went to sleep.

Even in sleep, though, she was aware of them—gully dwarves everywhere, slipping from hidey-holes, creeping closer to gawk at her in wide-eyed wonder, whispering and pointing, chattering among themselves. A few of them, braver (or stupider) than the rest, even crept near enough to snatch up the immobilized Aghar beside her and whisk him away.

"Where Highbulp go?" one among them whined in an old, wheezy voice that she recognized from a past time, from a past life. "Somebody better fetch Highbulp. He allus braggin' 'bout tamin' dragon. Tell him time for put up or shut up, 'cause we got dragon right here."

Verden twitched her tail and opened one eye, just a slit, remembering.

The Highbulp! This Highbulp couldn't possibly be that same obnoxious, arrogant little twit who had brought her to this fate . . . could it?

Dreams clung about her, and she could almost hear the evil, mocking laughter of a vengeful goddess. And she knew, even in sleep, that it could. The soundless whimper of outrage that formed in her mind was very like the calling resonance that another Verden Leafglow, in another life, had been given to communicate with certain other agents of the Dark Queen.

* * * * * *

Somewhere beyond Xak Tsaroth, beyond the broken lands fronting Newsea, beyond the mountains to the southwest, in a still, dark place, something huge moved. As though startled by a silent sound, Flame Searclaw opened dozing eyes and raised his great, spike-crested head. He turned, this way and that, searching. Green snake? he thought. How can you be alive? I sensed your death. Can it be that I

57

was wrong? Can it be that I may still have the pleasure of killing you, myself?

* * * * *

It took quite a while to find the Highbulp. Despite
his determined laziness and obvious clumsiness,
Glitch the Most could move when he had reason. He
had covered nearly half a mile of subterranean pas-
sageways before he found a suitable place to hide in
the bottom of what might once have been a slops
sump. Eventually, though, they found him. Then
more time was required to pull their leader out of
his hole so he could take charge.

When it was explained to the Highbulp that the
giant salamander was no longer a threat because his
throne had eaten it, he swelled with pride and
started for This Place. But when they added that his
throne was no longer a throne, but had turned into a
twelve-foot-long green dragon, they had to run him
down again and repeat the process of pulling him
from a hidey-hole.

Finally, though, they brought him back to This
Place, and Gandy greeted him at the portal. "Got a
dragon here," the Grand Notioner pointed across
the chamber, where the dragon was still sleeping.
"What Highbulp think we oughtta do?"

Glitch stared at the emerald form across the way,
ready to turn and run again. But the dragon didn't
seem an immediate danger, and he glanced around
at This Place. Gully dwarves were gathered here and
there, huddled in clusters at respectful distances
from the dragon, and most of them were looking at
their leader, waiting for leadership.

A few, though, were wandering around doing various things, and one group nearby was busy bending and unbending Tote. They were flexing his arms and legs, bending his middle, turning his head this way and that, poking fingers at his eyes to make him blink.

Glitch tipped his head and squinted. "What matter with Tote?"

"Him?" Gandy asked. "Got a cramp. All over. Head to toe. Some kin' cramp, huh?"

Glitch wandered over to get a closer look at the flexing of Tote, and Gandy padded after him, others following. "So what we do now, Highbulp?" the Grand Notioner asked again.

"Do? 'Bout what?"

"'Bout dragon! What else?"

Glitch turned and looked again, almost dissolving with sudden panic. For a moment, he had forgotten the dragon. "Dragon!" he gulped. "Run like crazy!" But when he turned to run, there were dozens of his subjects behind him. He bowled them over and went down with them.

Lidda had come down from the wall, and was hovering nearby. Now she shook her head. "Highbulp not good for much," she muttered, wading across tumbling gully dwarves to help her lord to his feet. When he was upright, she faced him and poked him in the chest with a stiff finger. "Got problem here, Highbulp," she explained. "What you gonna do 'bout it?"

Twenty yards away, the green dragon raised its head and looked around, hissing with irritation. "Will you little dolts keep it down? I just hatched, you know! I need some sleep!"

Glitch would have bolted again, but Lidda had him firmly by the ear, pulling him forward. "Dragon awake," she said, urgently. "Highbulp talk to dragon. Make it go 'way!"

"Lidda leggo!" Glitch wailed. "How come you bossin' Highbulp aroun'?"

"'Bout time somebody did," Lidda snapped. "Might make you 'mount to somethin'."

With Lidda leading him by the ear, Gandy prodding him with his mop handle and dozens of his subjects crowding behind him, Glitch the Most, Highbulp of This Place and Dealer with Dragons, reluctantly approached the irate creature. It wasn't as big as the dragon he had met before, only a third that big, but it was the same color, and it was still a lot bigger than he was. And it didn't look at all friendly.

Twenty feet from the creature, the party stopped because Glitch had his heels dug in and would go no farther. The dragon was still looking at him, contemptuously.

"Make dragon go 'way," Gandy urged.

Glitch waved a tentative hand at the thing. "Shoo!" he said softly.

The dragon raised a scaly brow. "What?"

His knees quaking, Glitch tried again. "Dragon shoo!" he chirped. "Go 'way!"

The dragon yawned. "No."

The Highbulp gulped, then tried one more time, a little more firmly. "Shoo, dragon! Scat! Go 'way, okay?"

"No," the dragon said, again.

"Oh, okay." Glitch thought for a moment. "Why not scat, though?"

"Because I belong here," Verden Leafglow said, resignedly.

"Fine," Glitch assured it. "We scat, then." He turned

to his subjects. "Ever 'body pack up! Time for go someplace else!"

"Don't be such an idiot," the dragon hissed. "I am . . ." It was a difficult thing to say, but she had no choice. "I am yours. I belong to you. Don't you understand?"

"Nope," Glitch admitted.

Verden shook her head in frustration. Not only was she delivered into the hands of these obnoxious creatures, but it was up to her to explain it to them. And there was nothing she could do about it. In her mind, a force greater than any power of hers demanded it.

"I am rejected," she said, hissing the words. "I have been given to you, to serve you as . . . as you please." Her eyes closed, her head turned upward and she wailed, "Goddess, release me! I can't stand this!"

But there was no response, no lessening of the curse that was upon her. She lowered her head, looking away. "I am unable to hurt you puny beings, any more than you can hurt me. I belong to . . . oh, gods! *Any* god! Help me!" The only response was an agonizing prod by her geas—the curse the dark goddess had put upon her.

With a shudder, she told the gully dwarves, "I *belong* to you little twits!" For a long moment, she turned away from them in revulsion, then her dragon head turned toward them again, big slitted eyes blazing with fury. "There! I've said it! Now leave me alone! I have to sleep and grow!"

Beyond her, in the big tunnel, another gully dwarf had appeared. Blip had just arrived on the scene. Both his hands were full of bashed rats, carrying them by their tails, and he was making his way past the mutilated remains of the salamander, his eyes wide with wonder.

"Wow," he said, gawking at the corpse. "Took care of that, alright." Then he stepped past it, turned and bumped into the nose of the green dragon just lowering her head to sleep. He froze for an instant, his eyes going huge, then screamed at the top of his lungs, spun around and ran, throwing dead rats everywhere.

"Gods!" Verden Leafglow twitched her tail in disgust, then went back to sleep.

Chapter 6
The Great Stew Bowl

It was a part of the goddess's punishment, Verden knew, that she was growing so fast. Day by day—almost hour by hour, it seemed, she gained in size and strength. In a matter of weeks, she nearly tripled her length. Her mass and physical power were multiplied by hundreds, and she could feel within her the capacity for breathing chlorine clouds, though within the confines of the gully dwarves' realm she was unable to do so.

From the vestigial nubs on her shoulders, great wings grew—wings that stretched almost from wall to wall of the great subterranean chamber when she spread and flexed them. She had attempted to exercise her wings properly, but the results had been disastrous. At first beat, the downdraft had sent every gully dwarf in This Place rolling and tumbling, and her geas had risen to punish her, to remind her painfully: Do not hurt them!

It was all part of the punishment. Until she reached full size and full power, she would not fully appreciate the exquisite humiliation of being powerless against the "least of the least," the Aghar. The goddess had not allowed her even the slight comfort of a lingering development or chanced the passage of time in which the short-lived creatures might have disappeared entirely.

Within the blink of an eye, it seemed, Verden Leafglow became a fully mature, fully-endowed green dragon. Enormous powers rested within her and festered there in the constant torment of powerlessness.

She had died once, before her rebirth. Now, relegated to servitude among the most contemptible of races, she would gladly have died again to escape the awful humiliation of it. Within weeks, she would have welcomed death. But death, like freedom, was denied her.

Throughout her growth, she was ravenous. The provisions for weeks of gully dwarf fare for the entire tribe were less than a single meal for her, and she was forced to hunt for herself, within the confines of Xak Tsaroth. By the time her growing slowed, there wasn't a giant salamander left in the ancient city, nor a fish, squid or giant eel in the submerged levels of it. Even the hairless, blind moles of the outer reaches—ugly creatures the size of cattle— were depleted in number.

At least, the constant, gnawing hunger had subsided a bit. Now, her existence settled into a monotony of misery as bumbling Aghar—now used to her presence—came and went about her, and Aghar children played slide-and-tumble on the scaly slopes of her flanks.

Powerless! The reality of it was a never-ending agony. She was commanded to serve them, but for the life of them, not a one of them had been able to think of anything they wanted her to do. It was as though she had become one with the stones, rubble and trash of This Place, except that they wouldn't leave her alone.

The Highbulp, finally convinced that the dragon posed no threat, had decided that her helplessness was all his doing. Except when he was sleeping or eating, he spent most of his time making life miserable for her. He was forever strutting and preening around her, bragging to anyone who would listen what a glorious Highbulp he was to have his own personal dragon, *again*. And having no throne now, he had taken to sitting on her nose at times.

Verden would happily have torn the little twit into a thousand bloody shreds and plastered the walls of This Place with him . . . if only she could.

But the Dark Queen's curse was total. Verden had no choice but to suffer the indignities, and no hope of ever being free again. Unless . . .

A memory from that other life tugged at her mind. A memory of the goddess's voice saying, "You seek mercy? Seek it from them."

But what Aghar would have mercy in his heart? It seemed hopeless.

For days at a time, she lay inert and immobile, suffering in silence, and many of the gully dwarves simply forgot that she was there. Not all of them, though. Glitch the Most was a constant nuisance to her, old Gandy kept hanging around being inquisitive, and a female called Lady Bruze came now and then to insist arrogantly that the dragon call in some rats for the stew pots.

Verden noticed that there was a real friction between the Lady Bruze and a younger female named Lidda. This one she recognized as the one who had shot the skewer at her.

With nothing much else to do, Verden observed gully dwarves.

They were as dull-minded as she had always thought. They were not exactly stupid, though. Rather, it seemed, they were just incredibly simple. And she began to see distinctive differences among them. Some, like Lidda and old Gandy, showed occasional signs of real intelligence, not always, but now and then, as though their minds held reserves that sometimes came into play for no apparent reason.

Just within the past few days, Verden had seen Lidda dragging a big, shallow bowl of heavy iron across the stone-paved floor, toward her. It had been a lot of work, but the little female finally had the thing in place near the dragon. Lying facedown, it was the shape of a large, shallow bowl. "Here, dragon," Lidda said, panting. "This for you."

"For me?" Verden had blinked at her. "What is that thing for?"

"'Case dragon want some stew," Lidda explained. "This nice, big thing for stew bowl."

It was ridiculous, of course, but it did show a sort of erratic intelligence.

And there were variations in personality. The Lady Bruze, for instance, seemed to enjoy ordering others around and making trouble for those who didn't respond. The Highbulp, on the other hand, seemed to take no special pleasure in exercising power over others. He did enjoy being the center of attention, but beyond that he didn't seem to care much whether any orders he might give were followed.

The Grand Notioner came closer to being concerned about the entire tribe than anyone else, though his concerns usually manifested themselves in subtle (for a gully dwarf) manipulations that made trouble about as often as they did good.

Patterns began to emerge. Even among these, the lowest of the low, there was good, and there was a sort of evil. Given their limits, the good was rarely *very* good, and the evil was nothing more than an occasional cruel streak or a fondness for little chaoses from which one or another might gain status. But there *was* both good and evil, though the great majority among them had very little of either, and even less interest in the difference.

By and large, each individual seemed to be just that—an individual.

Having nothing else to do, nor hope of any higher kind of association, Verden bided her time, studying gully dwarves. And though she—a mighty dragon, the highest order of life on this world—could never have admitted it, she found herself thinking in ways she had never thought before.

Since she was stuck with them, it would be a small matter to rule them, except that the goddess's curse pained her at the very thought of that. On the other hand, though, she could easily direct their lives toward a better way of life, which would be better for her, too.

But what she most wanted was simply to be free of them.

*   *   *   *   *

The Highbulp was becoming a bloody nuisance again. For a time, he had been the center of attention, and had loved every minute of it. But there came a time when even the sight of their Lord Protector sitting on the nose of a huge green dragon and preening himself became familiar to the combined clans of Bulp, and their attentions drifted elsewhere.

Realizing that the newness had worn off, Glitch the Most pouted for a while, then pondered the situation. And as usual when he pondered, he fell asleep.

He had been there for some time, snoring loudly between the eyes and the nostrils of Verden Leafglow, when Gandy wandered by, leaning on his mop handle. The Grand Notioner glanced at the Highbulp and the dragon, then glanced again. Glitch looked normal enough, curled up like a chubby child while echoing snores rumbled from his open mouth, but there was something about the dragon . . . Gandy stepped closer, and peered into a large, fierce eye, frowning in concern as though he saw tears there.

"Dragon got trouble?" he asked, curious.

"You might say that, yes," Verden Leafglow admitted. As she spoke, the Highbulp on her snout jiggled happily in his sleep.

"What kin' trouble?"

"This kind!" She narrowed her eyes, indicating Glitch. "This little oaf is driving me out of my mind!"

"Yep," Gandy said and nodded sympathetically.

"Highbulp can do that, alright. How come dragon put up with him?"

"I can't do anything else," she said. "Remember, I told you. I am under a curse."

"Oh, yeah," Gandy remembered. "That right. Dragon goosy."

"Not goosy!" she sighed. "I have a geas upon me."

"Got Highbulp 'pon you right now," Gandy observed. "Bein' nuisance, like usual. I got idea 'bout fix that."

Verden's nearer eyelid rose slightly. "Oh?"

"Sure," Gandy nodded. He stepped up on the edge of the iron stew bowl for a better view over Glitch. "Highbulp got too much time for foolin' 'roun'. Needs a wife, keep him in line."

"Oh," Verden sighed, disappointed. She had been hoping the old gully dwarf might—unlikely as it was—have an idea that would benefit her.

Suddenly, though, the Grand Notioner straightened and seemed to freeze in place. From the bowl where he stood, a rosy glow seemed to float upward, shrouding him with an eerie red radiance. He glowed, as though a lamp burned inside him, and his stance, his demeanor, his entire being seemed subtly changed.

Bathed in the soft, red glow, he seemed to radiate a power that no gully dwarf had ever had, or even imagined. He shifted and gazed up at her with a look she had never seen on an Aghar face—a bright-eyed, shrewd, almost compassionate expression that had real intelligence behind it. Abruptly, then, his eyes closed as though in sleep and the strange, reddish glow pulsed and danced around him.

His eyes remained closed, and the voice that came from him was not like the voice of any gully dwarf.

"You might do well to give thought to that idea, Verden Leafglow," it said.

She stared at the little creature, startled. "What did you say?"

"You heard me very well," he, or something within him, said. "You do want to escape your fate, don't you?"

"Of course I do. But how?"

"Nothing is ever hopeless, Verden Leafglow, so long as one is alive, even one who lives for a second time. The curse of a god is absolute, but even a geas might be . . . revised."

Chapter 7
The Prophecy

It was incredible. Verden felt suddenly dizzy, as though powers far greater than her own had entered her mind. Was this some more of Takhisis's cruelty? Did the dark goddess have further tricks to play upon her even more cruel than the one that she had played?

Yet she sensed no evil here. The "feel" of the strangeness that spoke to her was neither good nor evil, as she understood these qualities. Instead it was almost indifferent, except for a factor that was lacking in both absolute good and absolute evil. It cared! It cared for them, the little creatures to whom she was bound and it cared for her as well.

The sheer, sensed power of the emanation left her dazed. What kind of power, on this or any world, could it be except one of the gods? The dark goddess had disowned her. So who, then? Her eyes traveled upward, to the designs on the far wall—ancient designs surrounding nine metallic shields—nine counting the one under the glowing Grand Notioner's feet. Nine shields, of nine metals, representing the nine gods. She closed her eyes in confusion, then looked again at the glowing being before her.

"Revised?" she hissed. "A curse? Revised? By *gully dwarves?*"

"Of course not," the red glow said, amused. "The Aghar are as helpless to change a god's will as any mortal thing. But you above all, you with your skills at subterfuge and deceit, should know that even what cannot be changed can be viewed from many perspectives." The glow raised the Grand Notioner's arm to point at the inscripted wall with his mop handle. "A thrown spear, seen by its target, is only a dot, until it strikes. But seen from aside, it is a fleeting shaft that passes by and has no effect upon the viewer."

"This is no spear I bear within me," Verden pointed out. "It is a god's curse."

"The principle is the same," the voice said through Gandy's lips. "Like a spear, a curse is harmful only to the one standing where it strikes."

On Verden's snout, the Highbulp's snores became a snort and he rolled over, not waking up. "What does all that have to do with this wart on my nose?" Verden demanded. Glaring at the sleeping Glitch made her a bit cross-eyed.

"The dark way has failed on Krynn." The glowing

gully dwarf stood as though in a trance, and the strange voice from his lips sounded distant. "But chaos left chaos in its wake. Much remains to be resolved, and many weights must be shifted before a balance is restored. Small weights as well as big ones."

There was a pause, then the voice continued, more distant now as though its speaker had turned away. "From the least of the least," it said, "a hero shall arise, the first of his kind, at just such time as he is needed." For a moment there was silence again. Then the odd voice went on. "You have a role to play here, Verden Leafglow, and you will play it. But *how* you play it is vital to you."

"What does that mean?"

"To avoid the spear's thrust, the target must choose to step aside. No one else except the target can make that choice."

The eerie voice faded, and the reddish glow dimmed and was gone. Old Gandy sagged, leaning on his mop handle, and wavered on the "stew bowl's" edge as though he might fall.

"What choice?" Verden demanded.

The Grand Notioner's eyes popped open. He blinked and steadied himself. "What *what?*"

"What you were saying! What does it mean?"

"Oh." Gandy looked confused. "'Bout Highbulp need wife? Mean he oughtta get married. Wife might keep him busy. Keep him outta ever'body's hair."

He shrugged, turned and his foot slipped off the iron rim. He sat down hard on the edge of the bowl and it flipped up and turned over, covering him. There were panicked taps from inside, and Verden Leafglow shook her head, accidentally dislodging the snoring Highbulp. Glitch bounced on the stone beneath the dragon's head, let out a yelp, then rolled over and went back to sleep. Verden extended a talon to raise the bowl so that Gandy could crawl out.

The Grand Notioner muttered something unintelligible, dusted himself off and hobbled away. Verden glanced at the upside-down bowl, then stared at it. Her eyes went again to the sculpted wall across the chamber. The plaques on the murder holes were of various metals, each ornately decorated in the ancient Ergothian style in which a pattern could be seen in many ways, apparently all different, but all signifying the same concept.

The shields still in place on the wall depicted six of the nine deities the human monks of Tare had called the "Fundament Triad." The gods. Solinari was there, flanked by Majere and Paladine. Then Sargonnas, then three open holes, then Lunitari and Gilean. The two inverted shields, hanging below their openings, by their places in the circle she took to be Nuitari and Takhisis. They hung on their hinges, blank ovals with upside-down faces unseen, turned toward the wall. Those, and one hole with no shield.

Again she looked at the "stew bowl" beside her, and recognized it. It was the missing plaque—an oval shield of iron, with an intricate symbol worked into the metal. The symbol of the missing god.

"Reorx," she whispered, and the iron oval rang softly as though echoing the name.

Glitch the Most awakened abruptly, sat up and yawned mightily. "Time for Highbulp's breakfast, dragon," he said, glancing up at her. "You got stew?"

"Shut up!" Verden snapped. "Listen!"

He listened, then shook his head. "Don' hear a thing," he said.

But Verden heard something. In her mind now, and near at hand, was another voice, the taunting rasp of Flame Searclaw.

I have found you, green snake, the red dragon's mind purred viciously. *And I see you are still dawdling with those pathetic creatures. Shall I kill you first, green snake? Or might it be amusing to let you watch me fry your little friends before you die? It doesn't matter to me, green snake. I have found you, at last.*

Somewhere within Xak Tsaroth, somewhere not very far away, there was a roar of sound like a hundred dwarven forges, their bellows going full or like flames from a blast furnace whipping through stone corridors.

The Highbulp shrieked, bumped his head on Verden's chin and scrambled up her face, heading for shelter beyond her. He shrieked again and clung to her rising crest as she flexed massive sinews and stood, spreading her wings.

All of the frustration, the pent-up anger and humiliation within her rose to a crescendo in savage joy as green eyes glittered and slitted. She hissed a battle cry. She had been powerless, powerless to deal with the dim beings around her. But nothing in the curse upon her made her powerless against Flame Searclaw.

An intense joy like waves of wondrous heat flooded over her, and she picked up the Reorx shield and pressed it to her breast, only vaguely aware that she had picked up another gully dwarf with it. That one clung to her glittering scales and climbed, agile as a tree lizard, up her shoulder and along her neck, toward the clinging, burbling Highbulp.

Verden Leafglow pressed the iron shield to her breast, and it clung there, seeming to bond itself to her scales. It rested between massive emerald shoulders like a rust-red iron medallion on a field of green.

I asked for the help of a god, she thought. Reorx, I welcome your presence.

Verden Leafglow didn't wait for Flame Searclaw to come to her. With a mighty beat of spread wings, she rose and went to meet him.

A gaggle of fleeing, babbling gully dwarves, their shirttails smoldering, issued from the main corridor just as she reached it. With a chorus of shrieks, they hit the floor and skidded aside as the green dragon passed over them, inches above, and arrowed into the tunnel winding upward and away.

Stone surfaces shot past as Verden threw herself into the winding corridor, her swept-back wings whispering against the dark walls at each side, arms folded close and legs trailing alongside her whipping tail.

Atop her head, just at the rise of her great crest, two Aghar clung in wild-eyed desperation, bouncing this way and that as their fingers clenched her crest for dear life. Just past the first turn, the Highbulp almost lost his grasp until Lidda bit him on the ear to make him pay attention.

Another bend, and Flame Searclaw was there, huge and ruby red in the dimness, flames trickling from between his swordlike fangs. Nearly twice the size of the green dragon, he seemed to fill the tunnel. At sight of Verden he opened his mouth wider, readying another blast of fire when she slowed to meet him.

But Verden didn't slow. Instead she lashed her tail, put on a new burst of speed and, at the last instant, did a barrel roll in the tunnel to shoot directly under the surprised red, upside-down, raking him viciously with razor talons. Deep gashes appeared on his soft underbelly as she passed beneath him. The red roared and spat flames, but they had no target. Smaller, faster and more agile than the great red dragon, Verden Leafglow was now behind him, righting herself and coming around to attack.

Chapter 8
An Act of Mercy

Verden's thunderous departure from This Place had created a havoc of noise and confusion. Little vortices of wind howled and danced about the great chamber, flinging things here and there, flattening stew fires and raising a thick haze of dust. Clout, Blip and the others who had just entered, their backsides blistered and clothing charred, raised themselves and looked around in confusion. Something very large had passed above them, and now they couldn't see a thing for all of the dust.

Around them, querulous voices blended: "Wha'

happen?" "Where dragon go?" "Where th' Highbulp?" "Who ate my stew?"

"Ever'body hush!" Clout shouted. "Big, red dragon chase us in tunnel. Make fire on us! Where Highbulp?"

"Who?"

"What's-'is-name . . . th' Highbulp. Glitch! Where Glitch?"

"Who cares?" a voice whined. "Where my stew?"

A dim figure appeared in the haze, leaning on a mop handle. "Where Clout?"

"Right here. What Gandy want?"

"Clout say 'red' dragon. Where?"

"In big tunnel," Clout repeated. "Big, red dragon. Fire dragon."

"Gettin' be way too many dragons roun' here," Blip added firmly. "Highbulp oughtta do somethin'."

The roars of battle came then, echoing down the main corridor to shake the walls of This Place.

With no Highbulp in sight, Gandy took it upon himself to issue the emergency order. "Run like crazy!" he shouted.

Blinded by dust, gully dwarves ran everywhere—mostly into one another—and as the dust began to settle there were piles and tumbles of Aghar all over This Place.

* * * * *

Flame Searclaw was huge, far more massive than Verden Leafglow, and a ruthless and cunning fighter. The instant he realized that the green was behind him, he spread his wings, braked himself and lashed out with his great tail. Verden was just turning to attack, and the tail caught her off-balance. It thudded into her left shoulder below the wing, and her arm went numb. The second blow missed, but she had lost the advantage. She righted herself and saw Flame turning, clawing his way around in the corridor to face her.

Something tugged at her crest, and small feet kicked wildly in front of her right eye. "Get out of my way!" she shouted, shaking her head. High on her neck, Lidda clung and reached to pull the Highbulp up, away from the dragon's face. "Glitch get outta way!" she ordered. "Dragon busy!"

Almost blind with fright, Glitch accepted the tug and climbed up beside her. "Yes, dear," he panted.

Verden tried to press her attack on Flame, but now he was facing her, and the mockery in his voice was brutal. "You are soft, green snake," he chided. "And you have riders! Appropriate masters for one like you—gully dwarves!" With an evil chuckle, he opened his mouth and blinding fire shot out. On impulse, and out of spite, he aimed it high, directly at Verden's crest and the pair of Aghar clinging there.

Verden saw it coming, and her geas prodded her: they must not be hurt. She must protect them. At the last instant she stretched upward, drawing back her head, exposing her breast to the driving, killing flame. Reorx, she thought, I denounce evil. The dark ways are no longer my allegiance.

The fire struck, a roaring mass of white-hot blaze that crescendoed and mushroomed, filling the corridor. Verden was flung backward by the force of it, stunned and disoriented. She crashed against a wall, staggered for a moment, then straightened herself. Somehow, it seemed that she was unhurt. She looked down and realized that the iron shield on her breast had deflected the fire, turned it aside and thrown it back. The oval felt as cool as it had before, but now its surface was no longer rusted and stained. As though the ages had been burned away, it gleamed now, a mighty shield of polished iron.

Atop her, clinging to the dragoncrest, Lidda chirped, "What Highbulp say?"

"Wh-what?" Glitch stammered.

"Glitch say, 'yes. dear,' " Lidda reminded him.

"Did not."

"Did, too! Glitch wanna get marry?"

"Nope."

"Don' argue, Glitch!"

"Yes, dear."

"Reorx," Verden whispered, new understandings flooding her mind. In that instant of fire, she had rejected the Dark Queen who had punished her. More, she had accepted another god, a god of an entirely different color. Yards away, Flame Searclaw was shaking his head, trying to clear his vision. His reflected fire had nearly blinded him. Verden's long neck swayed, timing his movements, mimicking him, and her great haunches gathered beneath her, rippling with power. Flame swayed, searching blindly, then raised his head higher, and Verden launched herself at him. Low and fast, she went in for the kill. Even as the red's head rose, she plunged in under it, fangs and talons seeking his throat.

It was over in a moment. Great jaws closed on the underside of Flame's neck, the vulnerable area just above his shoulders, and a taloned claw closed a foot above. Fangs pierced scales, talons buried themselves in flesh, and the green dragon wrenched at the writhing neck, tearing it open. Dark blood sprayed and pulsed, and Flame Searclaw choked on his own scream. Bucking and thrashing, he tried to pull away, but Verden clung grimly, shaking him as a dog shakes a snake, ripping his throat wider and wider.

Thrashing red wings created raging storms in the confines of the corridor, then subsided to erratic twitching and went still. Verden drew back and studied the huge corpse sprawled in the dimness of ancient stone arches. "Reorx," she whispered. "I have stepped aside from the spear. Am I free?"

The iron shield at her breast throbbed. *It is for them to say*, something told her. *Ask mercy of them.*

She was aware again of the two gully dwarves, still clinging to her crest. She lowered her head. "Release me," she said.

For a moment, Glitch clung desperately, then he realized that the commotion was over. "Okay," he said. Releasing his grip, he clambered down to the floor and stood, trying to remember at least some of what he had just seen. He wasn't at all sure, but it seemed to him that he had just done battle with a red dragon and won! He began to swell with pride, and by the time he reached the dead dragon he was strutting and grinning. Lidda came after him, and took him by the hand.

"That all settle, then," she said. "We get marry right away."

He glanced around at her, puzzled. "We do what?"

"Never mind," she said, firmly. "It all settled."

"Highbulp kill a dragon!" he chortled, pointing at Flame Searclaw's dulling corpse. "Glorious Glitch th' Most, Highbulp an' . . . an' dragon-basher! Get ever'body, come see dragon Highbulp kill!"

He started to climb the corpse, so he could stand

atop it and be admired, but Lidda pulled him back. "Highbulp gonna let other dragon go?"

"Already did!" he reminded her. "Turned loose, got off an' . . ." he looked around at Verden, frowning. "Jus' as soon dragon get lost while Highbulp show off dead dragon," he said. "Don' need you here! Shoo! Go 'way! Come back later!"

"Glitch don' need dragon anymore," Lidda persisted. "Glitch great dragon-basher. Don' need dragon for keep aroun'."

"Nope," he admitted. "Jus' get in way, prob'ly."

Lidda gazed at Verden for a moment, something like true understanding shining in her eyes. Then she elbowed Glitch in the ribs. "Go 'head, then," she demanded. "Highbulp say, 'dragon is release.' "

"Okay," Glitch said. "Dragon is release! Don' need dragon anymore! Go 'way!" He waved an imperious hand. "Shoo!"

Verden's eyes widened. Within her, something fell away and she was unbound. The geas was broken. She was free! Free to do as she pleased. Free even to kill these miserable creatures if she chose! Still, Lidda had given her back her life. The little female gully dwarf—least of the least—had done an act of mercy!

Verden Leafglow turned away. Up the corridor, and beyond other connecting corridors, beyond the buried city of Xak Tsaroth, beyond the Pitt, spread a whole world that she had never seen in this life. It was out there, waiting for her.

Something clattered at her feet, and she looked down. The Shield of Reorx had fallen from her breast. With gentle talons, she picked it up and half-turned, holding it out to the gully dwarves. "Keep this," the green dragon said. "When you have children, give it to them."

She didn't look back again. Somehow, the sight of the Highbulp standing atop a slain dragon, looking smug and arrogant and actually believing that he, personally, had killed the great beast, was a little more than Verden Leafglow really wanted to deal with.

But in her mind as she crept around the upward bend, a silent voice like the voice of iron whispered. *The spear seen from aside passes by. But it is still a spear, Verden Leafglow. One day you will see my shield again. A gully dwarf—the unlikeliest of heroes—will bear it. In that time you will see a sign. When you do, you might choose to settle some old debts.*

Vengeance? Verden wondered.

Balance, the iron voice corrected. *From chaos, order may arise. But first there must be balance.*

PART 2

The Vale of Sunder

Chapter 9
The Wonder Of Spiration

"Before yesterday, somebody make all places," Scrib mused aloud, not really caring whether anybody was listening or not. "Rocks an' dribbles, leafs an' hills, mud an' holes . . . Somebody make all this stuff be. Even make sky, prob'ly. Somebody say, 'be sky,' an' sure 'nough, there sky is."

Around him his students shuffled their feet and one snapped, "So what? Who needs sky?"

"Gotta have sky," Scrib explained, straining at the concept. "All places under sky. 'Thout sky, no place for places be under."

Impressed with his own logic, Scrib squinted fiercely and wished that somebody might somehow remember what he had just said, so that somebody could repeat it back to him later. He knew he wasn't likely to stumble upon that bit of exquisite wisdom again.

As usual when he felt the need to teach, Scrib stood on a high place with his students gathered around him. Today's high place was a half-buried boulder in a marshy clearing, near the old Tall ruins that the tribe was occupying at the moment. The boulder was a good choice. A previous gathering, just the day before, had been dismissed early when it turned out that Scrib's rostrum was an active anthill.

The "students," as usual, were a dozen or so other gully dwarves who were here because they had nothing better to do at the moment.

Now one of them—a muscular young Aghar named Bron, who was usually in charge of the legendary Great Stew Bowl and, Scrib recalled vaguely, was related to somebody important—raised a tentative hand. "All that happen before yesterday?"

"Yep," Scrib said with a nod. "Sky, places, everything, all made before yesterday."

"How long before yesterday?"

Scrib screwed up his straggly-bearded face in thought. "Long time," he decided. "Yesterday before yesterday. Long time ago."

"What was long time ago?" a curly-bearded citizen named Pook asked.

"Long time ago somebody make everything," Scrib repeated patiently. He had noticed that some people's attention spans were shorter than others.

"Who did?" Pook wondered.

"Somebody," Scrib emphasized.

"Somebody do all that?" Bron pursued, skeptically. "Make everything? Places, sky, turtles? Even us?"

"Yep. Somebody."

Bron was on a roll now. "Make things, too? Like rats an' trees an' stew pots? An' . . . an' mushrooms an' bashin' tools . . . an' dragons an' bugs?"

"Yep," Scrib assured him. "Make ever'thing, make ever'body."

"Why?"

"Dunno," Scrib admitted. Of all the questions he sometimes heard, that was the toughest one. "Don' make much sense, does it?"

"Somebody pretty dumb, do all that for no reason," another student pointed out. This one was a young female named Pert, one of his regulars. Students came and went, and Scrib never knew who or how many might show up when he began a talk-and-tell. Participation in a talk-and-tell group required thought, and thinking was not high on most Aghars' lists of things to do.

But Bron and Pert, and a varying gaggle of others, were there more often than not, and Scrib sometimes felt gratified at their interest. Being a philosopher, probably the only philosopher the tribe of Bulp had ever had, unless one counted the Grand Notioner, was a tough job no matter how you mashed it. But being a philosopher alone would have been worse.

He didn't think of himself as a philosopher, of course. Being only a gully dwarf, he wouldn't have known what such a word meant, or even how to pronounce it. But he was obviously different from most of those around him. All his life, it seemed, he had been mystified by the things that others seemed to take for granted—like why is fire hot, and how come you fall down if you lift both feet at the same time, and what makes salted slugs become grumpy.

Then, one day, during the tribe's migration from That Place, which had been This Place until they left it, to the present This Place, which they hadn't found yet, they were filing across an ancient rope-bound bridge that spanned a wide chasm. The bottom of the chasm was full of ruined, abandoned buildings. Talls had lived in them once, but they were gone now.

They hadn't meant to stop. Once they were on the move, it was the way of all Aghar to not stop until the Highbulp said "stop," and the Highbulp was asleep at the time. Several sturdy gully dwarves had tied a rope around him, run a pole through the rope, and were thus carrying him while he slept.

But just below the dilapidated bridge was the crumbling shell of a large building with a daggerlike gold spire that still stood, its point only a few feet below the bridge.

Scrib had leaned over the side for a better look. The next thing he knew, he was dangling from the peak of the gold spire, which had pierced his flapping turkey-skin cloak when he fell.

It took them most of a day to rescue Scrib, and the Highbulp griped at him when he woke up. But in the process of un-skewering Scrib, they had explored the old village and found a lot of good tunnels and seeps, and a plentiful population of vermin. The Highbulp walked around, peering here and there while old Gandy trailed after him, and decided that this place was as good a This Place as anyplace else might be.

It had turned out, in fact, to be an excellent This Place. There were holes to scurry into, and water no worse than anyplace else they had been, and for the foragers there were nearby fields and caves where green things, yellow things and mushrooms could be found. The only serious drawbacks were frequent lightning storms, an occasional thundering herd of Talls crossing the bridge, and a one-eyed ogre who lived somewhere nearby and was thus a blight on the neighborhood.

All things considered, though, this place was a pretty good This Place, and it was Scrib's inadvertence that had led them to find it.

From that day, Scrib had been a changed gully dwarf. Life is like a bridge, he felt. Those who cross it without stopping to look wind up living somewhere else. He wasn't at all sure what that meant, but it sounded very wise. And where an idea that good and that persistent dwelt, there might be a clue as to how ideas can be leashed.

It was up to him, he decided, to expose his people to the wonders around them, and maybe to show some others how to do the same thing so he could take a nap now and then. Thus it was Scrib who, to the best of his ability, was leading the tribe of Bulp toward the light of reason.

Scrib had been spired.

"Somebody make everything," he continued now, ignoring Pert's low opinion of the grand maker. "Bound to be a reason. Somebody got somethin' in mind. Somebody make us, too, so must be a reason for us. Maybe that somebody our leader."

"Highbulp our leader," Bron pointed out.

"Highbulp really dumb," Pert said. "Nuisance most times, an' other times he snores. Highbulp nothin' but a worthless twit."

"Yep," Bron agreed cheerfully, "that Glitch alright.

Glitch th' Most. Glitch Dragonbasher, my dear ol' Dad. Pretty good leader."

"Only when Lady Lidda runnin' things," Pert snapped.

Unperturbed, Scrib spread his hands, holding them before him about three inches apart. "Highbulp great leader like this," he explained. "But Highbulp never make anything 'cept noise an' messes. Maybe *somebody* leader like this." He spread his hands to arm's length. "*Big* leader, maybe."

One of the students shook his head. "If we got leader that big, how come I never notice him aroun'?"

"You got me, there," Scrib admitted. The strain of thinking was beginning to wear him down. He decided they had accomplished enough for today. "That about it," he said. "Any questions?"

"Yeah," said Pook, raising his hand. "When we gonna eat?"

At that moment an alarmed voice somewhere near shouted, "Incomin'! Run like crazy!"

Scrib bounded from his boulder and headed for shelter with his assembly at his heels. In a moment the clearing was deserted except for a little cloud of dust and three gully dwarves—one whom had tripped on a root and two others who had tripped over him. They righted themselves and scrambled for safety.

From a hole in a clay bank, Bron peeped out. From the canyon walls above the ruined town came a low, rolling thunder, then Talls on horses appeared—a solid mass of armored humans astride great beasts, charging down on the rickety old bridge. There were dozens of them.

Just behind Bron, Pert crawled forward, trying to see for herself what was going on. But she was blocked from the entrance by his stocky shoulders. "Talls again?" she asked. Bron nodded, a gesture that was lost on her because she couldn't see his head. She found a stiff twig and poked him in the ribs with it. "Talls again?" she repeated.

"Yeah, Talls," he grunted. "Same as usual."

"How many?" Pert demanded.

"Two," he said. "Quit that!"

The armored charge across the old bridge was a drumroll of harsh sound, echoing down the canyon. But it didn't last long. Within moments the humans and their horses had passed, and were gone beyond the south rim. By ones, threes and fives, gully dwarves crept from hiding all along the canyon's floor, and went back to what they had been doing.

The occasional charge of mounted, armored men across the bridge above them had become an accepted occurrence in This Place. Nobody had any idea of who these Talls were, or why they kept galloping over This Place, but it had become just another mystery in a world full of mysteries. When it happened, everybody panicked instantly and dived for cover. But when it was over they stopped worrying about it.

Out of sight, out of mind—it was the way of gully dwarves.

It was something that Scrib had pondered on occasion, though. He accepted that armed hordes of formidable creatures might go thundering by above him now and then. But when it began happening every day or so, he couldn't help but wonder. And now he had an inspiration: maybe someone should go and see who those people were and what they were doing. Squaring his shoulders with determination, Scrib went in search of Gandy. Maybe the

Grand Notioner would have a notion about how to solve this mystery.

His trek up the canyon was interrupted almost before it began. The third building on the row facing the little stream still had a roof of sorts, and Glitch the Most, great Highbulp and Lord Protector of everybody who mattered, had made it his headquarters. Usually, that just meant that he slept there. But now the building was the scene of bustling activity.

Someone, it seemed, had found a crack in the rear foundation, and squeezed through looking for rats. Instead of rats, though, the explorer had found an old runnel, barely a foot wide, which led deep into the mountainside and emerged somewhere beyond at the bottom of a sinkhole.

It was a great discovery, and not to be ignored. Now at least half the tribe was gathered around, and there was some serious mining going on in there. Gully dwarves trooped in and out of the building, carrying out loads of broken stone and delved clay, while others within delved the fissure, widening it so that the pudgy Highbulp could get through to see what was beyond.

While supervising the project, Glitch the Most had gone to sleep and now lay curled up and snoring, right in the old doorway. The lines of miners going in and out bobbled there as each miner either jumped over their glorious leader or simply climbed him and stepped down on the other side.

But just as Scrib passed, Glitch turned over in his sleep. Two or three miners in transit tumbled through the portal and bumped into those immediately beyond. These in turn collided with others around them, and a moment later Scrib lay facedown in front of the house with a large number of gully dwarves piled on top of him.

"Rats," he muttered, finally getting to his feet after the pileup was cleared. He had been on his way to see the Grand Notioner, but for the life of him he couldn't remember what he wanted to see him about. So, having nothing better to do, he followed his nose into headquarters. Stew was being prepared, stew so fresh that some of its contents were still squirming.

Someone working in the tunnel had discovered a vein of pyrite, and the miners now were veering off into a new shaft in pursuit of shiny rocks. In honor of the occasion, the Lady Lidda had ordered the legendary Great Stew Bowl brought out.

The Great Stew Bowl was rarely used, because it was more than two feet wide, and made of solid iron. Just moving it from place to place required two or three ordinary Aghar, though a few among them—notably Bron—could carry the thing rather easily. For that reason, Bron was usually in charge of the Great Stew Bowl, and the reason Bron was as strong as he was may have been that he routinely carried the Great Stew Bowl when the tribe migrated from one This Place to another This Place.

But the discovery of pyrite was a special occasion, and the big, shallow bowl had been wrestled to a cook fire, where it brimmed now with bubbling, squirming delicacies.

It was two days later, when another thundering horde of humans rattled across the old bridge, that Scrib remembered his idea. Someone should go and find out what that was all about. Again he went in search of the Grand Notioner.

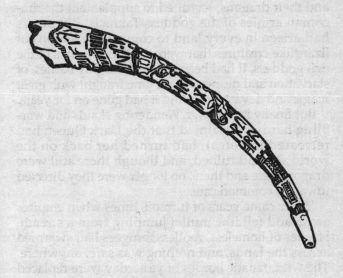

Chapter 10
The Fang of Orm

The Thousand Years War, so called because a former ruler of Gelnians—King Systole—had vowed that his people would fight for a thousand years rather than submit to the rule of the Grand Megak of Tarmish, was in its ninth year when the War of the Lance superseded it.

Dragons had ruled the skies through those dark times, and great armies had swept through every land—armies of humans, armies of elves, armies of dwarves and armies that were difficult to classify. Some in each land were followers of the Highlords and their dragons, recruited to supplement the draconian armies of the goddess Takhisis. But others had arisen in every land to combat the legions of lizardlike creatures that were the shock troops of the evil goddess. It had been a time of mighty battles, of starvation and desperation, a time fraught with great magic and devastation. And it had gone on for years.

But finally it was over. Wandering skalds and warbling bards proclaimed that the Dark Queen had retreated in defeat, had turned her back on the world she had ruined, and though there still were dragons here and there, no longer were they directed toward a common cause.

There came years of turmoil, times when empires arose and fell like mullet jumping from a stream. Hordes of homeless, rootless refugees had swarmed across the lands, and nothing was safe, anywhere. The wild, fanatic hordes of yesterday were replaced by a new breed of adventurers—mercenary warriors at the bidding of any who could afford their wages.

Organized insanity across a ravaged world replaced the random insanity of the turmoil. Now the war was a different kind of war. Both Tarmish and Gelnia had new rulers, and these were people unlike the kings and megaks of old. Somehow, during the chaos following the War of the Lance, both dominions had been infiltrated and claimed by outsiders. In both realms the old dynasties still were evident, but now they were no more than puppets.

Dominated now by a mysterious figure known as Lord Vulpin, the Tarmites had resurrected their threadbare Grand Megak from a foul cellar somewhere and put him back on his throne at Tarmish. The Gelnians, too, had a different ruler. Chatara Kral, a woman of mysterious background who had come with a private army of mercenary soldiers, named herself as regent over Gelnia. One thing remained as it had been, though. Tarmish and Gelnia, under whatever rule, refused to tolerate the existence of the other. The Vale of Sunder was back to business as usual: all-out war.

The origins of the disagreement between the city-state of Tarmish and the land surrounding it were lost in antiquity, but not the passions of it. Few wanderers through this land could tell a Tarmite from a Gelnian. They were the same kind of humans, cut from the same cloth. They spoke the same idioms, worshipped by the same rituals and claimed the same ancient ancestry, though each denied that the other had any such claim. Many were, indeed, related to one another by blood and marriage. Yet they were the bitterest of enemies.

Gelnian and Tarmite, neither would tolerate the other. And, as always, the flames of hatred were fanned by those who stood to gain. Always, in every land, there were those to whom conflict was the path to power and riches. Behind the tottering Grand Megak of Tarmish, like a towering dark shadow, stood Lord Vulpin, his hand in every intrigue, his thumb on every pulse, dreams of empire swirling in his cunning mind. And among the Gelnians, it was Chatara Kral who guided destinies now, as ward-regent to the infant Prince Quarls.

The origins of Vulpin and Chatara Kral were obscure. There were whispers in surrounding lands that the two were in fact brother and sister—the spawn of the evil Lord Verminaard, a Dragon Highlord of the recent War of the Lance. But in their own domains, nobody knew or dared to question where either of them came from or why they were here. It was enough, for most, that they spoke to the ancient hatreds of the region.

Now they faced off for control of all of Sunder. Vulpin stood in his tower overlooking the fortress of Tarmish, Chatara Kral amassed armies of Gelnians and mercenaries in the hills around. For months the Vale had seemed to hold its breath, awaiting the clash.

It was a standoff, a time of waiting. But Vulpin had made use of the time. Useful artifacts remained from the mighty war, and he had sent agents in search of such things. Even now, one such relic was on its way to him . . . if one called Clonogh could spirit it through the Gelnian blockade.

Among the secret documents of Krynn was a collection of scrolls, some very ancient, concerning a relic sometimes called Viperis, sometimes Wishmaker, and most often the Fang of Orm.

The scrolls once rested in the tombs of Istar, but somehow survived the Cataclysm and found their way to Neraka, and thence to Palanthas. Their last known resting place, prior to the War of the Lance, was the stone vault of the wizard Karathis, who sought immortality through the vesting of arcane powers upon the ambitious in exchange for portions of their lives.

The scrolls disappeared when Karathis was murdered by one of his customers, but their contents were known to the wizard's acolytes. They told of the Fang of Orm.

They say the fang grants wishes, but only for the truly innocent. And in granting wishes, the fang brings doom to its holder.

They say the Fang of Orm is not dead, but only asleep, and there remains a bond between the fang and its original possessor. When awakened, the relic still sends its ancient signal, and on some inconceivable plane of reality the creature from which it was torn still seeks it.

* * * * *

The man called Graywing crept silently from boulder to cleft, approaching the naked granite sheer that was the top of a shattered ridge. His senses were pitched to the windy crest, his eyes missing nothing as he moved, his ears sorting out the whispers of wandering wind and the calls of hunting birds soaring high above, his nostrils searching for any slightest scent that might betray enemy presence.

Such scrutiny was nothing new to Graywing. For most of his life, it seemed, daily survival had depended upon knowing who or what was near, before who or what discovered him. Descendant of Cobar plainsmen, he had come of age fighting Empiremen on the plains east of the Kharolis, then followed Falcon Whitefeather and the elf Pirouenne in their assault on Fe-Tateen.

Partly through his skill in guerilla combat, but mostly, he felt, through sheer luck, Graywing had become a captain of assault forces with the Palanthan Armies at Throt-Akaan.

Then that war, which settled many disputes in the northern greatlands, had ended. And now Graywing, like thousands of others whose entire experience was in battle, found himself hiring out as a lone mercenary. Hundreds of little wars had sprung up in the shambles of the great conflict, and there was plenty of employment. Men he had known for years now met on a hundred fields of battle, trying to kill one another for the wages paid by petty realms.

At least, he thought, I still can choose my jobs.

Somehow, the idea of doing battle for wages had never appealed to him. So he lived these days, as now, hiring out as guide and bodyguard for travelers.

At the crest of the ridge he crept to the lip of a stone outcrop and looked beyond. A wide, fertile valley lay before him, a valley that should be lush with ripening fields and rich orchards. Instead, as far as he could see along the lower slopes there were wisps of smoke—smoke from hundreds of separate campfires where little groups of armed men sat idle, waiting for orders. Beyond, in the distance, a squat fortress stood on a hill, and above it, too, hung the smoke of waiting.

Graywing's thick, corn silk beard twitched as his lip curled in a sneer. Blood would flow in this valley soon, and most of it would be the blood of fighters not personally involved in whatever conflict was growing here. Those who would bleed and die were mostly just men like himself, veterans with no skill but arms and no trade but war, men who would die for a few coins.

For long moments he studied the scene, practiced eyes seeking a route through the cordon of warriors. Then he backed out of sight, turned and looked to his own back trail. Again a sneer of distaste curled his lip. His employer was part of all this, of course. Clonogh was some sort of courier, he gathered. His destination was that fortress out there, and Graywing's job was to take him, and whatever secret thing he carried, there safely.

He didn't want to know any more than that about it, but he would be glad when it was done. Something about the courier made Graywing feel a little clammy. Whether it was the man's furtive manner—like a ferret slinking toward its prey, never straight forward but always at a deceptive angle—or possibly in the way the man's face seemed always hidden by the cowl of his dark cloak, or possibly the edgy, nervous way he guarded that leather pouch slung to his shoulder, Graywing didn't know.

It was as though Clonogh were a relic of another time—a lost, insane age when mages were everywhere and sorcery ran rampant on Krynn. Graywing didn't know whether Clonogh might be a secret sorcerer, but there was a quality about the man that raised his hackles.

He simply did not care for Clonogh. He would be glad to be rid of him when this journey was done.

Now, carefully, he made his way back to the crevice where he had left his employer. "There is a route through the cordon," he said, "but it won't be easy. There are sentries, and a dozen places where ambush would be easy. Suppose we have to fight? How are you armed?"

"You are armed," the hooded figure indicated the long sword at Graywing's shoulder. "I pay you for your skills, and for your sword as well," Clonogh said, his face a shadow within shadows. "You are my guide, and my protection."

"Fine," Graywing rasped. "If we run into trouble, it's all up to me. Is that how it is?"

"I pay you well enough," Clonogh purred. He picked up his walking stick—a fine, short staff of intricately carved ivory, slightly curved and delicately tapered—and got to his feet, hugging his leather pouch close to his side with a protective elbow. "I expect you to do your job."

Chapter 11
A Tall Order

With his headquarters no longer habitable because of rampant pyrite mining, His Bumptiousness Glitch the Most, Highbulp by Choice and Lord Protector of This Place and Anyplace Else he Happened to Notice, had moved his seat of leadership to an abandoned cistern behind the steeple tower of This Place. He was there, dozing on that ample seat, when Scrib brought Bron to volunteer for duty.

It wasn't Bron's idea. In fact, he had no idea what the idea was. Scrib had found him and said, "c'mon, le's go see Highbulp," and Bron had followed obligingly.

The descent to the bottom of the cistern was a bit harrowing, as the main access—a spiral of stone steps leading downward around the shaft—was temporarily blocked by throngs of gully dwarves with piles of rubble on every step. They were cleaning the gleaming baubles from the lesser stuff by smashing the ore with stones and throwing the rubble from the walls, to be picked up at the bottom after gravity had separated the trinkets from the chaff.

So Bron took the direct path, straight down the vertiginous wall. Scrib lost his hold on the wall twice, but Bron caught him both times. The second time, the muscular young Aghar flopped his teacher over his shoulder and carried him the rest of the way.

He still had Scrib on his shoulder, muttering and squirming, when he entered the august presence of Glitch the Most. Glitch was sound asleep, and beginning to snore. Respectfully, Bron pushed through the throng of gully dwarves gathering pyrite and kicked dust in his father's face to wake him up. The Highbulp snorted, opened grumpy eyes and raised his head. "What you want, Dad?" asked Bron.

"Want?" Glitch blinked his eyes, and squinted. "Me?"

"Yep. You. What you want?"

"Leggo my foot!" Scrib hissed behind him, squirming upside down in the younger gully dwarf's grip. "Lemme go!"

"Want stew, I guess," the Highbulp decided. "An' maybe a few fried snails."

"Okay," Bron said. He turned away and Scrib pounded on his back.

"Not why we came!" Scrib shouted, "Bron, leggo! S'pose to report for duty, not for stew!"

Confused, Bron stopped and dropped Scrib, who landed headfirst on the sandy stone floor. Bron turned and looked down at him. "Report for duty? What duty?"

Nearby, the Lady Lidda noticed the exchange and went to get Glitch some stew. If the Highbulp didn't get stew when he asked for stew, he tended to sulk.

"Highbulp need a scout," Scrib said, getting his feet under him.

Glitch blinked again. "I do? What for?"

"For see why Talls keep goin' over This Place, up there," Scrib reminded his lord and master. "Pay 'tention, dummy!"

"Oh," Glitch said, sagely. He hadn't the vaguest idea what Scrib was talking about.

"That'n easy," Bron told his mentor. "Talls go 'cross up there 'cause that where bridge is."

"Talls up to somethin'!" Scrib said. "Ought to find out what."

"How?"

"What?"

"How find out what?"

"Find out *what?*" Glitch asked.

"Somebody go see," Scrib explained to Bron.

"Oh." Bron scratched his head, then nodded. "Okay. Go 'head an' see."

"Go see *what?*" Glitch demanded.

"Not me." Scrib shook his head vigorously. "Bron go."

"Why me?"

"Why not?"

"Why not what?" Glitch roared, bringing all the gully dwarf activity in the place to a screeching halt.

"Why not Bron go look at Talls?" Scrib explained. "Highbulp say go look at Talls, see what goin' on.

Right, Highbulp?"

"Right," Glitch said, nodding. "Why?"

"Somebody ought to," Scrib pursued. "Highbulp say Bron go. Right?"

"Right, Bron go look at Talls."

"Already saw Talls," Bron reminded them. "See 'em alla time on bridge."

"But where Talls goin'?" Scrib pressed, becoming red in the face.

"Dunno," Bron answered. "Wan' me go see?"

Glitch had had enough. "Go see where Talls go!" he commanded.

"Okay," Bron said.

"Okay," several others nearby echoed.

Bron headed for the cistern wall, followed by dozens of other gully dwarves. Those who made it to the top on the first try trekked off toward the far side of the canyon and points beyond. The things they carried with them were whatever they'd had in hand when the order came to leave—a bag of mushrooms, a gourd, some rocks, a dead lizard, an extra shoe, and various other prizes.

Those who didn't make it up the wall simply forgot about it and found other things to do.

At the creek below This Place, Bron and his followers passed a gaggle of females more or less washing things. The wash included various utensils, implements, babies and garments, and the Grand Notioner, who protested loudly as several females scrubbed him down, immersing him repeatedly in the process. Gandy was very old and very wise, but some of the ladies had taken it upon themselves to see that he was bathed now and then, whether he needed it or not.

Pert was among the crowd washing clothes. At the sight of Bron she dropped the bit of fabric she was scrubbing, and stood. The garment, forgotten, floated away downstream. "Where Bron goin'?" she asked.

"Gotta look at Talls," Bron pointed eastward. "Highbulp say see where they go."

"Why?"

"Dunno," he said, shrugging. "Highbulp not real clear 'bout that."

"Highbulp not real clear 'bout anything," she observed.

"Right," he said. "Have nice day." With that he waded into the creek, heading for the other side. The creek was fairly deep midstream, and a number of Bron's sturdy troop went bobbing away downstream, scrambling for someplace to land. But he still had quite a few with him when he waded up the far bank, climbed the canyon wall there and set off cross-country in the direction the bridge road followed. In the distance ahead were low peaks, with a higher ridge beyond.

Most of them had no idea where they were going, and none of them knew why, but they were all true gully dwarves. Once set on a course, they would follow that course until either someone told them to stop or something more interesting came along. The strongest driving force of any Aghar was simple inertia.

* * * * *

That night, they rested in a shallow cave, making a meal of one scrawny lizard and various roots and berries gathered along the way.

"We a pretty good scout bunch, Bron. Lot of us here," said the one named Tag.

"Yep," Bron agreed. "Two."

"Where we goin'?" Tag wondered.

"Gotta look at Talls," Bron explained. "Anybody see any Talls?"

"Not lately," several of them said.

"Well, we keep lookin'." Chewing a root, Bron frowned. "Oughtta get rats," he mused. "Could make stew with rats."

"Saw a rat," one of them said. "Couldn' catch it, though. Need a bashin' tool."

"Maybe find a bashin' tool someplace," Bron decided. With that resolved, he lay back, curled himself comfortably and went to sleep.

Chapter 12
The Bashing Tool

Dartimien the Cat raised his head an inch as birds erupted from a treetop a quarter mile up the trail. Concealed in high brush, as nearly invisible as any human could be without the use of magic, he studied the slopes above, only his dark eyes moving. A red fox, its big ears twitching with caution, crept from the shelter of a deadfall log and froze in place, its eyes and nose testing the surroundings. Then, satisfied that it was alone, it scurried past within arm's reach of the hidden man, unaware that he was there.

Dartimien saw it pass. He saw everything, from

the slightest tremor of pine needles to the wheeling of a hawk in the distant sky. But he wasn't interested in foxes, hawks or pines. He was looking for people, and the birds up-trail had told him where those people were.

With a slight movement of his hand he signaled the four Gelnian assassins in cover behind him to be alert, and be silent. Their prey was near.

Dartimien the Cat was good at his work. A product of the teeming, squalid back streets of South Daltigoth, he had earned his nickname before he was eight years old. Like a hungry cat, he knew every back alley and crawlway, every sewer and garbage heap, and every loose shutter or broken lock within a mile. Fleet of foot, quick and lithe despite the hunger that was his constant companion as a child, he was as crafty and elusive as a stray cat, and so they had called him.

His skills had been expanded by a time of servitude to Ergothian fur hunters in the wilds of Bal-Maire, and by the time of the Great Turmoil he was a prime candidate for service as a nightraider in the Caergoth Legion.

Now, like countless others—almost a brotherhood of mercenaries—he did what he did best, in order to live. He was Dartimien the Cat—a hunter. He hunted.

From what he deduced, the Tarmites—those in the citadel out there in the valley—had found something to help them against the forces of Gelnia. An artifact of great magic, the rumors held. Whatever it was, they were waiting for its arrival. But to arrive, it first had to be smuggled through the Gelnian blockade. The purpose of the assassins was to find the smuggler and stop him. And Dartimien's job was to help them do that.

How many ways were there into the Vale of Sunder? Seven or eight, he guessed. Therefore, there must be ambush squads on that many separate trails, and there must be someone like him with each squad, to be its eyes and ears. But none of that mattered to him. This trail was his, and the birds told him that he was in the right place. Within minutes, he should see movement at the bend directly above, and then he would know how many there were for the ambushers to deal with, He would know, too, whether they had pack animals and, knowing that, he would know exactly where they would pass, and when.

He waited, counting heartbeats, and then there was movement above—exactly where he had known it would be. It was gone in an instant, but Dartimien the Cat had seen what he needed to see. He eased back through the brush, and turned.

"Two men," he said. "Both afoot. No escort, no animals. Follow me, *silently*, if you can! I'll show you where to wait."

"Where will you be?" a scar-faced veteran demanded. Like the others, like most of Chatara Kral's forces, the man looked out of place in the Gelnian colors he wore. "Can we count on those daggers of yours to—"

"Count on nothing," Dartimien snapped. "I hired on to lead you to a smuggler. That's all. What you do with him is no concern of mine. Now pay me."

"We haven't caught him yet," the Gelnian said. "You get paid when the job is done."

"I get paid now," the Cat purred. "If you don't trust me, you shouldn't have hired me."

"Then you can blasted well trust us, too!"

"No, I can't," Dartimien said, smiling. "And you know it."

With a muttered oath, the Gelnian slapped a handful of arrowheads down in front of him. They were fine, dwarven-crafted points, made of tempered nickel-iron steel—a better currency in trade than the coin of any realm. Dartimien picked them up, counted them, and put them away.

"As agreed," he said. "Now follow me. I won't give you your smuggler, but I'll show you where to get him for yourselves."

*   *   *   *   *

On the downward trail leading into the Vale of Sunder, Graywing called a momentary halt and crept forward alone to get the lay of the land. The trail ahead wound downward, in and out of stretches of forest so that only a turn here and there was visible to indicate the general direction of it.

The slopes in both directions were infested with Gelnians. Smoke from their many campsites hung like banners against the sky, and Graywing knew that there was other smoke as well. The blockade of Tarmish was strengthened by countless warriors of every ilk in the pay of the Gelnian regency. He had seen some of them on the roads leading toward the Vale. There were little bands of painted sackmen festooned with their deadly feathered darts, Abanasinian archers, swordsmen and mace-wielders from Estwilde and Nordmaar, little units of Nerakan infantry, plainsland horsemen of a dozen tribes and, among them, here and there, squads of Solamnic heavy cavalry, gaudy with armor and lance. Some still wore the raiment of knighthood, though reduced by circumstance now to the true first rule of chivalry: survive at any cost.

The orders of knighthood still lived in Solamnia, but there were few vacancies. Most "knights" now were free-lance fighters.

Graywing studied the smoke, and knew the placement of troops, but it was not those he could see that worried him. It was those he could not see, but knew were there, the Gelnian sentries and ambushers who would be lying in wait for any who tried to pass between the camps.

Tall and lithe in buckskins and soft boots, his great sword slung at his back with its hilt at his shoulder, Graywing at work was the very picture of the classic Cobar warrior. All that was lacking was his horse. The picture was not deceptive. With plainsman's eyes now, he studied the trail ahead and knew its secrets.

Once on the open valley floor, they would be past the blockade. From there, swift feet and a little luck would carry them to the Tarmite stronghold. But here on the slopes, cunning was required.

There, his eyes selected a forested crest overshadowing the faint path and *there,* and *there* . . . If assassins lurked, those were the places they might be found.

The most likely ambuscades he discounted. The Gelnians would know that Tarmish awaited outside aid, and they would assume that someone like him—someone the equal of their own best mercenaries—would be with those trying to get through. Therefore, the place of ambush would be selected by a specialist.

His eyes narrowed as he spotted the rock spur only a quarter of a mile away, an innocent-looking little rise beside the trail, so low and innocuous that no one would suspect an ambush there. If assassins awaited, that was where they would be.

Retrieving Clonogh, Graywing headed down the trail, the hooded courier following close behind him, his ivory stick now thrust through his waistband at Graywing's command. The stick's faint tapping could alert enemies a hundred yards away.

Graywing glanced back at his charge as the trail bent around the top of a forested ledge. What do you have in that pouch, Clonogh? he wondered absently. What do you carry, that is worth risking your life and mine to deliver?

At the high end of the rock spur, Graywing gestured and veered off the trail, Clonogh following close behind. The slope here was heavily wooded, and they ghosted from tree to tree, angling downward. Then Graywing froze, and halted Clonogh with a hard hand. Immediately to his left, the leaves of a ground-spreader rustled faintly and rhythmically, a tiny, repetitious movement like a man breathing.

They were there, lying in wait above the trail, and their "specialist" was truly expert at his craft. Senses even a hair less honed than Graywing's would never have found them.

Nothing moving but his eyes and his twitching nostrils, Graywing counted four of them waiting there. The count bothered him. Something told him there should be five, but he could find only the four. The Gelnians were facing the other way, watching the trail beyond the spur, and they were much too close! The nearest hidden assassin, so camouflaged that only his breathing betrayed his presence, was no more than two long strides from where Graywing crouched.

Soundlessly, he edged in front of the cowering Clonogh and eased his sword from its buckler. At that instant Clonogh's foot slipped. He danced for balance, stones rattled and all fury broke loose.

* * * * *

Like the cat whose name he bore, Dartimien blended effortlessly with his surroundings. Crouched at the toe of the rock spur, he seemed no more than part of the rock beside him. Still as a leaf in a calm, he watched the trail directly above and counted his heartbeats. The smugglers should have stepped into sight by now, should be at the mercy of the Gelnian assassins by now, but moments passed and no one appeared.

He was going to give them a minute more, but sudden intuition—like an extra sense that he had always possessed—raised the hackles on the back of his neck. The prey had somehow outsmarted the predator. The smugglers were not there! His eyes narrowing, he turned and saw them yards away, behind him. With a growl he spun around, daggers appearing in both hands as he stood. And at his movement, the ambushers turned, too.

The first move was so quick that even Dartimien barely saw it. The foremost smuggler—a tall, blond-bearded man with a feathered ornament braided into his hair at one side—leapt forward, his sword flashing downward in a deadly arc, and one of the Gelnians collapsed, spewing gore from a severed neck. Before the others could react, a second fell, gutted by a backswing. The other two scrambled back, got their feet under them and drew bright blades as the buckskinned warrior whirled full around, darted between them and struck again. One of the Gelnians fell. The remaining one scuttled back, stumbled over his own feet, then turned and ran.

Dartimien shifted one of his daggers and raised it to throw, then stopped himself. "This isn't my fight," he muttered, and faded into cover.

Graywing saw the third ambusher fall, and turned to aim a cut at the fourth. But terror seemed to have given wings to the man's feet. He scrambled backward, dodged the flashing sword, then spun around and fairly flew over the rock spur, onto the open trail and toward the brush beyond. In a moment he would be gone, spreading the alarm, and moments after that they would be up to their necks in enemies.

Graywing spun around, saw Clonogh still trying to get his balance, and ripped the ivory walking stick from the man's waistband. He heard Clonogh's gasp and the beginning of his shout, but by then he had acted. The ivory stick was stout, and had good weight. Barely pausing to aim, Graywing hurled it. It whistled through the air, flashed once in open sunlight, and thudded satisfyingly against the skull of the fleeing ambusher. The man fell like a rock, face down, and the stick caromed away into the heavy undergrowth beyond.

"Don't!" Clonogh shrieked.

"Got him," Graywing muttered. Then without formality he slung his sword, picked up his employer as one would lift a sack of grain, and sprinted down the trail. There was still a fifth man back there somewhere, and Graywing had no wish to be around when he saw what had become of his companions. That one, his intuition told him, was their "expert," and an entirely different sort than his fallen henchmen. Dealing with them had been easy. Dealing with him might take time that could not be spared.

Through flickering sunlight and shadow Graywing raced, letting the slope work for him. Within a few steps he was covering twenty feet at a stride, and the wind sang in his ears. Clonogh's strident wail trailed behind him, lost in the wake of their passage.

For a quarter of a mile he ran, and then another quarter, and the slope beneath him eased toward level ground. He burst from a tree line, through stinging brush and into a tilled field, and kept going until they were out of arrow range before he slowed his stride.

Finally, when he was sure they were in the clear, he stopped and set Clonogh on his own unsteady feet. The man's cloak had been whipped back, disclosing a totally bald head and a wrinkled, beardless face distorted now by rage.

"You fool!" Clonogh screamed at him. "You bloody, stupid barbarian! You've ruined me!"

Graywing stared at him, speechless for a moment, then his eyes narrowed to threatening slits. "What I did was save your life!" he snapped. "And your treasure!" He gestured contemptuously at the leather pouch still slung securely across the robed one's breast. "I've—"

"Idiot!" Clonogh shrieked. "You've ruined everything! I was to deliver the Fang of Orm to Lord Vulpin. Now it's gone!"

"You still have it," Graywing pointed at the sealed leather pouch, wondering if the man had gone insane. "It's safe in your pouch."

"Barbarian!" Clonogh howled at him, dancing about in his rage. "This pouch? This pouch is nothing! It was a ruse! The Fang of Orm is back there! You . . . you threw it away!"

121

"I threw it . . . you mean your walking stick?"

"Walking stick!" Clonogh was almost gibbering now. "That was no walking stick! That was the Fang of Orm, one of the most powerful relics in this pitiful world!"

* * * * *

In the blue of evening, Graywing crept alone up the slope, into the blockaded hills that ringed the Vale of Sunder. Moving like a shadow, he retraced his earlier racing route, looking for the scene of the failed ambush. Ahead he saw the rock spur where the assassins had waited, but there was no sign now that anything had occurred there. The bodies were gone, the trail apparently untouched.

Every sense alert, he moved from cover to cover, his eyes searching. Then a few yards ahead, where there had been no one a moment before, a slim, dark-garbed figure leaned casually against a tree. As Graywing tensed, his hand on his sword hilt, the man straightened and stepped forward. "Don't bother looking," a pleasant, musical voice said. "I already searched. It's gone."

Graywing squinted, feeling for an instant as though he were looking at a ghost. "Dartimien?" he breathed.

"Of course I'm Dartimien," the man grinned. "I always was. It's been a long time, Graywing, though I see you've lost none of your deft touch with the big blade. That was quite a mess you left here. Blood all over everything. Took me an hour to cover all the traces."

"Dartimien," Graywing repeated. "I thought you were dead, at Neraka."

"So did those goblins," Dartimien grinned. "They marched right over me. It was the last mistake they ever made."

"I'm glad to hear it," Graywing said. "Can't tolerate goblins. Besides, I always thought if anybody ever killed you, it should be me. What do you mean 'it's gone'? What's gone?"

"That white stick," the Cat said. "The one you cracked that Gelnian's skull with. I found everything else, and here you are searching, so I assume that's what you're searching for. What is it?"

"None of your business," Graywing said. Keeping a wary eye on the smaller man, he glanced aside, into the heavy brush, where the ivory stick had gone.

"I looked there," Dartimien said. "Believe me, it wasn't to be found."

With a movement so swift it fooled the eye, Graywing sidestepped and disappeared into the heavy brush. The artifact, the Fang of Orm, should be right there! But nothing was there. The stick had disappeared, as though it had never been. The only trace of any kind was a faint trail, as though rabbits had passed that way.

When he returned to the path, Dartimien the Cat was still there, lounging against a rock.

"I told you," the Cat purred. "Your stick is gone. I already looked."

"Those ambushers were yours?"

"They hired me for a job," Dartimien said. "I did the job. That's all."

"I knew there was an expert," Graywing muttered. Then he arched a brow at the smaller one. "Did you get paid?"

"Of course I got paid," the Cat snapped. "I always get paid."

"Well, because of you, I didn't!"

"A shame," Dartimien said. "Fortunes of war. Speaking of which, It's like a war zone around here. But when I was through here before, during the big war, there was a village, just over that hill. Want to have a look? We might find some halfway decent ale."

"Are you buying?" Graywing scowled.

"I suppose so. It seems only fair, under the circumstances. But tell me, truly. If that thing wasn't a walking stick, what was it?"

"The Fang of Orm," Graywing said. "It's a relic of some kind. A thing of magic. The Tarmites went to a lot of trouble to get it."

"It must be valuable, then. I guess that's what the Gelnians were after, too, though they didn't tell me." Dartimien cocked his head and raised one eyebrow, a boyish mannerism that made him seem, momentarily, harmless and prankish, though Graywing knew better. Dartimien was one of the most lethal fighters he had ever met. "Maybe we could find it, if we tried," the Cat mused. "It has to be somewhere."

* * * * *

Beneath a stone shelf above a human campsite, Bron and his followers were looking at Talls. It was an extremely boring activity. All the Talls had done since nightfall was roast some chickens, eat their supper, then roll up in their blankets and go to sleep. Bron had relieved the boredom by organizing a forage, and now the gully dwarves in their little cave were stuffing themselves on leftover roast chicken, washed down with Tall tea.

"How long Highbulp say we look at Talls?" the

chunky Tunk asked now, rubbing sleepy eyes.

"Didn' say," Bron said. "But Scrib say see what Talls do, an' they didn' do anything yet."

Tag crept close to peer at Bron's new bashing tool, a gleaming white stick he had picked up somewhere. It seemed to have pictures carved all over it, but none of the Aghar could figure out what they were pictures of.

"Pretty thing," Tag allowed, trying again to see into the teardrop openings in the wide end of the stick. The holes were a bit baffling. There didn't seem to be anything inside, but it was hard to be sure. Even in good light, the little hollow in the stick was as dark as night. It was an inky darkness that defied the eye.

Bron lifted the stick casually, feeling again the solid weight of it, the exquisite balance. "Pretty good bashin' tool," he admitted. "Wish I had a rat to bash, test it out."

The stick in his hand shivered slightly, and a large, beady-eyed rat scurried from cover nearby and ran across the opening of the cave. With a shrug, Bron swung his stick and bashed the rodent.

"Pretty good rat," Tag allowed, lifting the dead animal by its tail.

"Pretty good bashin' tool," said Bron, gazing at his stick fondly. Within the four little teardrop cuts at its heavy end, the blackness had given way to a smoky red glow. Now the glow faded and it was black again.

* * * * *

Somewhere, under a stony crag in a place at once very near and very far away, something stirred and shifted, something huge, massive and sinuous, responding to a momentary, tingling awareness. A great, flat head arose from inky coils, weaving this way and that, searching.

Not in a very long time had his lost fang called to him. The Fang slept, unless awakened by one who could demand its magic. It slept now, and Orm no longer sensed it. But for a moment, it had been awake. And in that moment he had known its direction, and been drawn toward it.

Ageless stone shifted and cracked as Orm moved. Beyond his cold, dry den, stones rattled and great slabs of granite fell away into the abyss below the crag. Where they had been, now was a jagged hole in the rock. And from this hole a great head—a dark, flat head, triangular like a blunt spearhead—emerged in starlight. Scale-circled eyes with slit pupils opened wide, and a long, forked tongue flicked out from the great snout, tasting the air. Dimly, still within the den, great rattles buzzed a dry warning as his tail twitched. The flat, scaly head rose higher and its lower jaw dropped open, hinging back to expose a huge, pale maw where a single, retractable fang as long as a man's leg flipped forward into striking position.

There was only one fang, the other replaced by misty blackness. The lost fang was still part of him, and in a way was always near, yet separated by a void that was neither distance nor space.

Only when its spirit lived could he sense it, but now he swayed nervously, searching. For a moment it had lived. Maybe it would live again. He knew the direction, and he was hungry. It had been a long time.

* * * * *

The gully dwarves were all sound asleep in their little cave when horns blared at the midnight hour. The bugle calls, repeated from camp to camp all along the line of Gelnian forces ringing the Vale of Sunder, echoed among the hills and became a mighty wail of discordant sound.

Bron awoke abruptly, scrambled upright, banged his head on the stone above him and sat down on Tunk, whose snore became a snort as his arms and legs flailed wildly about. In an instant, two gully dwarves had been kicked entirely out of the cave and were clinging sleepily to the ledge beyond, while the rest rolled and tangled in the darkness above them. It took a while to get it all sorted out, to discover which flailing appendage belonged to whom, but finally they were all awake and untangled, and all peering down in bewilderment at the human camp below.

The Talls were no longer asleep. Now most of them scurried around gathering their weapons, while the rest stoked up the fire and added wood. All along the slopes, other smoldering fires flared to full flame.

"What goin' on?" Tag asked, of no one in particular.

"Talls wake up," Swog pointed out. "Musta' been th' noise."

Torches moved in the forest, and a pair of liveried couriers appeared in the firelight below, bright-eyed and panting. "To arms!" one of them shouted. "Hear the words of Her Eminence Chatara Kral, Ward-Regent of Gelnia." He unrolled a scroll, while the one behind him raised his torch to light the characters on it.

"The Tarmite smugglers have evaded our sentries," the courier proclaimed. "It is certain that the pretender, the despised Lord Vulpin of Tarmish, now possesses the Fang of Orm. Men of the banner of Gelnia, to arms! Tarmish must be taken, ere the dark evil of the relic is unleashed upon the land."

The courier stood in silence for a moment, then rolled up his scroll. "This unit is assigned to the Third Regiment. Proceed immediately to your assembly area. We attack the fortress at Chatara Kral's command." With that he and his escort raised their torches and hurried off into the forest, bound for the next camp.

Beside the fire, a grizzled veteran of the Solamnic campaigns turned to the man nearest him. "What in thunder does all that mean?"

"Means the opposition has a trinket," the second answered. "Some kind of magical thing that can wipe us out if they get a chance to use it. So we're through waiting. Tomorrow we fight."

"Have you looked at that fortress down there?" the first snorted. "This siege is going to take a while."

* * * * *

In the little cave above them stood the gully dwarves. "Talls all awake, looks like. They up to somethin' yet?" asked Swog.

"Dunno," Bron admitted. "We keep lookin', I guess. Mebbe fin' out."

Chapter 13
The Pursuers

"It isn't there," Clonogh said, his desperate eyes gleaming in the shadow of his cowl. "As soon as that . . . that *barbarian* Graywing was gone, I cast a far-see spell back where it fell. The effort cost me dearly, but I tried. The Fang was gone."

"Someone took it, then," Lord Vulpin growled. "Did you see any who might have found it?"

"There was a man up there," Clonogh said. "I watched him. He hid the dead assassins, and their weapons, and covered every trace of the fight. And he searched all around. He was thorough."

Vulpin paced the little tower room. He was a great, dark figure whose steel armor and reticulated helm seemed as much part of him as the relentless ambition in his eyes. His billowing cloak flared with each turn of the wind through the open portals. He paused to look out at the foot of the slopes a mile away. The forces of Chatara Kral were still issuing from the forest, their banners bright under the morning sun. There were hundreds of fighters in the fields already, trooping toward the walls of Tarmish, and it seemed they just kept coming. "Describe him to me," he said. "The man you saw on the hillside."

Clonogh squinted. "A young man, though certainly not a child. Not a large man, but strong, as an acrobat is strong. Very slim, very quick in his movements. Dark hair, dark beard but not a full beard. Clean-shaven cheeks, chin beard and mustache, neatly trimmed. Dark breeches and a dark jerkin, high boots, and dagger-hilts everywhere. He must carry a dozen knives."

"I don't know him," Vulpin shook his head. "One of Chatara Kral's mercenaries, no doubt. You watched him?"

"I watched him as long as I could hold the seeing spell," Clonogh said, shuddering. "I told you. He searched the entire area. If the relic had been there, he would have found it. And if he had found it, I would have seen."

"Someone else, then," Vulpin muttered. He looked again at the armed forces gathering in his valley, preparing to attack. "I need that artifact," he growled. "And that barbarian of yours? Graywing? Is there any way he might have tricked you?"

"He knew nothing!" Clonogh said. "The man is a superb warrior, but in some ways a dunce. He thought the prize I carried was in my pouch. He thought the Fang no more than a walking stick, and when he needed it he used it as a weapon. He threw it away!"

"Protecting you and your . . . what he thought was your missive to me," Vulpin pondered. "Perhaps you should have trusted him, Clonogh."

"And perhaps it should have rained today," Clonogh spat. "But it didn't." He squared his narrow shoulders defiantly. "At least, whoever has the Fang now, it's not likely anyone capable of using it." Shadowed eyes, nervous eyes, glanced up at Lord Vulpin from the depths of his cowl. "If Chatara Kral has the stick, well, your sister is no more an 'innocent' than you are, my lord."

"But she could find one who is!" Vulpin rumbled. "I did." He strode across to a stone-framed portal overlooking the inner grounds of the fortress. Down there, hundreds of men scurried around, carrying defense ordnance to the outer walls, preparing for the Gelnian attack. Companies and battalions of Tarmites, their ranks swelled by Vulpin's mercenaries, marched here and there to reinforce the contingents on the walls.

But above all the turmoil, in a walled garden just below the tower of the keep, a young woman with a bucket and dipper was giving water to bedded flowers. Long hair like spun gold hung around her shoulders, and when she glanced upward her eyes reflected the blue of summer sky.

"Thayla Mesinda," Lord Vulpin said to Clonogh. "I chose her carefully, and have protected her since first you told me of the Fang of Orm. She is as pure as a rosebud, conjurer, and she will do exactly as I bid."

"Then so would the Fang, if we had it," Clonogh rasped. "But we don't have it. Tell me, my lord, if we get it back . . ."

"*When* we get it back," Vulpin glared at him. "And you, mage, more than anyone, should hope that it is soon."

"*When* it is recovered." Clonogh corrected, "exactly what wish will my lord demand?" He waved nervously toward the west, where Gelnian armies gathered. "Will you wish them all dead?"

"Yes!" Vulpin growled. Then, pausing, "No, not dead. Not all. Mindless slaves, to work my fields, to serve my table, to . . . to do whatever I demand of them." The tall man paced impatiently, his eyes glowing with anticipation. "A bodyguard of zombies, Clonogh! An *army* of zombies, to do my bidding! Tarmish is nothing, Clonogh. Tarmish, and all Gelnia, is but a base. From here I will sweep outward, land after land! An empire! The world for my empire! All I need is that single artifact. The Fang of Orm!"

Vulpin ceased his pacing. Eyes alight with ambition, he gazed out across the fields where armies now shifted into attack position. On a knoll behind the main lines, a bright pavilion was being erected. "*She* has it," he growled. "She must have it by now. We'll just have to get it back."

The shadows deepened beneath Clonogh's hood, as though the sorcerer was drawing inward upon himself. The Fang had such powers, and none knew it better than he. For years now he had studied the old scrolls, tracking down the ancient relic. "Wishmaker," some had called it in ancient times. For the man who controlled it, anything was possible.

Lord Vulpin turned to face the mage, his eyes like

points of glitter beneath the elaborate scrollwork of his helm. "You lost it, Clonogh. You will regain it for me. Out there is Chatara Kral. You will go there, and retrieve it."

Clonogh flinched at the command, as though stung by a whip. "My lord," he pleaded, "you know the cost of my magic."

"I know," Vulpin's stare held no compassion, no relenting. "Each spell costs you a piece of your life. A year, or three, or five. You made a bad bargain for your magic, Clonogh. But it was your bargain, not mine. Your bargain with me is this." He drew an amulet from his robe. It was a small, glass sphere with a single, bright speck of light inside it. Teasingly he tossed it upward, caught it in a casual hand and tossed it again. He enjoyed it when the mage whimpered. "Your living spirit, Clonogh. I hold your very existence in my hand and my price for its return is the Fang of Orm."

"Pray your sister doesn't have it," Clonogh muttered. "Or, if she does, that she doesn't learn its use before we get it back."

"What if she does?" Vulpin squared his shoulders, seeming to fill the portal where he stood now, looking out at the Gelnian army. "Where is she going to find an innocent among that mob?"

In a hushed voice, Clonogh spoke a transport spell and was gone.

"Another year or so lost, Clonogh?" Vulpin muttered to no one but himself. "My, how time does fly."

* * * * * *

At the forest's edge, small things moved among the shadows and small, curious faces peered out at the broad fields where armies of humans were doing mysterious things.

"Talls def'nitely up to somethin'," Tag decided. "Runnin' 'roun' like crazy out there."

"All keep lookin' at that big building," Tunk observed. "Wonder what in there?"

Bron squinted, shading his eyes with a grimy hand. "Wish we had a better look," he muttered.

The ivory stick in his fist shivered slightly, its wide end radiating a smoky, reddish glow, and abruptly they were no longer there. Where there had been a gaggle of gully dwarves, now there was only the still forest of the slope.

* * * * *

In a place of stone and silence, Orm opened slitted eyes and raised his great, flat head. He peered here and there, weaving impatiently. Again he had sensed his lost fang, but again it was only for a moment. Within the den behind him his mighty tail twitched, and husk-dry rattles buzzed. Someone was playing with him! These quick, taunting tastes of his fang, so brief, too brief for him to gather himself for a strike. Someone or something was goading him!

But whoever it was, would pay. To awaken his fang at all, required at least a vestigial intelligence. Its holder must be capable of wishing. And the weakness of intelligence, he knew, was its tendency to dwell upon its own thoughts. Sooner or later, a test of the fang must linger long enough for him to strike. Angry and hungry, Orm waited.

* * * * *

Scrib the Philosopher was on the verge of a great discovery when the flood came. The thought had started with a thing he noticed about mushrooms. Added to a pot of stew, they could give a pleasant flavor to the stuff, but only if the proper proportions were used. Too little mushroom, and nothing was achieved. Too much, and the stew tasted distinctly like wormwood. It had to be just the correct amount.

Only rarely, though, was that "correct amount" of mushroom achieved. Wouldn't it be nice, Scrib had pondered, if somebody should happen to remember from one stew to the next how much mushroom should be included?

Like most Aghar, Scrib had almost no concept of numerical comparison. If anyone in the tribe knew how to count past two, no one was aware of it because there was no way to express such a notion. It was the nature of gully dwarves not to count for much.

But they did understand quantity, and Scrib had noticed that truly fine comparisons could be made on this basis. A bear was bigger than a rat, and a bug smaller than a bird. Talls were bigger than gully dwarves, and fire was hotter than sunlight and the Highbulp snored louder than anybody else.

Stew pots were of varying sizes, ranging from half a turtle shell or a dented helmet found on a Tall's battlefield to the Great Stew Bowl, which was far older than yesterday and had something to do with the Highbulp's legendary dragon.

Squatting on the sandy floor of the old cistern, Scrib drew doodles in the sand, sticking out his tongue in concentration as he labored with a stick, making circles of various sizes. By a stretch of imagination, the circles might be seen to represent stew pots.

By the time he had his circles completed, he had almost forgotten the rest of the equation, but he hit himself on the head a few times and it returned to him: *mushrooms!*

Mushrooms, numerically, had the same limitations as anything else. There could be one, or more than one. But in quantity they could be likened to a handful of dirt, or a mouthful, or a spadeful, or a pouchful.

A handful of mushroom would probably be too much for a mouthful of stew, but maybe not too much for a pouchful. Laboriously, Scrib drew squiggles inside his circles, hoping the squiggles might somehow resemble mushrooms.

And as he worked, a great understanding began to dawn upon him. If everybody knew that a circle meant a stew pot and a squiggle was so much mushroom, he thought, then anybody should be able to flavor stew by studying doodles in the sand.

Somehow the idea seemed to just miss the mark, but Scrib felt he was definitely onto something except that now he couldn't find his doodles because they were under water. So, in fact, were his feet, and the water was rising.

Thus Scrib was well on his way to inventing the cookbook and, incidentally, the written word, when the flood came.

Ever since their arrival at This Place, the tribe of Bulp had been mining a crevice behind one of the old buildings. The crevice had been very narrow, and clogged with rubble, but they had cleaned it out and widened it in their search for pyrite—pretty yellow rock that the Highbulp was convinced must have some value.

The crevice led back into the hillside, to an old

sinkhole with a lake at the bottom of it. The fact that the lake became deeper each time it rained in the hills, and it rained often in this season, seemed of no consequence, since the gully dwarves had all the water they needed in the little stream that flowed through the gorge of This Place.

Then, yesterday, there had been a particularly violent storm in the western hills. Lightning had danced a frenzied pattern on the high places, and the thunders had echoed like the roll of great drums. Then the entire western sky, along with the hills, had disappeared behind a slate-gray curtain of rain.

The highlight of the day had been when a huge, one-eyed ogre came stomping and muttering down the canyon, carrying a battered cudgel in one hand and part of a horse in the other. The gully dwarves had fled ahead of him, diving into hidey-holes to watch him go by. His running commentary as he passed indicated that he had been rained out. His cave, up in the hills somewhere, was full of leaks, and he had packed his possessions and was moving to a better climate.

By evening the little stream had become a roaring torrent, but it seemed to have reached its peak.

Today had dawned bright and cheerful, except for some ominous rumblings somewhere nearby. Glitch the Most, Highbulp and Legendary Dragonslayer, had awakened hungry and cranky, and promptly announced that he was tired of living in a cistern and wanted his breakfast out in the sunlight.

The simple demand had turned into a major undertaking. First the heaped pyrite had to be cleaned from the cistern's stairs, then several dozen gully dwarves were required to get the Highbulp to the top. Somewhere along the line, Glitch had developed vertigo, and he kept blacking out and falling off the stairs.

Directed by his wife and consort—the Lady Lidda—they had finally blindfolded Glitch, then worked in teams to get him to the top. Some pulled, others pushed, while still others swarmed below to catch him if he fell.

"Glitch a real twit," the Lady Lidda had declared, climbing the sheer wall to meet her lord and master when he emerged. "Still our glorious Highbulp, though."

Another problem was the Great Stew Bowl, which was still at the bottom of the cistern. The big iron bowl was just plain heavy.

Sometime in the past, in a fit of inspiration, Bron had fashioned a sturdy leather strap for the thing. The stew bowl had protrusions on its rim—a pair of iron rings on one side that might have been half a hinge, and a hook-shaped knob directly across that might once have been part of a catch. The strap, stretched across the mouth of the bowl from one to another of these fixtures, had made the bowl fairly easy to carry . . . for Bron. Few others among them could even lift the thing.

After several attempts by various people, to hoist the bowl out of the hole, the Lady Lidda went and found the tribe's burly Chief Basher, Clout.

"Clout," she ordered, "Go get Great Stew Bowl."

"Okay," Clout muttered, yawning and getting to his feet. But before he could start on his errand, his path was blocked by the Lady Bruze, his wife.

Hands on her hips, Lady Bruze glared at Lady Lidda. "Lotta nerve!" she snapped. "How come you boss Clout aroun', Lady Lidda? You wanna boss somebody, go boss what's-'is-name. Th' Highbulp."

"Go sit on a tack, Lady Bruze," Lidda suggested graciously. "Need Great Stew Bowl out of hole. Clout can go get it."

"Okay," Clout said. Again he started toward the cistern, and again the Lady Bruze blocked his way.

"Tell Bron go get it!" Bruze said, glaring at Lidda. "Great Stew Bowl Bron's problem, not Clout's!"

"Bron not here, though. Highbulp send 'im someplace."

"Where?"

"Dunno, but Highbulp's orders. So Clout go get stew bowl."

"Okay," Clout sighed. He started again for the hole, and his wife grabbed him by the ear.

"Lady Lidda got no business tell Clout what to do," Bruze insisted. "Clout stay here!"

"Okay." He sat down, rubbing his sore ear.

"Still need Great Stew Bowl," Lidda pointed out. "How 'bout Lady Bruze tell Clout go get it?"

"Lot better," Bruze conceded, backing off a step. She pointed toward the cistern. "Clout, go get Great Stew Bowl."

With a pained expression, the Chief Basher got to his feet again. "Yes, dear," he said.

Clout was gone for a time, then finally emerged from the cistern, sweating and puffing, carrying the iron bowl on his shoulders, and several of the ladies set about concocting a batch of stew.

Left alone in the hole, Scrib the Doodler squatted on dry sand, on the verge of inventing a written language.

It was then that the sinkhole up in the hills reached capacity and its walls gave way. The gush of water that roared through the crevice and out into This Place was a mighty torrent, spewing tumbling gully dwarves ahead of it. Within seconds the entirety of This Place was a raging cauldron of cold water, and the cistern was filling up.

The water was almost to the top when Scrib bobbed up and scrambled frantically for solid ground. "Wow!" he panted. "Some kin' brainstorm."

Not far away, the Highbulp found himself totally awash in floodwater, which seemed to be everywhere.

"'Nough of this!" he roared. "This no fun at all! This place no good! All over water! This place uninhab . . . unliv . . . a mess! Not fit to live in! All pack up," he ordered. "This place not This Place anymore. We go someplace else."

* * * * *

It was a grim, soggy, deserted village that Graywing and Dartimien the Cat found when they reached the chasm.

Scouting around, they found faint traces of recent habitation, though not exactly human habitation. "Gully dwarves!" Dartimien spat, gazing around at the ruins. "Nothing but gully dwarves, and even they have gone."

Graywing had paused by the bank of the swollen creek. He squatted there on his heels, studying faint traces on the muddy ground. It looked as though rabbits might have passed this way, very much like the sort of trail he had seen in the brush after the Fang of Orm had disappeared.

Scowling, he stood and glanced around at Dartimien. "Do you suppose?" he asked.

"At this point," the Cat said, "nothing would surprise me."

"Then I guess we'd better go have a look," Graywing suggested. "That faint trace . . . can you follow it?"

"Like you can follow a herd of horses, barbarian," the Cat grinned. "Or a toothsome wench. I swear, sometimes I believe you plainsmen can't see your hands in front of your faces."

"And you alley-crawlers can't see past the ends of your arms," Graywing snapped. "So you concentrate on where we're going, and I'll concentrate on what's ahead."

Chapter 14
The Designated Hero

Almost since the day seven years ago, when the Tarmite slavers had taken her, Thayla Mesinda had led a sheltered life. No more than a scrawny, coltish little girl then, she had been spared the squalid fates of most female Gelnians taken captive by the raiders. It might have been the innocence of her frightened blue eyes, or the flaxen hints in her unwashed hair, or it might have been pure chance that singled her out. But within minutes of her arrival at Tarmish, she had been hustled away by robed celibates and ensconced in her own, private quarters in the tower keep.

She had been selected by Lord Vulpin, they told her, and would say no more. With time and proper nourishment she had blossomed into a lovely young woman. She had been fed and schooled, protected and pampered, and she still had not the slightest idea what she had been selected for.

Her world was a comfortable apartment in the jutting fifth level of the tower, where wide ramparts skirted the upper spire rising to Lord Vulpin's haunts. The great ramparts gave a wide, walled balcony to Thayla's chamber, and she spent her waking hours there in good weather. Her companions were the flowers she nourished there, the songbirds that came to trill and twitter and sometimes to rest on her outstretched finger, and the tight-lipped, robed celibates who unbolted her door each day to bring her meals and clean clothing. There were always three of them, all very old, and she had the feeling that each was there to keep a wary eye on the other two.

Beyond the balcony was the rest of the world, vast and intriguing, so near she could almost reach out and touch it, yet impossibly remote—beyond the sheer drop from her balcony, beyond the locked and barred portal of her lonely apartment.

Often she longed for association with the people of the fortress and of the fields and hills beyond—for a chance to go down and mingle with them in the courtyards and on the walls, to hear their voices around her, to feel the warmth of their fires. She wished she knew the names of the sweating men who labored in the stalls and marched to and from the battlements, and the women who came and went among them.

Sometimes she literally ached for companionship—

people who were not like the wizened, silent robed ones or the curtailed crones who taught her a smattering of the arts, or that ominous, frightening presence in the tower above.

Often she dreamed of a hero who would come to take her away from all this, though she had very little idea who or what a hero might be. It was a vague word, contained sometimes in the stories of the old women who schooled her: hero.

Heroes, she deduced, were those who came to rescue young maidens from captivity. Heroes were those who fought against evil. The more she dreamed, the more convinced she became that there would be a hero for her, too. There *must* be.

Yet each day was like those before, filled only with the robed old celibates with their silent glares and their baskets and bundles, the occasional "teachers" and now and then a glimpse of that dark, formidable figure on the tower above—the regent Lord Vulpin. He had spoken to her a few times, through the grillwork in her door, but each time it was only the brief promise: do for me what I command when that hour arrives, and you will be rewarded.

His presence was like a cold wind on a balmy day, and each time she glimpsed him, or heard his voice, she dreamed again of an unknown hero.

Sometimes it seemed that the only real things in her world were the dreams and the flowers that lined her balcony and the birds who came to call. Aside from those, her only companions were loneliness and boredom. But things would change, she assured herself. A time would come when the sameness of the days would be altered, and then her hero would come for her.

Thus it was with a mounting excitement and a

sense of destiny that she watched strange armies taking the field beyond the fortress. There were thousands of armed men, some afoot and some mounted on great, prancing beasts, moving to surround the battlements while horns blared and drums rolled in the distance.

Something entirely new was happening, something unforeseen, and Thayla Mesinda watched eagerly. Maybe, somewhere in that threatening horde, was the hero of her dreams. She was standing at the stone railing, gazing outward, when feet scuffed the pavement behind her. She turned, and gasped.

Where there had been no one a moment before, now there were at least a score of little people—short, almost-human creatures not much more than half her size, huddled in a motley mass on her balcony, gaping around with startled eyes.

As she turned, one of them—a fuzzy-bearded little person slightly larger than the rest with sturdy, broad shoulders, and an ornate ivory stick in his grimy hand—gawked at her. "Oops! Ever'body run like crazy!"

With a furious scuffling of small feet, the creatures erupted from their cluster. Some scurried for shelter behind flower vases and benches, some ducked into shadowed corners, and some collided with one another, rolling and tumbling this way and that. At least two squeaked with panic and dived over the edge of the balcony, clinging there high above the courtyard until others could pull them up.

Within seconds, there wasn't a single one of them in sight, though she knew that every bit of shelter around her was packed with them.

Curious, Thayla Mesinda stepped across to a potted shrub and parted its fronds. "Hello," she said to the wide-eyed, pudgy face staring back at her from the gap. "Are you a hero?"

Tunk nearly fainted from fright when the Tall girl confronted him. He gulped, went pale and trembled violently. The chattering of his teeth almost drowned out the frantic, muffled whisper just below: "Tunk! Get foot out of my mouth!"

"Well, are you?" Thayla repeated. "Are you a hero?"

"Nope, don't think so," Tunk managed. With a sickly, placating grin he pointed toward a rosebush. "Maybe better see Bron 'bout that. Bron might be one."

Thayla stepped to the rose bush and walked part way around it, peering. Just beyond it, soft, scurrying sounds told her of someone moving, trying to stay out of sight. She paused, then turned quickly and went around the other way. The one with the ivory stick was there, gawking up at her, nose to locket.

"Are you Bron?" she asked.

"Yep, guess so," he quavered. "Pardon, just passin' through."

"You're the hero, then," she decided. Somehow she had expected heroes to be larger, and maybe better-dressed. And it had never occurred to her they might be anything other than human. But she was in no position to quibble over details. "How did you get here?"

"Beats me," he admitted. "There we were, jus' mindin' own business, lookin' at Talls. Then . . ."

"At what?"

"Talls," he repeated. "Like you."

"Oh," she said, not understanding at all. A suspicion tugged at her mind. "Did Lord Vulpin send you here?"

"Th' Highbulp send us," Bron explained. "Highbulp say, 'Bron, go look at Talls. See if Talls up to somethin'.' So here we are. You folks up to somethin'?"

She shook her head. "I don't think so. Uh, you said the . . . ah, the *Highbulp* sent you?"

"Yep. Glitch th' Most. Th' Highbulp. Real famous person. Ever'body know him."

It sounded just bizarre enough to be true. No one had ever mentioned where heroes came from, but they must come from somewhere. Somebody must send them. "Then are you here to take me away?"

"Dunno," Bron admitted. "Highbulp didn' say."

"You probably are," Thayla decided. "You are my hero, here to rescue me from captivity."

"Oh," the gully dwarf said. "Okay, if you say so."

"It won't be easy," Thayla reasoned. "How many are with you?"

Bron glanced around at the thoroughly populated balcony. Every conceivable hiding place was occupied by gully dwarves. He had no idea how many there were, but he gave her his best estimate. "Two," he said.

* * * * *

From their encampments in the hills, Chatara Kral's forces moved down into the valley, assembling at staging areas north and west of Tarmish Castle. Most of the commanders and approximately a third of the gathered warriors were Gelnians. The rest were men from many lands, set adrift by the great turmoil of recent years.

By the dozens and hundreds they had come, drawn by the promise of cash and the lure of loot.

Companies of barbarian horsemen, squadrons of varied infantry and several entire armed brigades of once Imperial troops answered the call, as well as several platoons of Solamnic heavy cavalry and countless individual warriors of many breeds.

With the end of each new war in the decade of darkness, many had returned to their homes and taken up their plows and their hammers. But many more had not. Mercenaries of all kinds roamed the lands these days, seeking employment or loot, whichever came first.

A lone, armored horseman and his squire paused at the verge of forest fronting the Tarmish fields, and studied the panorama just ahead. By his armor, weapons, the magnificent dark war-horse on which he rode and the practiced ease with which he sat his saddle, the plated one might once have been a knight of one of the great orders, or, more likely, a free-lance candidate for knighthood who had chosen a solitary road instead. No banner flew upon his ensconced lance, and no device of heraldry adorned his attire. But he was no less a formidable figure for all that.

His "squire," afoot, was a lithe, cloak-wrapped dandy with a trimmed, pointed beard and dark hair that curled in little ringlets above his hooded eyes. His manner, as he attended the reins of his "master," was brusque and curt, noticeably lacking in subservience.

Dartimien the Cat had played many roles in his time, but this was his first experience as a knight's steward.

At the forest's edge he knelt, studying the ground. "They came this way," he said. "It looks as though they went right into that encampment. Would gully dwarves do that?"

Astride the great horse, Graywing raised the heavy visor of his borrowed helm and scanned the assembling army ahead. "Not if they could help it," he said. "But maybe they got here first. This is a new camp."

"Well, if they did," Dartimien stood, brushing leaves from the knee of his immaculate, dark britches, "they're up to their necks in humans now. There must be two legions out there."

"Then I suppose that's where we must go, too," Graywing sighed. "I don't like it much, to tell you the truth. What do you think?"

"Your decision," Dartimien said, gruffly. "You're the one with the horse."

"And three hundred pounds of itching armor," Graywing snapped. "Remember, you had your chance to be the knight, here. I offered."

"Some offer," the Cat sniffed. "You know I can't stand horses."

Somewhere behind them, on the slopes above, a confused Solamnian mercenary, naked except for his stained linen undergarment and destitute except for a carefully-written receipt on a scrap of tanned buckskin, was nursing a bump on his head and trying to find his way out of a deep cleft in the rocks. The last thing he remembered before awakening in this predicament was pausing to relieve himself in a laurel thicket. The buckskin receipt itemized all of his belongings and promised their return at some unspecified time.

Neither Graywing nor Dartimien bore the wayward knight-errant any ill will, but they had decided they truly needed his horse, armor, weapons and trappings far more than he did at the moment. A visored knight and his squire might attract less attention in this valley of warriors than two mismatched individuals without credentials.

"There is a little canyon running through the camp," Graywing pointed. "It isn't much more than a ditch, but gully dwarves might hide there."

Dartimien squinted, peering into the distance. His city-bred eyes could read the trail of a beetle or follow the flight of a bee, but he had learned that the Cobar's sight was far superior when it came to distances. Dartimien's eyes were like a cat's eyes. He saw intensely what was near, and his night vision was excellent. But Graywing, the plainsman, had eyes like a hawk. What seemed too far to see, to Dartimien, Graywing saw clearly.

"I'll take your word for it," the Cat conceded. "What's the best way to get there?"

"Straight through the encampment, I'm afraid," Graywing said. "There's a worse problem, though. The gully runs directly behind that big pavilion with the banners atop it. There. Do you see it? Where the lone oak tree stands. That's probably the tent of someone important."

"You might say that," Dartimien sighed. "That's Chatara Kral's headquarters."

* * * * * *

The "gully" was actually a fan of little canyons, most of them only a few feet deep. Eroded by years of seasonal rainfall, they carried the rivulets that drained this entire quadrant of the valley, carrying waters away to a little creek that wound across the valley like a meandering ribbon among tilled fields.

Brush and scrub forest screened the gully, with larger trees standing here and there along its shoulders. Beneath some of these, decades of runoff from the fields had eroded away the soil, leaving hidden caves among the roots. The burrowing of animals over the years had enlarged some of these into sizeable holes, and it was in one such opening that the wandering tribe of Bulp had stopped to rest.

Now Scrib and Grand Notioner Gandy peered from screening brush as hordes of grim-looking Talls swarmed as far as they could see. Men tended stock, set stakes, hauled wood and gathered around countless breakfast fires. Teams of foresters and ox-drivers shuttled from the nearby forest, bringing timbers for the shaping of rams and the building of siege engines.

"Where they all come from?" Gandy quavered, clutching his mop handle staff. "Not here last night."

"Dunno," Scrib shook his head, then sighed, trying to stretch the aches out of his spine. Trying to see everything that was going on beyond the brush, was becoming a pain in the neck. From his shelter he could see a dozen other gully dwarves (or parts of them) through the matted brush. Fully half the tribe seemed to be awake now, and coming out to gawk at the altered scenery.

But not everyone was awake. Despite the noise of the human encampment all around their hiding place, they could distinctly hear the muffled snores of Glitch echoing from the burrow below them.

"Somebody better pop a gag in Highbulp's mouth," Gandy muttered. "Be jus' like that twit to wake up hollerin'."

The word was passed back, from gully dwarf to gully dwarf, and abruptly the snoring below went silent. The scuffling sounds that followed were far less intrusive than the Highbulp's snoring had been.

The Lady Lidda crept up between Gandy and

Scrib, followed by a younger female, the one called Pert. They peered with dismay at the countless Talls beyond. For a moment they were as stunned as everyone else had been, as anyone would be, awakening to a world that suddenly swarmed with humans. But then the details of the scene began to fascinate them. So many Talls, with so much armor and so many ominous-looking weapons!

Like all female gully dwarves, they immediately began to think in terms of forage.

Somewhere a trumpet blared, and men near its source formed themselves into rows and ranks, long spears gleaming in the morning sun. Not far from the verge of brush stood a huge, bright-colored structure of seamed fabrics, held upright by ropes and poles. Guards with spears and pikes surrounded it. Just beyond it, men in bright livery paraded great horses in a roped-off enclosure, while other men came from lean-tos, carrying huge loads of varied contrivances of leather and iron.

"Wow!" Lidda breathed. "Lotsa good stuff."

A flap in the pavilion was opened, and Talls set poles to hold it up, forming a roofed entry. From this issued more Talls, dozens of them all wearing the same bright colors and all carrying wicked-looking blades. They ranked themselves in two lines outside the entrance, all facing outward. Behind them came a coterie of servants, followed by a magnificently-garbed woman whose brilliant robe and kilt were outshone by the exquisitely-polished, embossed steel armor of her bejeweled helm, breast plate, buckler and shin plates. At her side hung a businesslike short sword with gem-encrusted pommel and guard.

"Look," Scrib whispered. "Lady Tall."

Nearby, Gandy blinked rheumy eyes and turned toward him. "How you know that a lady?"

Scrib had no good answer for that. "Shape like a lady," he said finally.

"Rats," Gandy allowed.

Which reminded them all of breakfast.

The Lady Lidda pursed her lips and squinted, deep in thought. "Wonder what they got in there?" she whispered, pointing at the great pavilion.

"Might be some stuff they don' need," Pert said. She edged aside, trying for a better view, and stopped. There was a large, sandaled foot in her way. She gaped at the foot, and turned slowly, looking upward. Beyond the foot was another foot, and just above them the fringes of a dark robe, which extended upward to a shadowed cowl.

A human! An old Tall in a dark cloak, standing right there beside her!

"Uh-oh," Pert breathed. "Ever 'body! Run like crazy!"

In an instant, the brush was full of running, tumbling gully dwarves, scrambling in all directions. Guards near the pavilion gaped at the sudden turmoil, then advanced on the run.

Pert, scuttling away from the old Tall in the cowl, scurried between the legs of a confused piker and dived for cover under the fringes of the pavilion. Several others were right behind her.

Somewhere the Grand Notioner squealed.

"Gully Dwarves! A whole swarm of them!" shouted a deep voice.

"Caught one!" another shouted. "Let's take 'em . . . Ow!"

"What happened?" some other human called.

"Little bugger hit me on the nose with a stick!

There it goes! Catch it!"

"Well, this is no gully dwarf!" the first voice growled. "You! You in the hood! Let's see some identification!"

"They're hard to catch!" a man swore, crashing through a thicket. "Pim! To your left! There goes one!"

"Forget the cursed gully dwarves!" the first voice commanded. "Reassemble. We have a prisoner here!" There was a pause before the same voice began asking questions. "Who are you? What's your name and how'd you get past the sentries?"

"Clonogh," a wheezing, ancient voice said. "Please, sir, I'm only a poor traveler. I've lost my way."

"Traveler, huh? Well, we'll just let the captain of guards decide what to do with you. Come on, move!"

"Would you look at that?" a guard noted. "There were gully dwarves all over, and now there isn't a one in sight! How do they do that?"

"Forget the gully dwarves, I said! Reassemble! Move this prisoner out of these weeds!"

"Some prisoner," another guard spat. "That shuffling old geezer is eighty if he's a day."

PART 3

The Bulpian Chronicles

Chapter 15
Dragon Beholden

Accompanied by her bodyguard—a matched dozen frost-bearded giants from the Ice Mountains—and by her Gelnian officers, Chatara Kral strode through her encampment. Tall, lithe and statuesque, with eyes as black as night and a great mane of raven hair that curled and flowed from the base of her lacquered helm, she was a striking figure. Everywhere she passed, men turned to stare in awe, then lowered their eyes. It was known that Chatara Kral brooked no insolence, and no man in his right mind was ready to face the wrath of the tundra giants who flanked her as she walked. Even an ogre, it was said, was no match for such men in combat.

New sunlight sparkled on the gems encrusting the ward-regent's sword and visor, and cast patterns of reflection from her mirror-bright armor. Her flowing cloak was rich with color, all the heraldry of the royal house of Gelnia emblazoned in its weave. As ward-regent, Chatara Kral had proclaimed herself the voice and the will of the infant Prince Quarls, last survivor of Gelnia's last great house.

In Gelnia, Chatara Kral's word, even her slightest gesture and whim, was law.

After making the rounds of the encampment, where men labored to prepare an attack on the Tarmite stronghold, the regent led her assemblage to a log-walled little stockade at the western perimeter. Along its final hundred yards, the path was lined with gruesome trophies—the still, dangling forms of crucified men, and here and there tall, upright poles crowned by the severed heads of decapitated prisoners.

Some of these unfortunates were Tarmish warriors, captured in the hills. Others might have been spies, traitors or saboteurs, or simply Tarmish farmers caught in their fields when the Gelnians advanced. Most of them, in fact, were guilty of no greater offense than having displeased Chatara Kral. Nevertheless, at the hands of the regent's Nerakan inquisitors they had gladly confessed to any and all crimes suggested to them.

Chatara Kral barely glanced at the trophies as she passed. She went directly to the little stockade and was admitted by bowing guardsmen. Inside the gate, the chief inquisitor bowed low. "Have you come to see the old spy, Excellence?" he asked.

"I have," she said. "What have you learned from him?"

"Considerable," the chief inquisitor said, grinning. "He is very old and has little strength. He required only the slightest prompting to talk to us."

"And is he truly a spy?"

"Oh, indeed he is, Excellence. His name is Clonogh, and he was sent directly by the Lord Vulpin, in search of some relic that has been lost."

"Relic?"

"Something he calls the Fang of Orm. It seems this Clonogh attempted to deliver the thing to Lord Vulpin, but he somehow lost it, instead. He claims it is a thing of magic, Excellence."

Chatara Kral's dark eyes glittered beneath her visor. It was almost too good to believe. Vulpin *did not* have the Fang of Orm.

The chief inquisitor led her to a reeking cell and gestured. "That is the spy, Excellence."

Chatara Kral looked at the feeble, old body stretched between the timber arms of a torture rack. "That man is ancient!" she rasped.

The chief inquisitor chuckled. "He swears his true age is thirty-seven," he said. "He says he has been aged by magic."

"He looks dead," the regent observed.

"Very nearly so, Excellence. We are a bit surprised. A man so feeble should have perished an hour ago, yet he still lives. I inquired about that the last time he was conscious. He says he cannot die because the Lord Vulpin holds his life in contract."

"My brother is still up to his old tricks, it seems," Chatara Kral muttered. "Very well. Put this Clonogh into the cellar. If he can't die, then he can rot there. But tend his wounds. He might be a handy pawn to play when we take the castle."

She watched as burly Nerakans freed the bonds from the old man's wrists and ankles, threw a noisome blanket over him and carried him out of the stockade. The "cellar" was a hole in the ground, a hundred yards away from the stockade. It was covered by slabs of stone, and its only access was a hinged iron grate in the top.

Outside the stockade, the ward-regent of Gelnia felt as though a weight had been lifted from her. Throughout her preparations for the siege of Tarmish, there had been the foreboding sense that Vulpin might turn the tables at any moment. With the Fang of Orm in his possession, there was magic he could use.

Her best advisors had been able to tell her little about the Fang of Orm, except that it was extremely dangerous. All of them had agreed that the person who possessed it had the power to win wars. And her spies had alerted her that it was on its way to Vulpin at Tarmish.

But now, it seemed, Vulpin did not have the relic. The thing had been lost before it could be delivered.

She turned to her coterie of officers. "Complete all preparations before the sun sets. Tomorrow we attack Tarmish."

Nearby, an armored lancer had paused. Dismounting, he made various adjustments in the fittings of his armor while his "squire" inspected the trappings of his great war-horse. A knight-errant preparing for combat, the little group fit right in with their surroundings. But of the three, the only one concentrating on preparedness was the horse.

"That was Clonogh," Graywing said. "He's older than I thought, and he's a mess with all that blood on him, but I'm certain it was him."

"Then maybe he knows where the Fang of Orm is," Dartimien suggested. "Maybe we should talk to him."

"We can't," Graywing growled. "Didn't you see? He's dead."

"Look around you, plainsman," the Cat purred. "Those wretches on those poles are dead, and those in that pile out there behind the stockade. When people die in that place, they either display them or throw them out. They don't lock them in cellars, with Nerakan guards at the grate."

"You could be right," Graywing admitted, gruffly. "Well, then, if Clonogh isn't dead, let's go talk to him."

"Easy enough to say," Dartimien squinted, studying the bleak, open area around the cellar hole. "But how do we do it?"

"We just do it," Graywing said, gritting his teeth. Dressed in three hundred pounds of armor, even a shrug was an effort. He wondered, as he had wondered many times before, what kind of people Solamnians were, that so many of them could choose to spend their lives in such fetters.

He had fought with Solamnian knights in the past, sometimes against them and sometimes alongside them, and still he wondered what made them tick. When he was much younger, he had thought of the armored knights on their armored horses as "clanking churls." But that was before he first saw a charge of heavy cavalry, lances aligned and hooves a'thunder.

He had discovered that those "clanking churls," with their massive armor and their great, battle-trained mounts, were as efficient and formidable a war machine as anything human and horse could be.

Still, he would be glad to get rid of these massive trappings as soon as possible, though right now they served a purpose. It would be hard to find a better disguise for rummaging about a hostile encampment. Everyone expected to see knights, but few men had the temerity to ever stop and question one of them.

Atop the stone-slab dome of the "cellar," two burly Nerakan guards squatted on their heels, playing a round of bones. During the regent's inspection, the two had remained at rigid attention. But now boredom was setting in. Their task as guards wasn't to keep anyone out of the hole. No one in his right mind would want to get into the hole. Their purpose was to guard against escape by those inside, and at the moment there was only one prisoner—a feeble old man so tormented that he was nearly dead.

The two didn't even notice the approaching knight until morning sun cast his shadow across them, and then they only glanced up, squinting. "Wha'dya want?" one of them growled.

"Oh, all sorts of things," the knight said, cheerfully. "I want fame and fortune, beautiful women and fine horses, and maybe even a quiet little kingdom somewhere to call my own. What do you want?"

The bones stopped rolling. Both of the guards shaded their eyes, squinting up at him as though he had lost his mind. Slowly, they rose to their feet and hefted their axes, their eyes flicking here and there over the armored juggernaut before them. The trouble with knights was that it was hard to tell where to hit them, if one needed to do that. "State your business here!" one of them demanded.

"I want you to open that grate," Graywing said. "Otherwise I'll have to do it myself."

"You want us to—" the Nerakan's voice ceased abruptly and his eyes rolled upward in their sockets. Beside him, almost simultaneously, the other guard twitched violently and blood gushed from his mouth. Then they both crumpled, facedown and unmoving on the stone. In the back of each of them stood a businesslike dagger, sunk to the hilt.

"I never did care for Nerakans," Dartimien said, kneeling to recover his weapons.

In the reeking hold beneath the grate they found Clonogh, more dead than alive but still breathing. Again Graywing was struck by how old the mage seemed, far older than he had only days before.

"Wrap that tarp around him," he told the Cat. "We'll get him on my horse, behind the saddle, then look for a hiding place until he recovers his wits."

"I thought we were after gully dwarves," Dartimien muttered.

"We're after the Fang of Orm," the plainsman rumbled, his voice sounding hollow within his unaccustomed armor. "He knows more about it than I do."

Fortune seemed to be with them for a time. No alarm was raised as they brought Clonogh out of the cellar, wrapped him like a roll of bedding and slung him across the war-horse's rump. Graywing climbed aboard and they started eastward, toward the bushy draws where they might find some cover.

Ranks of pikers marched past, yards away, and a drumroll of hooves arose nearby where a company of hired Solamnians maneuvered. People came and went about them, stepping aside to allow the "knight" passage. Then, halfway to the draw, a patrol of Gelnian guard broke stride and veered toward them as its commander shouted, "You. there!

Halt and identify yourselves!"

Before Graywing could react, Dartimien dodged around the horse and swatted its haunch, behind its armored skirt. "Break for cover!" The Cat shouted. "I'll join you when I can!"

* * * * *

It was almost noon, and the armies of Gelnia were moving in on Tarmish, when a great shadow swept over the landscape. Everywhere men looked upward, then turned and ran in blind fear. Years had passed since the great war, when dragons had ruled the skies, and for most people it was years since they had even seen a dragon. But the sight of a dragon in flight had lost none of its impact. Nothing else in the world could inspire such bone-chilling fear in every living thing. Now in the sky above the Vale of Sunder, great wings flapped lazily, and struck cold terror into the hearts of all who glanced aloft.

Verden Leafglow had been asleep for a time, snugly ensconced in a high mountain cavern. In the way of her kind, she sought solitude when there was nothing to do, and finding it, she slept. This sleep amounted almost to an intermittent hibernation, broken only by occasional forages for food. A dragon's nap could last for many seasons, and for one such as Verden Leafglow, who had died once and been reborn from her own egg, and whose memories were of supreme betrayal, sleep was an alluring alternative to unpleasant reveries.

But now she was awake, though she wasn't sure why. In her dreams it had seemed that she was being summoned—as though a voice that wasn't a voice at all kept telling her that she had a duty to attend to,

an obligation to be met. And when she swam from
the oblivion of sleep into harsh wakefulness, the
urgency of it lingered. Somewhere, out there below
the mountains, a destiny was nearing full flower,
and she must play a part in it.

Now she swept across the breezes above a wide
valley, her great, amber-green eyes searching the
puny sights below. High sunlight glistened on a huge,
bright-scaled body that once had been as green as a
spring leaf but now was rich with rosy highlights. She
was aware of the changes that had occurred during
her hibernation, and in a way she understood why
they had come about. Once the servant of an evil goddess, she had borne the colors of that deity. But she
had been rejected by her god, and in rejection had
accepted another—a puzzling, almost reticent sort of
god, but one not so harsh, not so driven to vent his
powers upon the world below him.

Among the lowest of the low, Verden Leafglow
had taken control of her own destiny, and regained
her honor. And in doing so, she had accepted an
obligation to the god Reorx, to do . . . *something* . . .
when the time came. Something about helping a
hero, who would rise among, of all creatures, the
Aghar. The bumbling, dull-witted gully dwarves.

Such a thing was absurd, of course. No gully
dwarf could ever be heroic. Still, Verden had worn
the shield of Reorx in battle, and had felt gratitude
in a way. And now her breast tingled in the area
between her massive shoulders where that shield
had once clung. Deep within her exquisite con-
sciousness, she could feel the shield calling to her.

And the call was like a god's voiceless voice. *The
small one will need assistance soon*, it said. *Find him and
be ready.*

167

Assistance? Verden suppressed a hiss of irritation. She and her kind were the most powerful creatures ever to live on this world of Krynn. Yet, through fate and the whims of a fickle god, Verden Leafglow had found herself subservient to the most doltish of the sentient races—the gully dwarves—not once, but twice, in two separate lives. And now she remained beholden to, of all things, a gully dwarf!

In a former, more evil incarnation, she would have simply rejected the thought. No one less than a god could force a dragon to honor any obligation if she didn't feel like it. And the god Reorx, the god she now grudgingly accepted as her god, seemed not inclined to force his subjects to do his will. Rather, he simply expected of them that they would do the right thing, by choice.

A part of her sneered at the concept. She was, after all, a green dragon. Every instinct of her kind told her to hold all other creatures in contempt, to seek her own satisfactions and never concern herself with others. Yet another part of her was aware of the debt of service she owed, and accepted it. It was that same part of her that had been at work over the years, altering her color, warming the cold green of her scales with tinges of rosy bronze.

Now I'm arguing with myself, she thought, her eyes narrowing in a sneer of contempt. A waste of time. When I know what is asked of me, then I can decide. For now I need only see what is here.

The valley below her was wide, a fertile basin surrounded by forested crests. Tilled fields lay like a tapestry on its floor, and near the center of it, on a barren rise, was a solid, massive fortress of stone.

On the flats around the fortress were large encampments, and armies were on the move, surrounding the fortress, their units moving up for attack as great siege engines were trundled into place behind them.

The contestants were humans, of course. Of all the races on Krynn, many engaged in combat now and then, but it was only humans who truly started wars, wars that too often engulfed the other races around them.

Spiraling beneath the high sun, Verden swept over the fortress for a closer look. The place was packed with people, all scrambling about now in panic at the sight of her. She saw the walls, the battlements, the tower . . . and there her senses detected the presence of magic. But it was no magic of this world.

Circling closer, her eyes followed the sense of magic to a garlanded balcony halfway up the tower keep. There were gully dwarves there. Her eyes focused on one of them—a gaping, wide-shouldered little dolt with a stick in his hand. But the stick was no stick. Though it seemed only an artifact of carved ivory, it radiated an intense, cold taste of deadly, latent magic. Beside and slightly behind the gully dwarf was a young human female. She was half again as tall as the little Aghar, but he seemed to be trying to shield her by his stance. And though he was quaking visibly with abject fear, the hand with the stick was raised in ridiculous challenge.

So that is our "hero," Verden thought, almost chuckling at the absurdity of it.

Then the distant, voiceless voice came to her again. *Heroism isn't in appearance or stature, Verden,* it said. *Heroism is in the heart. One who is willing to try to be a hero, is a hero. It is the intent that counts.*

"Reorx?" Verden said aloud. "Do you speak to me?"

You understand about heroes, Verden, the voice said

within her. *You didn't have to come, but you are here.*

Swerving, she sped toward the source of the soundless voice, a gully near the center of the largest human encampment. Below her, people scattered like fallen leaves in a breeze, but she ignored them. She concentrated on the brush-covered ravine, and then she saw them. More gully dwarves. A whole tribe of them, hiding amidst humans!

With a hiss, she recognized a face, a bewhiskered, pudgy little face that combined arrogance and idiocy in its rough features. The little creature even had the old crown she remembered, a crown of rat's teeth, askew on its graying head.

"Glitch!" Verden hissed aloud. "You little twit, I thought you'd be dead by now."

Beside the old Highbulp a female gawked upward at her, then blinked and waved a cautious hand. It was Lidda.

"I don't know if I can stand this," Verden muttered.

It's your choice, Verden, the soundless god-voice said. *Stay, or go, as you wish.*

Now she saw where the voice came from. Among the pathetic belongings of the tribe of Bulp lay a rusty old iron bowl, with a strap across its rim. It lay facedown, but she knew what it was. Somehow, after all these years, the little dolts still had the shield of Reorx.

"So what am I supposed to do?" Verden asked the voice within her.

Your presence has begun it, the silent voice of the old shield said. *Rest now, and wait. You will know when you are needed.*

A craggy hillside to the west beckoned her, and she soared toward it on mighty wings. A small herd of elk grazed there in a hidden clearing, and just above was a cozy cavern overlooking the Vale of Sunder. Verden ate her fill of elk, then crept into the cavern and curled herself for sleep. But even with her eyes closed, she could still see every movement of the creatures below, as though she were there among them.

Now that the dragon was out of sight, the humans had reorganized their forces and the battle of Tarmish had begun.

I could put a stop to all that, she thought, sleepily. It would be easy. I could . . .

Of course you could, the silent voice within her agreed. *But then nothing would be resolved, only interrupted. Only through their free will, unfettered, will they fulfill their destinies.*

Even as Verden dozed, the scanning image in her mind roved the valley below, showing her detail after detail of the puny doings of the lesser creatures. Twice she was roused by surprise, and bitter old memories, memories almost forgotten, came to life again. When the vision scanned the tower keep of Tarmish, she saw the face of Lord Vulpin. And again, when her view roved the trundling ranks approaching the fortress, there was another face, that of Chatara Kral. Thus Verden understood the darkness of the evil that had befallen this embattled realm.

Both of those faces were familiar. Though she had never seen them before, she knew them. Faces of evil reincarnate, they bore the features of their common sire.

"Verminaard!" the dragon hissed.

The dire memories were so livid, it was as though no time had passed at all, as though the dread days of the War of the Lance lived again, and Verden was part of it, as she had been then. Verminaard! Dragon Highlord, liege lord of all the forces of the Dark Queen, next to her the very symbol of evil.

Chatara Kral and Vulpin, the heirs of that evil. But there could be only one heir supreme. So that was what this puny conflict was all about. The children were in contest on this field, to determine which of them should don the mantle of their father. One would live and one would die, and from the victor would spring new evils yet unimagined.

Verden was fully awake now, and in her dragon mind an idea grew. It would be fitting, almost poetic, if both betrayers succeeded, and in succeeding, failed.

Destiny, the voice within her whispered. *You have a destiny, too, Verden Leafglow.*

Rested now, she studied again the armies in the valley below, and the castle that was their objective.

Infiltration and subversion, she mused, her great, green eyes glowing slightly. Throughout her service to the Dark Queen, these had been the skills of her specialty. In a dozen campaigns with the Dragon Highlords, Verden had become adept at the furtive talents. She had become something of a specialist in infiltration. She had served as a saboteur.

Wouldn't it be interesting, she mused. And a voice within her—a voice not her own, repeated, *destiny*.

Chapter 16
The Breakout

Pert, Lady Lidda and a gaggle of other females had begun a forage of the big pavilion, where interesting bales and crates were stacked along the walls. But the expedition was cut short when the Lady Tall with the bright attire returned, along with a lot of her followers.

"Prepare to break camp," she ordered. "Our next sleep will be at the gates of Tarmish."

Suddenly the pavilion was full of busy Talls, hurrying about, poking here and there, moving packs and bales. The Lady Lidda decided it was a bad time to visit. "Everybody scat," she whispered. The command was relayed among those behind her. Within moments a dozen gully dwarves had burrowed out, under the sides of the pavilion, and were scurrying through the brush, back to where the tribe waited.

"Lotta good stuff back there," Pert noted, sadly. "Might be spices an' corncobs an' yard goods . . . an' maybe shoes an' ribbons an' stuff."

"An' maybe a comb," the Lady Bruze mused. "Could use a good comb. Clout been gettin' fleas a lot lately. Shoulda' stayed longer."

"Easy come, easy go," Lady Lidda said. A troop of mounted Talls thundered past, shouting and pointing, almost on top of them, and the Aghar ladies dived for cover beneath spreading brambles. "We better do our shoppin' later," Lidda decided. "After th' rush."

At the dugout bank, gully dwarves were bustling around busily, gathering up whatever came to hand—sticks, used bird nests, pieces of fabric, bits of gravel, a surprised tortoise. Pert glanced around, bright-eyed, and asked, "what goin' on?"

Most of those around her ignored the question, having no answer to it, but two or three paused. "Highbulp say pack up," one explained. "Didn' say what to pack, though."

"Highbulp say time to leave here," another added. "Say, all these Talls aroun' here, neighborhood gone to pot."

The Lady Lidda went in search of Glitch, while other ladies scattered here and there, becoming involved in the collection of whatever was being collected. The legendary Great Stew Bowl went trundling by, on its way to the pile of goods. Its trailing edge almost dragged the ground, and nothing but feet showed beneath it. Pert squatted to peer under it, then turned away, disappointed. She had hoped it might be Bron under there, carrying the big iron thing. But it was only a grumbling Clout. Apparently he had lost his best bashing tool somewhere, and he wasn't happy about it.

Come to think of it, Pert didn't recall seeing Bron lately. She wondered now where he was. Vaguely, she recalled Bron saying something about the High-bulp wanting him to go and look at Talls. Cautiously, she climbed a few feet up into a scrub tree and looked around. Just beyond the brush, on all sides, there were Talls everywhere—unimaginable numbers of them, doing all sorts of mysterious things. But she didn't see Bron anywhere.

Directly below her, Scrib wandered by, carrying a shard of dark slate in one hand and a piece of soft limestone in the other. He had found that when one was rubbed against the other, it left an imprint. Now he strolled happily along, oblivious to anything around him, drawing squiggles on his slate. Pert came down from her tree and fell into step with him, staring at the incomprehensible doodles. "What Scrib doin'?" she asked.

"Makin' a list," he said absently.

"List of what?"

"Stuff," he said, shrugging. "This,"—he indicated a squiggle—"a mushroom." He pointed at a larger symbol. "This more mushrooms. An' this a cloud, an' this a stick, an' this a whole lotta rats."

"How much rats?"

"Two," he explained. "Lotta twos."

"You see Bron lately?" she asked.

"Nope." He glanced upward, tilted his head in

puzzlement, then drew an elaborate doodle on his slate.

"What that?" Pert wondered aloud.

"Dragon," he said. Then he seemed to freeze in place. He dropped his slate and chalk, and his eyes bulged out. "Dragon? Dragon!" Scrib pointed at the sky. "Dragon! Ever'body run like crazy!"

Others echoed the alarm, and abruptly the brush was alive with scrambling, scurrying, colliding and tumbling gully dwarves. One glance was enough for Pert. She looked where Scrib had pointed, and her eyes went wide. There, coming across the sky, was a behemoth on mighty wings, a huge, sinuous creature that seemed to be looking directly at her. She chirped, fell, rolled and scrambled upright, then fled in terror.

The cavern beneath the tree roots was packed solid with gully dwarves when she got there, and more were trying to pile in, burrowing among those already there. The space within was obviously full. For each one who managed to push his way in, another popped out. As Pert skidded to a stop, the Highbulp, Glitch the Most, tumbled past her, head over heels down the sloping bank. Just behind him, the Lady Lidda shouted, "Glitch! Get back here, stupid!"

Pert was almost bowled over as Lidda raced past her, going after the disheveled Highbulp.

But now it was too late to run. On wide, gliding wings, the dragon loomed over them, its huge head swinging this way and that as it scanned the area below. More than thirty feet in length, with a wingspan of at least that width, the great beast cast a racing shadow that seemed to cover everything.

Glitch had just gotten to his feet and looked

upward. The dragon looked back at him and a muted hiss came from it like an expression of disgust. Beside Glitch, the Lady Lidda stared at the beast, then grinned and waved at it. As though vastly annoyed, the dragon turned away, banked majestically and zoomed off toward the west.

"That dragon our dragon," Lidda told the Highbulp, who seemed to have frozen where he stood. "Glitch 'member dragon?" Turning, she waved again. "Bye, dragon," she called.

Pert might have been interested in all that, but she wasn't paying much attention to them at the moment. She was standing next to the pile of collected goods, just inches from the Great Stew Bowl. And it seemed to her that the Bowl was humming softly.

* * * * *

With the unconscious Clonogh across his saddle, Graywing spurred the war-horse. The animal launched itself into a belly-down run that rained gravel upon the Gelnian guards closing in behind. For a moment, the plainsman thought he had escaped, but the feeling was an illusion. Behind him bugles blared, and ahead, several companies of troops turned, spotted him and began closing in.

In an instant, there were dozens, and then hundreds, of pikemen, archers, lancers and footmen moving to encircle the lone knight, and directly ahead of him a squad of Solamnic knights-errant spread in a solid arc of armor and lance points, waiting to receive him.

On a proper plains horse, light-geared and Cobartrained, and without all the heavy armor encasing him, the warrior might have eluded the trap. But, though his armor gave him protection from arrows and spears, he was no knight, and no match for those who were.

Still, he had to do something. Lifting his great lance from its saddle boot, he leveled it, braced himself for battle, touched the horse's reins and charged.

He had no idea where Dartimien had gone, nor any time to worry about him. The Cat could take care of himself.

The sheer audacity of the charge caused the line of horsemen ahead of him to pause, and waver slightly out of position, but they corrected immediately. Faced with a madman, the Solamnians would deal with him as a madman. There was only one open way through the camp, and they wheeled to block it, forming a solid rank of iron men on iron horses, each with eight feet of deadly lance ready to impale their prey.

It was what Graywing had hoped for. With a shrill war cry he shifted his grip on his own lance, raised it and hurled it like a spear. In the same instant he veered his horse to the right, angling away from the open path, directly into the thickets along the draw.

It was a chance in a thousand, he knew, but it was the only chance he had. The instant he was shielded by brush, he swiveled around, lifted the inert Clonogh, slung him over his shoulder like a sack of seed, and threw himself to the side, diving out of his saddle. The horse thundered on, crashing through the brush, and Graywing lit with a mighty clatter of armor, and rolled into deep brush.

He didn't know, or care very much, whether Clonogh was alive or dead. Breathless and aching from his fall, the Cobar worked frantically to shuck himself out of several hundred pounds of plate steel and binding pads. He slung his sword on his shoulder and straightened his belts. His sweat-soaked, leather-bound jerkin became a pack for the armor, and his long shield a sled. Onto it he loaded Clonogh, wrapped in his blanket like a caterpillar in its cocoon, with his extra sword—the knight's sword—atop him to serve as a tie-bar for the strips of armor thong that held him in place. Towing the shield-sled with a hard fist, Graywing snaked through the brush, staying low, moving at right angles to the direction his horse had gone.

Only yards away now, men were crashing through the thickets in hot pursuit. Graywing let the first mob of them go by, then shifted his position, moving almost soundlessly—not through the brush, but under it.

He was nearing the bank of the nearest draw when horsemen thundered by, just a few paces away, and turned for another sweep of the brush. With a muttered oath, Graywing loosened his sword buckler and braced himself. Returning, they would be right on top of him.

Then he heard cries of terror, and the sound of horses running in confusion. For a long heartbeat he waited, listening. Then he raised his head. All around, searchers were fleeing in all directions, and a huge shadow swept across the brush. He looked up, directly into the face of an enormous dragon gliding across the sky, barely above the tree tops.

Seized by the instinctive dragonfear natural to all creatures, Graywing ducked into the screening brush, locked a fist into the "sled's" towline and slithered deeper into the thicket. Just ahead was the bole of a big, stubby tree. Abruptly, the earth seemed to crumble beneath him. He fell on his face and his free arm shot downward into a warm, squirming mass of movement. Something—or someone—bit him on the finger and a muffled voice said, "Keep hands to yourself, clumsy!" He recoiled, and more soil sheared away, dropping him headfirst into a hole that hadn't been there a moment before.

All around him were muffled, startled little cries of alarm and outrage.

"Somebody broke th' ceiling," someone said. "Who there?" another wondered. "Somebody clumsy," still another decided. "Highbulp clumsy," a new voice chimed in. "You got Highbulp there?" "Can't tell," the first said. "Dark an' dusty in here."

Choking and blinded, almost suffocated by the falling dust and the press of warm, small bodies around him, Graywing felt himself being hoisted and boosted from hand to hand as dozens of small hands hustled and jostled him toward a source of light.

"Pretty big somebody," a voice in the darkness said. "Lot bigger than Highbulp."

"Big no excuse for pushy," another snapped. "Not 'nough room in here as is."

Graywing was unceremoniously ejected from the hiding cave, into the filtered light of the draw. He coughed, tried to get his breath, and opened dust-grimed eyes. He was lying on his back under a canopy of limbs and a tiny, ancient-looking creature stood over him, poking him with a stick.

"This not somebody," the Grand Notioner Gandy announced, finally. "This just a Tall." He peered down again at the choking, dust-covered man, then whacked him on the head with his mop handle.

With an oath, Graywing rolled away, trying to clear his eyes. All around him, gully dwarves, panicked at his sudden appearance among them, turned and scurried away. Several dozen of them climbed the brush-covered bank, started to flee beyond, then turned back when they saw the chaos of armed Talls just beyond. Graywing was just getting his feet under him when a flood of panicked Aghar poured from the bank, knocking him flat again. In a blink, he was awash in gully dwarves, tumbling over him, falling on him, almost burying him in their frenzy.

Glitch the Most recovered from his fear-freeze in time to see the swarming pile of his subjects tumbling around in the bottom of the draw. Entirely forgetting the dragon of moments before, he strode to the melee and demanded, "What goin' on here?"

Most of those in the tumbled pile ignored him, but two or three glanced around. "Who want to know?" one of them asked.

"Me!" Glitch snapped. "Your Highbulp!"

"Oh, yeah," several of them agreed. "That right. You ol' Glitch."

"Right!" he grumbled.

The tumble of gully dwarves began to sort itself out. "What Glitch want to know?" somebody asked.

Glitch pondered, trying to remember what he had asked. Then he snapped his fingers. "Oh, yeah. Why th' pileup here? Have a fall?"

"No, thanks," one of them said. "Jus' had one."

"Don' go up there, Glitch," another pointed at the dirt bank. "Talls ever'place up there."

"Go down there, then," Glitch decided, gazing down the draw. "Ever'body come on. Time to move out." With an imperious gesture, the glorious leader of all Bulps started down the draw, tripped over his chief doodler and sprawled flat on his face.

"Glitch a clumsy oaf," several of his subjects

noted, selecting objects from the collection stack to carry with them on their journey.

Scrib, down on hands and knees searching for his slate and chalk, barely noticed that the Highbulp had tripped over him. He knew the utensils were here somewhere, and he wanted to recover them, to have a look at his picture of the dragon. It was the first time he had ever seen a dragon, and he wanted to be sure he had it right. Searching, he crawled right into the remainder of the recent tumble, bumped his head against something solid, and looked up— directly into the angry eyes of a prostrate human.

"Oops," Scrib said, backpedaling frantically. From a few feet away, he had a better view of the Tall. The man lay belly-down, with several gully dwarves just getting to their feet around him. Atop him, standing between his shoulder blades, Clout gazed around absently, then looked downward. "What this?" the Chief Basher wondered.

A few steps away, old Gandy leaned on his mop handle. "That a Tall," he said.

It took a long moment for it to soak in, then Clout chirped, gaped and made a huge leap that landed him several feet away from the man, on the rim of the Great Stew Bowl. The big, iron shield rose, flipped and landed faceup, with Clout beneath it. Gully dwarves scrambled to lift the thing and get him out.

By the time they had completed the task, the fallen man, forgotten for the moment, was sitting upright in the sand, watching in amazement. Graywing had seen gully dwarves before, and heard about them. But he had never really believed most of what he had heard. It was difficult to imagine how creatures so thoroughly dim-witted could exist.

But he began to believe it now. They had evicted him bodily from a collapsed cave, rapped him on the head, then fled in panic from him. Then they had ganged up on him, knocked him flat and pinned him down, then literally forgotten all about him, and all in a matter of minutes. Now, as the little creatures turned toward him by threes and fives, gaping and gawking, he had the distinct feeling that it was about to start all over again.

"Just hold everything!" he ordered, raising a hand.

They gaped at him, and some turned to flee. "I said hold it!" he barked. "What in the name of all the gods are you runts doing?"

"Us?" It was a paunchy, gray-bearded little individual with a crown made of teeth askew upon his head. "Nothin'. Jus' leavin'. Bye."

"Hold it!" Graywing repeated.

"Okay," several of them said, readily.

"What Tall want?" a bright-eyed little female queried.

They were leaving, they said. Therefore, they might know a way out of this place. On impulse, Graywing said, "I'm going with you. Where's Clonogh?"

"Where what?"

"Clonogh! Oh, never mind." Standing, he stepped to the cavern entrance among the tree roots and peered inside. In the dim recess was half of a knight's long shield, with half a shrouded load strapped on it. The other half of each was buried in gravel and topsoil.

Finding his towline, he heaved at it and brought out his "sled." He scooped soil from it and knelt to listen. Within his blanket-shroud, Clonogh was still breathing. "Alright," he said to the crowd of gully dwarves around him. "Which way?"

Before Glitch, or anyone else, could think of a good argument, they were on the move, working their way down the bottom of the dry slough. Graywing walked among them, towering over them even though he was crouched as low as he could to stay out of the sight of Gelnians and mercenaries just beyond the dense brush. Most of the gully dwarves, he had no idea how many there were of them, seemed to have either accepted his presence or forgotten that he was there. They trudged along in true gully dwarf fashion, going this way and that at random but generally following the lead set by their leader. Graywing had to be careful not to step on any of them, or trip over them as they scurried about their line of march. The Cobar's sharp eyes roamed here and there, looking for any sign of the ivory stick he had seen so often in Clonogh's hand, the Fang of Orm. But there was no sign of the artifact, nor of any container in which it might be hidden.

Still, each step was taking him farther from the hostile encampment of the Gelnian forces, and he still had Clonogh, or what was left of him. He hurried along, constantly on the alert, dragging the shield-sled after him. But he noticed, after a time, that it seemed to grow heavier with each step.

He turned, stared at his burden, and stifled a cry of anger. At least a dozen gully dwarves had crawled onto the sled, including the one with the big, iron shield. Several of them were now asleep back there, snoozing contentedly atop his loaded sled.

"Gods," Graywing muttered, gritting his teeth. "How did I get into this?"

Chapter 17
The Tower of Tarmish

In the instant when the dragon swept over Tarmish, Thayla Mesinda's trio of guardians, carrying the day's rations in trays and baskets, unbolted the door to her apartment. At the sound of the heavy door opening, Bron hissed, "Ever'body run like crazy!"

Thus it was that the first thing the three robed ancients encountered was a flood of scurrying gully dwarves, sweeping around and under them as they fled for cover. Before the guardians could react, they were bowled over, pummeled by scampering feet and tumbled back into the stairway corridor. Baskets and trays flew everywhere, and one of the guardians disappeared down the stairwell, a tumble of flailing arms, legs, bright robes and clinging gully dwarves.

When the other two got their wits about them and peered into the bright apartment, there wasn't a gully dwarf in sight. But there was something else. Just past the outside portal, on the balcony, Thayla Mesinda—seeming to have some extra arms and legs now—crouched in terror. And just beyond, low in the sky, was a huge dragon, floating majestically on great, extended wings.

The two guardians goggled at the sight, then turned and fled, back the way they had come.

On the balcony, Bron had been trying to bolt for cover, but everywhere he turned the human girl blocked his way, trying to hide behind him. Cornered and desperate, Bron turned to face the dragon, brandishing his bashing tool.

But the dragon did not attack. Instead, it only looked at them for a moment, then wheeled and soared away.

"Wow!" Bron breathed, watching it go.

"Golly!" Thayla Mesinda echoed, then looked down at her designated hero with approving eyes. "You're pretty good, for a . . . for whatever you are," she said. "You scared it away."

The dragon circled and wheeled above the amassed Gelnian hordes outside Tarmish, then flapped its wings lazily and soared away toward the forested hills.

When it was out of sight, Bron sighed with relief and looked around, wondering where everybody had gone. He saw Tunk, or at least the rear end of Tunk, squirming and kicking at the base of a low, bronze chest. Tunk had tried to dive under the thing to hide, but the crack was too small. Now his head was stuck, and the rest of him was struggling to free it. Pook peeked from behind a heavy, open door in the interior room, and Swog was climbing out of a flower pot. Around the corner, Tag and a few others emerged from beneath a daybed.

"Two," Bron counted them, frowning in concentration. "More than two. Thought there were more than that, though. Where ever 'body else?"

"Some of 'em went out this door," Pook said. "Some Talls, too."

"Don't need any more Talls," Bron said, squinting up at the girl beside him. "Already got one. Real nuisance."

Thayla strode to the open door. Beyond was a narrow, smoky corridor with stone stairs leading upward to the left and downward to the right. "I guess this is the way out," she said. "Come on."

Bron frowned at her. "Come on, where?"

"Out," she explained. "You are here to get me out of this place, aren't you?"

"Dunno," he answered.

"Well, you are! That's what heroes do. So come on, get me out of here."

"Okay," Bron said, shrugging again. None of it made any sense to him, but the female Tall seemed to understand the situation. "Ever 'body come on," Bron said. Holding his bashing tool before him like a shield, he peered into the corridor beyond the heavy door, then stepped through. With the others following him, he turned right and started down the winding stone stairs.

But a few steps down he stopped, bracing himself as some of those behind, gawking around at the mosaic of the tower's stonework, piled into him.

"Why Bron stop?" someone asked.

"Somebody comin'," he said. "Sh!"

"What?"

"Sh!"

"Why Bron say, 'sh,'?"

"Shut up!"

"Oh. Okay." The chattering subsided. Somewhere below, faint noises grew, coming nearer.

"Better go other way," Bron decided. He turned, tripped over Tunk and sprawled on the stairs, then picked himself up, muttering.

"We can't go up," Thayla argued. "I'm sure the way out isn't up there. It has to be down there."

"Somebody comin' down there," Bron explained. "We go up."

"I don't think we're making much progress toward escaping," the girl noted. But she turned, lifted the hem of her skirt prettily, and led the way. At the open door they had just come from, two or three gully dwarves veered off, curious, but Bron called them back. "We already been there," he said. "Le's go some other place."

The sounds from below were growing louder. There definitely was somebody coming. A lot of somebodys.

The stairs wound steeply upward, following the interior wall of the tower. At the top was a plank landing, a short passage lighted by guttering torches. At the end of the passage was a large, iron-bound door.

The Aghar pulled up short there, gawking at the closed portal. "Oops," one of them said. "Dead end."

"Maybe can dig through," another suggested. "Or jus' break it down. Bron pretty strong. Bron, break down door."

"Okay," Bron agreed. He backed away, took several running steps, and braced himself. He thudded into the heavy timbers and bounced off. Backpedaling, he took two or three other gully dwarves with him. They skidded to the edge of the landing and rolled down several stairs before overcoming their momentum.

"Oh, for pity's sake," Thayla sighed. With a dainty hand she grasped the door's ornate bar and pulled. The portal opened readily, swinging wide on oiled hinges. Thayla stepped through, the gully dwarves following.

The room they found themselves in was circular in shape, occupying the entire top floor of the great tower. Open portals looked out in all directions. and those on the east wall led to a narrow, railed balcony.

"Lord Vulpin's quarters," Thayla murmured, wide eyes darting here and there. The tower loft was richly furnished. The walls between portals were lined with fine trunks and chests of enameled hardwood, some of them bound with gold filigree, some with lustrous leathers. Near the western portal stood a large, brass telescope of the finest mountain dwarf design, set on a silver tripod. Across from it stood a single, elaborately-carved chair of darkwood and bronze and lush satin cushions.

"Wow," Tunk breathed, climbing to the seat of the tall chair. "Pretty nifty."

The sounds from the stairwell had grown louder, and now they could hear the distinct echo of angry Tall voices, coming closer.

Thayla turned to the door, but before she could close it a horde of gully dwarves tumbled through.

"Hey, there!" Bron waved at them from the ledge of the west portal. "Where ever'body been?"

"Downstairs," several of them explained.

"Got company comin'," Tag said, pointing at the open door, where the echoes of human voices had become a loud babble. Rising through the voices was the distinct clatter of unsheathed weapons. "Which way's out?"

"Dunno," Bron admitted. "Maybe not any."

"Oh," several of them said.

"Then what we do?" Tag wondered. "Hide, maybe?"

"Why not close the door?" Thayla Mesinda suggested.

"Good idea," Bron said. "Somebody close door."

Obediently, half a dozen of them hurried out, and a moment later the door slammed behind them. There was a pause, then the sound of small fists pummeling the planks. Thayla shook her head in disbelief, went to the door and opened it. The gully dwarves piled in, looking sheepish. "Oops,"one of them said.

The human girl slammed the door and dropped its heavy bolt into place, just as the first of Lord Vulpin's tower guards came into sight on the stairs below. Their shouts were drowned by the closing of the portal.

Bron had dragged a big, wooden chest across to where the telescope stood. Climbing up on the chest, he pressed an eye to the instrument's glass, then hissed in fright and threw himself back. In an instant he was flat on his back on the floor, his eyes wide with alarm.

Thayla Mesinda stared at him for a moment, then stepped to the glass and looked. The instrument was of the finest quality, crafted by skilled glaziers in the mountain fortress of Thorbardin. Through its lenses, the Gelnian army in the fields below seemed to be only a few feet away.

"It's only a far-seeing glass," she told Bron. "Not magic." Curious, she swiveled the glass here and there, studying the hordes of armed men closing in on the fortress. There were thousands of armed warriors of all kinds, moving in tight, choreographed ranks and files. Closest among them were massed companies of archers and spearmen, flanked by units of heavily armored cavalry, formidable lancers on huge war-horses, and troops of plains raiders on swift mounts. Great companies of footmen, with shields, swords and axes followed the assaulters, and behind them came clusters of men and draft animals, each cluster tending one of the tall siege towers that trundled majestically along, inching their way ever nearer to the walls of Tarmish.

"I believe they're planning a war," Thayla said to herself. "I wonder why?"

Bron had clambered onto the chest again, and Thayla stepped back from the telescope. "Here," she said. "Take a look. It won't hurt you."

"Wow," Bron breathed, scanning the view. "Lotta Talls."

Someone was pounding at the barred door now, and muffled voices came through. "Gully dwarves," a human said. "I saw them. They can't be much of a problem."

"But they're in Lord Vulpin's quarters," another voice objected. "There's no telling what kind of mess they might make in there. Somebody should go tell Lord Vulpin."

"His lordship is busy," a deep voice growled. "He's at the walls, setting up his defenses. He has no time for gully dwarves."

"But the girl is missing, too," a thin, aged voice piped up. "She must be found!"

"So, we'll find her," the gruff voice snapped. "She can't go far. But first let's get those little pests out of Lord Vulpin's chambers! Get that door open!"

"It's bolted," another voice pointed out.

"Then unbolt it, imbecile! Get some prying bars up here. If that doesn't work, we'll break it down."

Chapter 18
Fortress Infested

Dartimien the Cat took good advantage of the momentary confusion following Graywing's flight into the brush. Dashing directly beneath the belly of a knight's rearing mount, he whirled and pointed back the way he had come. "That way, Sir Knight!" he shouted. "Don't let that man escape!"

As the armored rider and his followers veered to follow his point, Dartimien scuttled aside, disappeared beneath the flaps of a wares tent and reappeared a moment later swathed in the long, dark robe of a Gelnian priest.

He bowed solemnly as a company of footmen raced by, then swung flat-handed at the officer bringing up the rear of the line. The edge of his hand took the man in the throat, and Dartimien caught him as he fell. In the space of a heartbeat he had dragged the armsman into the wares tent. When he emerged again, a moment later, it was as a platoon officer of the Gelnian guard.

For a moment he watched the wild, blind search in the nearby brush, then he turned away and harshly beckoned to a pair of stragglers. "I want each of these sheds and tents searched, immediately," he ordered them. "Those thieves may have hidden contraband here. Look for a carved ivory stick, three or four feet in length. It's tapered and curved, much like a maenog's horn. Search for it, then report back to me here."

The guardsmen saluted, and began their search. With that part of the encampment covered, Dartimien marched across to the main armory and searched that himself. The two guards at the gate had hardly noticed his approach, and didn't notice anything at all thereafter.

There was no sign of the Fang of Orm. The Cat emerged into sunlight, clad now in the bright cloak, plumed helm and light plating of a captain of lancers. Thus attired, he approached the headquarters pavilion of Chatara Kral and confronted the captain of guards at the entrance. "Why was I summoned here?" he demanded.

The huge frostman stared at him for a moment, then shook his head. "How should I know?" he rumbled.

"If you don't know, then who does?" Dartimien pressed, squaring his shoulders and managing to look down his nose at the big Icelander, who towered head and shoulders above him.

"Ask them inside there," the giant said. "They don't tell us anything."

As though the hulking brute didn't exist, Dartimien strode forward, and the big man hastened to step out of his way. The other guards, seeing their leader pass the visitor, also gave way.

Once inside the great tent, Dartimien ducked aside and disappeared among the bales of provisions stacked there. In the open center of the place, Chatara Kral herself was directing a conference of commanders who were planning their assault on Tarmish. But none of them saw or heard the silent intruder as he made his way around the pavilion, poking here and prodding there.

He was just completing his search of the place when there were shouts and screams outside. "Dragon!" someone shrieked, and other voices joined in. The conference in the pavilion broke up as people there rushed to look outside, then scurried back in, their frostman guards nearly trampling them in their panic.

"Dragon, huh?" Dartimien muttered to himself. "Wonder how the barbarian managed that? Well, one diversion is as good as another." He crept through an unguarded flap, and straightened his cloak. He watched with surprise as a great, green, or almost green, dragon swept away toward the forested hills. "There really was a dragon," he muttered. "How about that?"

Pausing only long enough to glance toward the wares tents, where his appointed searchers cowered under a tilt-up shed, he turned and went the other way. They hadn't found the Fang, either. They would have had it in hand if they had found it.

"You, there!" a voice called. Dartimien turned to face the giant from the pavilion, one of the frostmen of Chatara Kral's personal guard. The huge man wore a long necklace of steel chain over his bearskin jerkin, and held a heavy axe in his hand as lightly as Dartimien might have clutched a dagger. "You didn't identify yourself," the frostman growled. "Who are you?"

The encampment around them still was a scene of panic. People and animals were still reacting to the fearful passage of the dragon. But apparently this monster had a one-track mind. It was not at all distracted.

Dartimien gazed up at the brute, curiously. "Did you see a dragon out here?"

"Yeah," the giant rumbled, frowning. "They didn't say there'd be dragons when we took this job. If any more of those things show up, I'll look for work somewhere else." He paused, and his frown deepened. "Who did you say you are?"

Dartimien was tempted to gull the giant with some elaborate tale, but decided against it. Within a minute or so, the camp would be settling into its routines again, and it wasn't worth the risk. So he merely shrugged. "I'm an intruder," he admitted. "I don't belong here and I'm probably an enemy. But I'm just passing through."

With an oath, the giant raised his axe and swung it, but it clove only thin air. Dartimien had ducked under the cut. Before the frostman could reverse his swing, the Cat dived between legs the size of tree trunks, catching the giant's dangling steel necklace as he went. Behind the giant he rolled, sprang to his feet, planted a soft boot against the brute's buttocks and kicked, at the same time heaving at the necklace. With a roar, the giant did half a somersault and crashed to the ground, headfirst.

It took the frostman only seconds to recover, but it was enough. Dartimien the Cat had disappeared.

In the rope corrals near the brushland, chaos lingered. Hundreds of horses, still in panic from the dragon's approach, were racing around, pitching and rearing, breaking their hobbles and charging the ropes. The melee was beyond the capability of a few dozen horse-handlers, so other men from several sub-camps had run to lend a hand.

All around the encampment, mercenaries of all kinds scowled at one another. "Nobody told us there'd be dragons," several muttered, over and over. "Definite breach of contract, bringing in dragons," others pointed out.

In the general turmoil, no one noticed one more volunteer, helping with the horses. Dartimien moved among them, carefully selecting a fine pair of plains-bred mounts already wearing saddles and gear. These he collected by their reins. He calmed them by whispering in their ears and breathing in their noses as he had seen plainsmen do. Then he led them away. Once in the heavy brush bordering the sloughs, he turned northwestward, following faint tracks in the sand.

Gully dwarves scattered here and there as he intercepted the Bulp migration, but he ignored them. After a moment, they ignored him, too . . . or forgot about him. Leading his horses, he rounded a bend in the dry watercourse and found Graywing waiting for him.

"I wondered where you'd gone," the plainsman said. "I don't suppose you found the Fang."

"It isn't there," Dartimien shook his head. "I looked."

"Well, these little *Aghar* don't have it, either." Graywing took the reins of the two horses, looking them over with expert eyes. "Good," he muttered.

* * * * *

Inside the tower, Tunk fidgeted on Lord Vulpin's cushy chair. "Talls don' sound too happy," he noted.

"I think we're trapped," Thayla Mesinda said.

"This a nifty thing!" Bron chortled, still playing with the telescope. "Highbulp ought to see this." He swung the glass this way and that, then stopped, staring. "Hey!" A wide grin spread across his face. "There Gandy! An' ol' Glitch an' Lady Lidda an' . . . there Pert, too!" He jumped up and down on the chest, waving his bashing tool. "Hi, Pert! Hi, Dad! Hi, ever'body!"

"Oh, hush!" Thayla said. "They can't hear you. They're not here. They're way out there."

"Oh," Bron subsided, his grin fading. "Not here, huh?"

"No, they're not here."

"Wish they were," Bron said.

In his hand, the "bashing tool" glowed faintly.

* * * * *

Dartimien leaned over the loaded shield-sled and pulled back a flap of blanket to peer at the shriveled face of Clonogh. "Is he still alive?" he asked.

"I don't know how, but he is," Graywing said. "But I guess we don't need him anymore. It looks like the Fang of Orm is lost for—"

As though a curtain had been drawn, the world around them winked out and they were in another place. Stone walls framed large, open portals, overlooking broad fields beyond. And the place was packed with gully dwarves. The horses went wild. "What the blazes?" Graywing stepped back, drawing his sword, then gaped as his eyes fixed on the most stunning young woman he had ever seen—fixed, but only for an instant. For standing next to her was a gully dwarf, holding the Fang of Orm. There seemed to be gully dwarves everywhere.

"There it is!" Graywing hissed, focusing on the Fang.

"That's it!" Dartimien said.

"Run like crazy!" a gully dwarf shouted.

Someone was pounding at a heavy door, but now the rending of timbers and the rasp of parting hinges were drowned in bedlam as a room full of gully dwarves ran for cover, bounding and leaping, tumbling and rolling in a packed chamber with nowhere to run.

Graywing saw Dartimien go down beneath a tumbling pile of Aghar, and leapt aside as a tide of terrified little people swept past. He reached the human girl, got an arm around her and lifted her just as a tumble of flailing gully dwarves boiled beneath her. With a leap, the plainsman gained the top of a tall, teakwood chest, and from there the saddle of a pitching, kicking horse.

Leaning to gather the beast's reins, he hauled the girl up behind him, just as the heavy door ahead of him burst open. Beyond it were armed men, crouched to enter, but he saw them only for an instant. They were bowled over and swallowed up by a bounding tide of gully dwarves spilling out the door and across the landing beyond.

Somewhere near, Dartimien shouted, "Get off me, you little dolts!" A pile of gully dwarves erupted upward. Graywing tried to hold the horse, but it shrilled in terror and charged the open door, and all he could do was hang on. Behind him, the girl clung like a monkey, her arms wrapped around his middle. A second horse, riderless, was just behind them.

In the space of a heartbeat they were pounding across the plank landing and down a steep, curving stairway, engulfed to the hams in a rising tide of fleeing gully dwarves, bits of armament and tumbling, inverted Tarmite soldiers.

Somewhere behind him, the plainsman heard Dartimien's angry shout: "Graywing! Get back here, you barbarian! I saw her first!"

* * * * *

Somewhere on a distant plane, Orm blinked huge, slit-pupiled eyes and hissed in frustration. Again the lost fang had called, but again the call had lasted only an instant.

Great, scaled coils writhing in serpentine irritation, Orm waited. The call had come. It would come again. Sooner or later there would be a long moment of life, stimulated by someone's concentration. It would be enough. Orm needed only a moment, a lingering, consistent moment of wishery by whoever held the fang. Then Orm would have the path across the planes. Then Orm would strike.

Frustrated and seething with dark anger, the great serpent waited.

* * * * *

When Bron crawled out from beneath the Tall chair, everything seemed relatively peaceful. There were gully dwarves scattered here and there, picking themselves up and staring around in puzzlement, but most of the sudden crowd seemed to have gone somewhere else.

Bron took a deep breath, shook dust out of his hair and his clothing, and picked up his bashing tool. "Wow," he muttered.

Somewhere above him, Tunk said, "That some kin' party, Bron. Didn' last long, though." The chubby Aghar extracted himself from the chair's cushions and stood up, jumping on the seat. "There what's-'is-name," he pointed. "Th' Highbulp. Hi, Highbulp."

A cabinet drawer hung open across the room, and Glitch the Most peered out of it, rubbing his eyes with a grimy fist. "What goin' on?" he grumbled. "What kin' place this?"

Nearby, a fallen tapestry seemed to be coming to life. Its folds twitched, humped and muttered. An edge of it lifted, and the Lady Lidda crawled out, followed by Gandy and several others. The last one to appear from there was Pert, who gawked at her surroundings, then smiled happily at the sight of Bron. "Hey, Bron," she chirped. "Been lookin' all over for you! Where you been?"

"Bein' a hero," he explained.

"Bein' what?" Pert started to lean against a large, iron turtle, then jumped back as the turtle moved behind her. It was the legendary Great Stew Bowl, and under it was the dour Clout. He looked more unhappy than usual.

Bron helped Clout out from under the iron shield, and knelt to look the shield over, carefully. It seemed to be unharmed. As an afterthought he glanced around at Clout, who seemed unbroken as well. "Here, hold this," he handed the ivory bashing tool to the Chief Basher, and raised the Great Stew Bowl by its leather strap. It was almost as big as he was, but he was used to carrying it around.

"This a pretty good bashin' tool," Clout judged, brandishing the ivory stick. "Where Bron get it?"

"Found it, someplace," Bron answered, then turned abruptly as a groan sounded from a heavily-loaded metal "sled" resting aslant against one wall. Carrying his shield, Bron approached the object cautiously. On top of the rig rested a large, bright broadsword with strings tied to it. The bindings served as lashing for a blanket-wrapped package beneath, and it was this package that seemed to be groaning.

Curious, Bron untied some of the lashes and lifted off the broadsword. It was as long as he was tall, and quite heavy, but it fascinated him. "This a Tall's bashin' tool," he told the others, who were gathering around him. "Talls call it 'sword.' "

"Clumsy thing," Lady Lidda pointed out. "Too big for rat killin'."

"Maybe good thing for hero, though," he lifted the sword high, panting at the effort. It was heavy, but Bron was strong.

"Good thing for *what?*" his mother asked.

Attracted by the repeated groans, Gandy hobbled to the blanket-wrapped package and pulled back a flap. Beneath it, a hairless old human blinked rheumy eyes and groaned again. Gandy whacked him on the head with his mop handle and dropped the flap.

"Nothin'," he muttered. "Jus' a Tall."

A thin shriek of anger grew beneath the blanket and they all backed away. The blanket sat up, fell away, and there was an ancient man there, rubbing his aching head and muttering curses as he glared around at them.

"Oops," Gandy said.

"Maybe bash him again, with this?" Clout suggested.

The old human gaped at the gully dwarf's bashing tool and lunged to his tottering feet. "That's it!" he rasped.

"Right," Glitch the Most declared. "That 'bout it. Ever'body run like crazy."

Clonogh stood, aching, swaying and naked atop a travel-scuffed shield as the big room suddenly emptied itself. Before he could react, the gully dwarves were gone, out the broken door and down unseen stairs beyond.

Blinking and swaying, Clonogh stared around him. He recognized the big room with its stone-framed portals. It was Lord Vulpin's tower chamber. "How did I get here?" he wheezed.

But just at the moment there was no one around to explain it to him.

* * * * *

The tower stairway, from loft to ground level, made three complete circuits of the tower and ended in a wide alcove lined with guard quarters and facing on the courtyard. All the way down, the great flood of fleeing gully dwarves had picked up speed, carrying the horses and riders along with them. As a result, when they reached ground level they shot through the alcove and burst out into the crowded courtyard like a flash flood, bowling over everything and everyone in front of them.

They were halfway across the main court before their momentum slowed and the gully dwarves in front had a chance to look around. When they did, they saw surprised human warriors everywhere they looked.

"Talls!" one of them shrieked. "Ever'body run like crazy!"

Gully dwarves went everywhere, spreading like a ripple of chaos as they went. Men shouted, draft horses reared and pawed the air, a team of oxen bolted and a wagonload of hot oil vats overturned, scalding people right and left.

Graywing finally managed to get his horse's attention by sawing at the reins, and gaped at the spreading havoc all round. In all his years, he had never seen anything like it.

Behind him Thayla gasped. "Mercy!" she exclaimed. "I'm afraid Lord Vulpin isn't going to like this at all."

"Lord Vulpin?" Graywing started, then stopped as a deep, angry voice rang over the chaos of the courtyard. Just ahead and above, on the ramparts between the main gate battlements, a big, dark figure stood—a large man encased in dark steel armor, plumed helm and flowing cloak. The man was pointing directly at them, and shouting.

"He has the girl!" Lord Vulpin roared. "Get him!"

Despite the chaos of the courtyard, armed men heard the command and drew their weapons, closing in on Graywing.

"Mercy!" the girl chirped.

"Mercy is where you find it," Graywing growled.

Hauling at the reins, he kneed the horse into a belly-down turn and headed back toward the sheltered alcove beneath the tower.

With attention diverted from them, the gully dwarves of Bulp sought shelter, and took it where they found it. Dozens of them plunged into gutters and sumps, seeking the storm sewers below. Others took refuge in the larders, the armories, and in every crack or crevice of the old fort's foundations. Within moments, Tarmish was completely infested by Aghar, as thoroughly as though they had been living there for years.

In the shadowed alcove, Graywing set the girl down, then wheeled the horse and charged the open portal just as a platoon of foot soldiers reached it. He hit them like a summer storm, a thundering fury of singing sword blade, flashing hooves and Cobar battle cry. Through their ranks he swept, then turned and hit them again before they could recover. Once more through the ranks, and the area outside the alcove was free of belligerents. There were still soldiers there, but those that remained were down and not likely to get up again.

Once more within the alcove, Graywing swung down from his horse. "That should hold them for a few minutes," he muttered. He found the girl cringing in the shadow of a doorway. "Is there another way out of here?" he demanded.

"I don't know," she said. "I'm a prisoner . . . or I was, anyway. Who are you?"

"Graywing," he said. "Who are you?"

"Thayla. Thayla Mesinda." Wide, unreadable blue eyes gazed up at him, and he felt as though he might drown there. "Are we trapped here?"

"I'm afraid we are. But I'll think of something."

"Oh, don't worry about it," she said. "I have a hero, you know. His name is Bron."

"Bron?"

"He's a gully dwarf. He's here to rescue me from all this."

"A *gully dwarf?*" He gaped at her, thinking he must have misunderstood. "Gully dwarves aren't heroes, girl. Gully dwarves aren't much of anything. They're just . . . just gully dwarves."

"This one is different," Thayla assured him. Then her eyes widened. "Look out!"

Graywing spun around. A green-clad Salacian mercenary had crept into the alcove, and was drawing his longbow. The steel-pointed arrow was aimed straight at Graywing's heart, point blank from three paces away.

Before the draw was completed, though, the man's throat was full of flashing dagger. The bow and arrow slipped from numb fingers and the man pitched forward, facedown in his own blood.

"You should try watching your back, now and then," Dartimien suggested wryly, stepping from the stairwell. "You can't count on me to save you every time." The Cat stepped past Graywing then, brushing him aside as though he wasn't there. He executed a courtly bow to Thayla Mesinda and when she returned the curtsy he grinned and took her small hand. "Hello," he purred. "I'm Dartimien, and you're beautiful. I assume you have been waiting for me all your life."

"Now, hold on!" Graywing snapped, and the girl gasped, looking past him.

A pair of soft-footed Tarmite axemen had crept into the alcove, and now launched themselves from the shadows, broadaxes aloft.

The first one had Graywing cold . . . until he tripped over a knee-high iron shield and crashed facedown on the pavement. Like a panther, Graywing was on him, dispatching him with a whistling swordstroke. The second Tarmite ducked aside, swung back his battle-axe. . . and toppled like a tree. From behind the iron shield, a broadsword had appeared, flashing in a roundhouse swing that took the Tarmite across his shins. The toppling man began a scream, which ended abruptly as one of Dartimien's daggers found its mark.

Then the two warriors' jaws dropped open in unison. From behind the shield, a young gully dwarf emerged, dragging a bloody sword that was far too big for him. "Pretty good bashin' tool," he said, indicating the broadsword. Several other gully dwarves, peering at him from the stairway, nodded their wide-eyed agreement.

"You? You did this?" Graywing goggled at fallen Tarmites, and the little person with the shield and sword.

"Dunno," Bron said, raising the big sword. He stared at it in fascination. "Must have."

"Look at that!" Dartimien pointed at the second fallen Tarmite. "Look at his legs . . . his feet!"

The gully dwarf's swing had amputated both of the man's feet. The severed feet still stood where they had been.

"Oh, yuck!" Thayla shivered.

"Forget feet," Graywing growled. "You," he pointed a stern finger at the puzzled gully dwarf. "You had the Fang of Orm. I saw it. Where is it?"

Bron looked around, vaguely puzzled, then he shrugged. "Beats me," he said.

From beyond the alcove, a bull voice roared, "I

want that girl! Now!"

"Here they come," Dartimien pointed.

Just beyond the alcove, shielded footmen were advancing quickly in a solid rank, closing on the tower arch.

Graywing braced himself for combat, and a flashing dagger from Dartimien's hand found a gap in the shield rank. A man there fell, but soon others took his place. Bron gaped at the advancing humans, and quickly disappeared behind his big, iron shield. In the shadows of the stairway, small feet scampered as gully dwarves hiding there scurried for the cover of a storm drain.

The stone that fell from the sky then was the size of a fat shoat. It crashed among the advancing footmen, smashing some of them, and showering the rest with shards of stone as it exploded loudly against the pavement. A few yards away another huge stone fell, then came several more, here and there in the courtyard.

Men shouted and screamed, and their voices were drowned out by a thousand battle cries just beyond the high walls. More stones fell, lofted by catapults and trebuchets beyond the walls, and thrown spears whistled through the sky and clattered down among them.

Bron poked his head out to see what was going on, then headed for the storm drain, carrying his shield and dragging his sword. He looked like a two-legged turtle with a long, steel tail. "Run like crazy!" he shouted.

"Best advice I've heard lately," Dartimien muttered. He reached for Thayla's hand, but missed it. Graywing was already lifting the girl, flinging her across his shoulder. Graywing ran off. With an oath, the Cat followed.

The Gelnian army had begun its assault on the fortress of Tarmish, and the open courtyard and its alcoves were not healthy places to be.

Chapter 19
The Road To Rune

In a place of shadows, small shadows moved. Here ancient, mildewed granite walls stood half-buried by rubble and silt, somber testament to the antiquity of the unseen structures high above. Great pillars of rough-cut stone towered at intervals along the walls and across the fields of rubble. Dark monoliths stood here and upon their sweeping shoulders rested Tarmish—the fortifications, the habitat, the entire culture of the people of this place. Here in a time long forgotten, generations of human toil had carved foundations from the virgin stone, foundations upon which future generations could build a fortress.

No one remembered now how these monoliths had come about, or who had shaped them. Over time these reminders had been so despised by the people above them that they had been ignored and eventually forgotten. For those ancient people who built such underpinnings had been neither Tarmite nor Gelnian, but the common ancestors of both.

For any Gelnian to admit such ancestry would have been unthinkable, for it would have been an admission of kinship with the hated city dwellers of Tarmish. And of course no Tarmite would even consider that a Gelnian—one of those despised rural folk who were good only for tending the crops that kept the city fed—might be even remotely a relative.

Thus the foundations of Tarmish—a dim catacomb of tunnels, vaulted passages and great chambers among stone foundations—went unnoticed, generation after generation. If anyone thought of the cavernous cellars at all, it was only as the place where storm drains led, and where sewers discharged.

Yet now, suddenly, these nether regions were occupied. The new tenants crept here and there, cautiously, exploring their surroundings by the muted light that came from grates far above. Here and there, little bands of Aghar roved the shadowy corridors, exploring. None of them were quite sure where this place was, or how they came to be here. But such abstract reflection was of little interest. The fact was, they were here, and until somebody told them otherwise, they would stay here.

It was a place. That was enough to know about it. It wasn't This Place, of course. For any place to be This Place, the Highbulp must designate it as such.

But nobody had seen the Highbulp just lately, or anybody else of any authority. The Lady Lidda wasn't here, any more than the Highbulp was. Nor was Clout, the Chief Basher, or Clout's wife, the Lady Bruze, who might have taken charge had she been around. It was the nature of the Lady Bruze to take charge every time she had a chance. But she was as absent right now as the rest of Bulp's notables. Even old Gandy, the Grand Notioner, was among the missing.

Others seemed to be missing, too, but nobody was exactly sure who, or how many. There was a lot to see here, and having nothing better to do, most of the lost tribe of Bulp set out to see it. For a time, Scrib followed along with the general pack, peering here and there, as awed as the rest at the magnitude of the ancient construction. "Big stuff," he muttered, circling a monolithic stone pillar that rose from rough rubble into the echoing shadows far above. It was like the countless other pillars in this catacomb, but larger, and it captured Scrib's attention by its sheer size. "Somebody make all this big stuff, sometime," he said, nodding sagely. "Long time before yesterday."

Hands clasped behind him, he shuffled around the great, standing cylinder of the monolith.

Though roughly crafted, without the fine work of a column that was intended to be seen, the massive, carved stone fascinated him. Shrouded in centuries of accumulated lime, mildew, fungus and filth, it was nearly a hundred feet in diameter, and at least twice that tall. Though the Aghar had no concept of such architecture, the massive column was the central support for the Tower of Tarmish, high above. It was, in fact, the root of the great tower and its solid core of stone extended to the very floor of the tower's highest bastion.

At a bulge in the dark, grime-coated surface, Scrib paused, peered more closely, and rubbed the moist, sticky surface with an inquisitive finger, which he then stuck into his mouth. Cocking his head thoughtfully, he smacked his lips. "Not bad," he decided. "Taste kinda like mushroom." He took another taste, and was crowded aside by dozens of other curious Aghar, who had been following him around the base of the column, all of them gawking like tourists. Scrib had tasted the mildew, so now they all wanted a taste, and all from the same bulge.

"Nice," one of them commented. "Pretty good goo."

"Heady li'l vintage," another nodded in agreement. "Del'cate arom . . . boqu . . . don' smell too bad, if you hold nose."

"Hint of musk," somebody else judged. "Well aged an' full-bodied."

"Bit on th' sandy side," a string-bearded individual pointed out. "Like raw bird craw."

"Nothin' but mildew!" a female grumbled. "Mildew is mildew. Okay for taste, but not food!"

"Some folks got no palate," somebody observed. "This make pretty good spice for stew."

"Don't have stew," Scrib muttered.

"Got a point there," somebody agreed. "Anybody got stew stuff?"

Obediently, dozens of gully dwarves searched their pockets and pouches. Among the treasures discovered were several old bird nests, most of the mummified remains of a lizard, twenty or thirty nice rocks, a forgotten shoe, a fur ball recovered long ago from some cat's abandoned den, a shriveled ogre-finger, a single scissor and a putrefied pigeon egg. But nobody had any food.

"Rats!" several remarked.

"Oughtta be rats around here," one suggested. "Anybody got a bashin' tool?"

"Clout usually has bashin' tool," somebody said. "Where Clout?"

"Not here," several of them reminded him. "Maybe we better find a bashin' tool."

"Maybe we better find Clout," somebody suggested.

"Don' have any stew pot," a female complained. "Bron carries stew pot, but Bron not here either. Gettin' so ya can't count on anybody anymore. Bron not here, Clout not here, Highbulp not here."

"Better find Bron, too," they decided. "Anybody see Bron lately?"

With a purpose established, squads of gully dwarves set off in various directions to begin their search. And a dozen or so of the ladies organized a forage, to see what else they could find that might be useful. Still musing over the mildew-covered bulge on the stone column, Scrib glanced around. "Where everybody goin'?"

"Lookin' for Clout an' Bron," somebody told him. "Need a bashin' tool."

"Gonna bash Clout an' Bron?" Scrib asked, puzzled.

"Need meat for stew."

"Gonna cook Clout an' Bron, for stew?"

But there was no answer to that. Most of them had gone off in search of their missing members, and those who remained hadn't understood the question. With a shrug, Scrib turned his attention again to the bulge on the column. Where the mildew had been scraped away, a metallic surface glowed dully.

"What this?" Scrib mused.

A helpful passerby peered at the metal, then stuck out his tongue to taste it. "Not brass," he said, his dwarven senses at peak. There were those who speculated that the Aghar—the gully dwarves of Krynn—might be distant cousins of the true dwarves. No true dwarf, of course, would have tolerated such a thought for an instant, and it was unlikely that any gully dwarf had ever thought about it. To the Aghar, true dwarves—or "swatters"—were just as mysterious and unfriendly as Talls. But there were common traits between the dwarven and Aghar races, and one was a taste for metals. "Got zinc in it," the passerby decided. "Mus' be bronze. Pretty old, but still bronze."

Jostling the helpful one aside, Scrib rubbed some more mildew off the surface, and squinted at the metal beneath. There were markings on it—row after row of strange little doodles carefully inscribed.

One of them, repeated several times, resembled the squiggles Scrib had drawn earlier, representing mushrooms. And there were squiggles of many other kinds, as well. Intuition crept up Scrib's spine, making his hair itch.

A few times in his life, Scrib had encountered "Talls," or humans, and "swatters," the true dwarves of the mountains and the hills. Both races, to a gully dwarf, were mysterious, dangerous creatures, quite beyond comprehension in most ways. But Scrib recalled vaguely a thing he had noticed before. Both humans and dwarves seemed to be able to make squiggles talk.

"This a message?" he breathed, excitement flooding through him. "Maybe somebody leave instructions."

"Instructions for what?" several interested Aghar wondered.

"For us!" Scrib snapped. "All kinda squiggles here. All mean somethin'. Been tryin' to tell you, squiggles mean stuff . . . See?" He pointed impatiently. "This kin' squiggle mean 'mushroom.' Here, an' here an' here. Mushroom."

"Lotta mushroom," somebody said. "How many?"

Scrib counted the squiggles that, to him, meant mushroom. There were several of them. "Two," he decided. "An' lotsa other kin' squiggles, too. Like worms an' trees an' li'l boxes. An' this one look like a storm. Somebody tryin' to tell us somethin' here."

"Maybe say it gonna rain," someone suggested, helpfully.

"Gonna rain worms an' boxes," another elaborated.

The voice they heard then seemed to come from everywhere and nowhere. Though as soft as a disgusted mutter, it was a very big voice, and seemed to fill the shadowy reaches of the cavern. "What a bunch of nitwits!" it said. "Those are runes, you little idiot. Don't you know about runes?"

Eyes wide, the gully dwarves stared around in the gloom. "Who that?" somebody squeaked.

Little winds stirred the dust of the old cellar and great wings whispered softly in the shadows above. All eyes turned upward, gawking in terror. It looked as though great parts of the shadowed ceiling had detached themselves and were descending—a sinuous, graceful flow of shadow among shadows slowly took form as stunned Aghar eyes traced the outlines of huge movement. With wings spread wide, rippling along their edges, and its great, graceful tail

217

sweeping this way and that, the dragon seemed to fill the recesses above.

"D-d-dragon?" Scrib whispered, terror in his eyes.

"Craze like runny!" a panicked Aghar shrieked.

Frenzied gully dwarves scurried about, running blindly in circles, then froze in place as the big, irritated voice rasped, "Stop that! Stand still! Do you want me to step on you? Gods, what a bunch of little ninnies!"

Huge, reptilian feet, feet with gleaming talons like great, curved blades, touched down as gently as feathers among the fear-frozen Aghar, and the dragon settled its weight and folded its wings. A scale-armored head bristling with spikes swung this way and that on a long, sinuous neck, peering at each of them in turn, as though memorizing them. The little creatures seemed frozen with terror.

"Who's in charge here?" Verden Leafglow asked, as pleasantly as her natural aversion to the insipid little creatures permitted. Time and experience had brought about profound changes in the green dragon—time, experience and the attention of a god. Reorx had given her a new way of thinking, and she settled more and more into it. Once she would have killed every gully dwarf in sight without giving it a second thought, just for the fun of it. But many things had happened since those times, and a gully dwarf had once shown her a mercy. Now, strangely, she felt inclined to tolerate the despicable creatures—so long as they didn't irritate her too much.

For a moment none of them responded. Most of them, in fact, were too terrified to move even their lips. Then one of them stuttered, "Wh-what dragon say?"

"I asked who's in charge here," Verden repeated.

"Dunno," the gully dwarf said. "What's-'is-name usually in charge. Ol' G-glitch. th' Highbulp. Highbulp not here now, though."

"Where is he?"

"Dunno. Someplace else. M-may-maybe dragon go s-someplace else, too? Might fin' Glitch."

"I don't intend to go off searching for some nitwit gully dwarf!" Verden snorted.

"Okay," the unfrozen one said. "Then *we* go someplace else. No p-problem. Bye, dragon." With a shudder he turned, started to run and collided with another gully dwarf. The collision seemed to trigger a chain reaction. By the tens and dozens, fear-frozen Aghar found their feet, running and colliding in all directions. Where there had been silent, still gully dwarves, now abruptly there were noisy, panic-stricken gully dwarves scurrying, colliding. tumbling and falling like dominoes, everywhere.

Verden Leafglow raised her majestic head, shaking it in disgust. "Gully dwarves!" she hissed. The hiss became a roar. "All of you, stop it! Stand still!"

Obediently all the commotion ceased. With a fore-claw the size of a giant's rapier, Verden singled out Scrib and tapped him on the chest. He goggled at her and nearly fainted. "You," she said. "How are you called?"

Scrib blinked, swallowed and shrugged. "Any ol' way," he said. "Mos'ly jus', 'Hey, you!' that g-good enough."

"I mean, what is your name?" Verden snapped.

"Oh, that," Scrib said. "Name S-scri-scr . . . uh . . . Scrib. Pleased t' meet you, dragon. Bye."

"Come back here!" Verden snapped. "Show me what you have found."

"Okay." Scrib began emptying various pouches

and pockets in his clothing. "Got a m-m-mar-marble," he said. "An' piece of string, an' a t-t-turtle t-tooth an' some rocks. Ol' flat b-black rock an' sof' white one. An' part of a lizard, an'—"

"Gods," Verden muttered. "I don't care what's in your pockets, I want to see the runes you found."

"See wh-what?"

"The runes! The . . . the 'squiggles!' "

"Oh." Scrib brightened. Someone was showing interest in his discovery. And even though that someone happened to be a dragon, still he was pleased. And it didn't seem as though the dragon meant to kill him, at least not right away. "There," he pointed a grimy finger at the bronze surface gleaming dully beneath its coating of mildew. "Squiggles," he pronounced. "In my bes' judgm . . . opin . . . looks to me like stuff 'bout mushrooms."

"It has nothing to do with mushrooms," Verden grunted, peering at the ancient inscriptions.

"Not mushrooms?" Scrib was a bit deflated. "What, then?"

"It's a sign," Verden said.

"Sign?" Scrib stood on tiptoe, trying to see past the dragon's huge muzzle. "Yep, mebbe so. Sign is doodles that talk. Swatters got signs in Th'bardin. Say stuff like, 'Fourth Road,' 'No Tresp . . . tres . . . keep off,' an' 'No Aghar Allowed.' Talls got signs, too. Signs say 'Solace Three Miles,' an' 'Eat at Otto's' an' 'No Aghar Allowed.' " Enthralled, he planted a foot on the dragon's lower jaw, between her jutting fangs, grabbed a great nostril and hauled himself up onto the beast's snout. There he knelt, leaning precariously to get a closer look at the bronze plate.

"Get off my nose!" Verden snarled. With a yelp Scrib tumbled from the dragon's snout. He landed on a huge forepaw and cringed between scaled "fingers" the size of tree roots.

Ignoring the little oaf, Verden scanned the ancient inscription:

> Upon this rock be balance found. Let harmony reside here, on the fulcrum of the shining stone. Eternal the heritage of high and low.

Verden puzzled over it, then lifted a delicate talon to chip away bits of the mildew-fouled surface below the bronze. The gully dwarf, clinging frantically to her finger, bounced and chattered in terror.

Beneath the ancient coating of the column was pure, white quartz. Unmasked, it seemed to glow with a life of its own.

"It *is* a sign," the dragon breathed. "This is the sign Reorx promised."

Unburdened by any significant attention span, Scrib instantly forgot the terror of a moment before and clambered up the dragon's arm for a better view. Perched on her gigantic shoulder, he peered at the ancient column. "What sign say?" he asked.

"It says this is the point of balance," Verden said, mostly to herself. "The fulcrum. It says the harmonies rest here."

"What?" Scrib demanded, baffled. In his eagerness he climbed higher, clinging to Verden's eyelid as he tried to find footing on the scale-slick bridge of her nose.

"It says this is the shining stone!" the dragon thundered. "Get out of my face, you little nitwit!"

With a flip of her head she sent Scrib flying. He lit, tumbled and rolled, and sprawled at the feet of the Highbulp, Glitch the Most, Highbulp by Persuasion and Glorious Defender of Various places, who had just arrived, followed by portions of his scattered tribe, and by some humans.

Most of them were so taken with Scrib's acrobatics that for a moment they didn't notice the dragon towering nearby.

But then the three humans, sharp-eyed among the bumbling Aghar, saw the monster and Thayla stifled a shriek. Dartimien and Graywing both moved to protect the girl, Graywing's sword whistling as he drew it, the Cat's hands abruptly full of daggers. But before they could shelter Thayla, someone else was there. With a mighty heave, Bron the gully dwarf raised his big, iron shield and brandished his broadsword beside it. "Sh-shoo!" he ordered. "Dragon shsh-shoo! Scat, dragon! G-go 'way!"

The little creature's eyes were the size of Solamnian shoebuttons in a grimy face now pale with fear, but still he stood his ground.

Verden's great head swung around casually, and she studied the puny creature with interest. Reorx had told her that one day she would meet a gully dwarf hero, but she had never truly believed it. The idea was too preposterous. And yet, here was a gully dwarf, trying to protect another person. The ugly little creature was actually threatening her, *ordering* her away!

This was indeed the one. The shield he held before him was that same shield that had protected Verden from Flame Searclaw's dragonfire, long ago in the tunnels of Xak Tsaroth.

As Verden gazed at the shield the insignia on it seemed to come alive, to realign itself, to take new shapes and patterns. No Aghar would have recognized the elaborate design as a picture of a face.

Even humans might have seen it only as an intricate pattern of contours. But to the dragon's eyes it was a visage. To Verden Leafglow, who had lived twice, the tracery was more than a just a likeness. In the patterns on the ancient shield Verden saw the face of a god, of Reorx himself.

Once again the green dragon, who had once served a darker god, found herself in the presence of a god. But Verden Leafglow was no longer exactly green. Rich, warm hues now tinged the verdant scales of her mighty form. And the god before her now was not that vindictive deity of her first incarnation. In the shield Verden saw the face of Reorx, wielder of the hammer of heavens, Reorx the life-giver, the creator of balances.

Within the dragon's mind a voice like distant, rolling thunder murmured. *You have come to the fulcrum, Verden Leafglow. In this place issues must be resolved. High and low lurk here, awaiting balance. Those less than you will decide the outcome, Verden. But it will be for you to seal the choice when it is made.*

"I'll have my revenge?" the dragon breathed.

Revenge is a dark thing, the silent voice whispered. It really was not a voice at all, just thoughts that came unbidden within her head, and had words of their own. *Vengeance creates vengeance but clear retribution can balance scales. You were promised a gift, Verden Leafglow. That gift is what it always was . . . the freedom to choose.*

"I don't know what I'm expected to do," the dragon breathed.

This conflict is cluttered, the distant thunder murmured. *One might begin by tidying things a bit.*

The voice faded. The shield held by the trembling gully dwarf was again only a shield. Behind it, three humans and most of a tribe of Aghar gaped at the huge beast confronting them. But now Verden Leaf-glow knew her task.

One of the human males—the big one with the sword—was edging aside, crouching to attack. Verden pinned him with her eyes. "Don't even think about it," she suggested. But even as she turned toward him, something flashed in the dim cavern and a sleek dagger thumped into her scales, an inch from the softer tissue over her heart. The weapon hung for a moment, suspended from its needle-sharp point, then clattered harmlessly to the floor.

At that moment, the green dragon she had once been would have begun a slaughter, and its first victim would have been the second human male—the slighter one, with the dark garments. Even now, he was balancing another dagger, ready to throw it.

But she was not the dragon she had been long ago, and she controlled the anger that rose within her. "Stop that!" she hissed. "What do you think you're doing?"

The man hesitated. "Well, ah . . . I guess I'm throwing knives at you," he admitted, frankly. "I'm trying to kill you, you see."

"Why?"

"Why?" He lowered his throwing arm, puzzled. "Well, because that's what I do. I mean, you're the enemy, aren't you? You're a dragon."

"And you kill dragons?"

"Of course I do!"

Verden's eyes narrowed, in what no human would have recognized as mirth. "And how many dragons have you killed so far?"

"Actually," Dartimien the Cat admitted, "you're the first dragon I've ever met. At least, socially."

"That's obvious," Verden said. "You're still alive. Do you have a name?"

"Dartimien," he said.

"I'm Verden Leafglow," the dragon said. "And you?" Her gaze shifted again to the other man, who was still looking for an opening to use his sword.

"Ah . . . Graywing," the warrior said. "Pleased to meet you." His eyes roved over her, and stopped at a chink in her scales, below the left wing. He crouched, raising his blade.

"Forget it," the dragon warned. "Who is that little dolt with the big shield, and what does he think he's doing?"

Behind the Aghar, the human girl said, "This is Bron. He's a hero."

"My, my," Verden muttered. "A hero? You don't say."

Emboldened by the accolade, Bron raised his shield higher and waved his broadsword over his head. Its weight almost overbalanced him. "Dragon go 'way!" he said. "Scat!"

Ignoring him, Verden said, "There's a war going on around here. Are any of you involved in it?"

"What war?" some of the gully dwarves muttered, mystified.

"Not by design," Graywing said.

"We're just passing through," Dartimien added.

"Then you won't mind if I simplify things a bit?"

"Help yourself," Graywing shrugged. "But I warn you, we'll fight if you—"

"You'll get your chance," the dragon assured him.

Dartimien frowned. "What do you mean by that?"

"You'll see," the dragon hissed happily. Then the cavern seemed to shimmer as a powerful spell resonated soundlessly, outward to echo in the recesses,

225

then inward upon its source. For an instant Verden Leafglow towered over them, seeming to fill the vaulted cellar with her presence. Her spell was a simple one, that she had used many times. Yet now it seemed slow, as though someone, somewhere, was drawing substance from it. Verden concentrated. She shimmered, became a dim outline in the gloom, and condensed into a drifting vapor. The vapor flowed upward toward an air duct and vanished through it.

Graywing shuddered. "I hate magic," he rumbled.

"Magic is alright," Dartimien argued. "Might be handy sometimes. What I hate is dragons."

Among the goggling gully dwarves, small voices were raised in wonder. "Dragon gone?" "Where dragon go?" "Get off my foot, clumsy!"

A little gully dwarf female stepped forward, gazing proudly at the puzzled Bron, who had lowered his shield and sword and was peering around in bafflement. "No big deal," Pert assured them all. "Bron tell dragon to go 'way, so dragon go 'way. Bron a hero."

"That's ridiculous," Dartimien snorted.

"It is not!" Thayla Mesinda said. "He *is* a hero. I told you that."

Chapter 20
Bron's Dragon

Drained of his strength by the demands of his spells, Clonogh lay alone in the tower of Tarmish, cursing the fates. Hatred coursed through him as he remembered that dim-witted little Aghar who had been so close at hand—almost seeming to offer him the magical relic he so desperately needed—then had run away with it. To Clonogh it had seemed almost that the gully dwarf was taunting him, though he knew that gully dwarves lacked the subtlety to taunt. Taunting was cruelty, and gully dwarves had no cruelty in them. Cruelty was a form of evil, and gully dwarves simply had no capacity for evil. They could no more do an intentional wrong than do an intentional right.

"Gully dwarves just happen," so the common saying went among other races. Gully dwarves were just gully dwarves. There was little more to say. The creatures operated on simple inertia. Once started, on anything, they were difficult to stop. And once stopped, they were reluctant to start.

A bit of insight presented itself to Clonogh, though he was too weak and tired to give it thought. Gully dwarves were innocent. They were innocence personified. They could never be anything else.

Clonogh shoved thoughts of gully dwarves aside and concentrated on someone who was truly evil—the power-mad tyrant, Lord Vulpin. Clonogh's loathing of the man raged within him. Vulpin held Clonogh's life in his hand. And Vulpin did taunt him, constantly.

The man was half of a double evil. The other half was Vulpin's sister, Chatara Kral. Clonogh knew their origins. Both Vulpin and Chatara Kral were spawn of the Dragon Highlord Verminaard, archenemy of the Dragonlance War.

They were like their sire, those two—both crazed by an insatiable thirst for conquest. It was their manipulations—both of them, that had brought Clonogh to the state he found himself in now.

As always, when cataloging his enemies, the mage cursed old Piraeus, that long-dead sorcerer who had yielded up the secrets of magic to him so long ago, yielded them all but one! Somehow Piraeus had withheld from Clonogh the power to resist the ravages of his own spells. Just in a matter of months now, Clonogh had become old, incredibly old, old beyond death but unable to die.

Piraeus, before he died, had tricked him. Magic always demands a price, and Piraeus had known that. It was a necessary part of any spell, a secret inflection, a directing code to cause the spell to draw its energies from elsewhere, other than from its user. But in Piraeus's revelations the shielding magic had been withheld. Instead, in each spell the old trickster had substituted a different sort of inflection—the shield-code of a dragon spell.

The code worked . . . but only for dragons. It was useless to anyone else, except in the presence of dragon magic.

Clonogh wished he could see Chatara Kral beheaded. He wished he could see Vulpin disemboweled. He wished the sky would fall on all gully dwarves. He wished that the ancient mage Piraeus might burn forever in the torments beyond death.

Mostly, he wished that he could wish. If only he could have captured that bumbling Aghar who carried the Fang of Orm in its grimy hand, he could have forced a wish from it. The Wishmaker responded to innocence. And nothing, he realized now, was more innocent than a gully dwarf. The creatures were detestable, despicable and deplorable, of course, but more than anything else they were *innocent!* They fairly reeked of innocence. They simply weren't smart enough to be otherwise.

One wish! A single wish, made by an innocent, could have saved him! It would have been enough. That wish would have restored his own youth and delivered his enemies to him for his amusement.

But wishing without the Wishmaker did no good.

Beyond the tower, all around him, he heard the sounds of battle. Chatara Kral and the Gelnian hordes were not settling in for a long siege. That would have required patience. No, they were attacking the Tarmish stronghold in force. The air was filled with the crashing of hurled stones, the clatter of weapons and the voices of men striving in mortal combat.

Unable to do anything about his plight, so weak and frail he was hardly able even to move his fingers, Clonogh closed his eyes in resignation. Then he opened them abruptly. Somewhere, around him, arcane forces were brewing. He could sense them, feel them in his bones, forces nearby, near enough that their power wafted over him.

Magic! But not his magic. Not the sorceries that he could command or had known when he had the strength to exercise spells. The magic here was not human magic. It was a powerful, alien magic as different from his own as iron bonds differ from silk threads. Dragon magic! Somewhere within his mind's hearing, a dragon had cast a spell.

With the last of his will, Clonogh focused his thoughts, concentrating on the sorcery he sensed, drawing its tuned vibrations into himself, willing its shield powers to fill the holes in his own magic, to mend him and brace him and make him complete.

The power of the dragon spell flowed around him and he drew from it as a sponge draws water, absorbing those patterns that he required.

In a moment it was gone, but the moment was enough. Like a leech in stagnant waters, Clonogh had ridden the turbulent energies and sucked from them the sustenance he required. For an instant he marveled that it had come at such a time—in his hour of greatest need, magic had turned for him, and his grasp on it had been sure. It was almost as though some god had intervened, he thought. But the thought did not linger. He had other things to think about now. A glance at his pale, skeletal hands told him that he still appeared incredibly ancient. But now it was only appearance. Within the husking shell of him, he was as powerful as any youth.

Energized and rejuvenated, feeling strong and fit, Clonogh stood and gazed around through renewed eyes. A catapult's stone crashed against the tower, spraying its interior with shards and dust, but Clonogh cared nothing about it. An energy like steel veils flowed about him, and nothing touched him. He strode to the west wall, pulled down a tattered tapestry there and with strong hands tore it into segments, which he bound around his nakedness with pieces of sash.

Beyond the shattered doorway, at the top of a descending circular stair, he found a dead mercenary clad in the colors of Lord Vulpin's tower guards. The man seemed to have been trampled by a horse. Clonogh took the man's boots and put them on his own feet, then paused curiously, gazing down at the corpse. With only the slightest hesitation, the mage pointed a finger and muttered a minor spell. Before his eyes, the guard's body writhed and shriveled, collapsing inward upon itself until only skeletal remains lay there.

Clonogh took a deep breath, stood thoughtfully for a moment, then nodded. "Good," he muttered. He had made a strong spell, and for the first time, the spell had done him no harm. He was protected now by dragon magic.

A memory presented itself in his mind, the memory of that old mage whose secrets Clonogh had taken from him so long ago. That old mage who, even in death, had avenged himself by tricking his killer.

231

"I win," Clonogh said. "Now I truly have the power!"

Beyond the tower, a battle raged. All along the ramparts of Tarmish, men struggled frantically to maintain their defenses. Below, beyond the walls, hordes of Gelnians stormed forward under the cover of their bombarding catapults and trebuchets.

Another great stone impacted the tower, and whole sections of it collapsed, but Clonogh sang a spell and the portion where he stood—the floor beneath his feet, the portal and the stairwell—remained intact. Like a bizarre, misshapen finger pointing at the sky, the wreckage of Lord Vulpin's tower stood above scenes of chaos. The structure was only a skeleton of itself now, but it remained sturdy. Vaguely, Clonogh marveled at the ancient engineering that had raised such a structure.

Of more immediate interest, though, was the Fang of Orm, somewhere below, probably still in the hands of some detestable gully dwarf scurrying through the rubble. For that relic, Lord Vulpin had robbed Clonogh of his spirit. For that same relic, Chatara Kral had ordered the mage tortured. For the Fang of Orm and the power to use it, a few minutes ago, Clonogh would have given his soul. Now it meant less to him, though he still wanted it. Now he had magic of his own, unburdened by the pain of instant aging.

What he wanted now was revenge. And in the Fang of Orm rested delicious vengeance.

A chorus of screams arose now from below, and Clonogh turned full around, watching with bemused interest as a great dragon swept from the sky to glide across the ramparts of Tarmish. In its wake, on the ground, attacks and defenses collapsed as men by the hundreds ran in all directions, trying to escape. Dragonfear spread and rippled among them. Where Crealic mercenaries manned repelling catapults atop a wall, the dragon swept low, its huge claws ripping downward to destroy the defenses. Spears and javelins bounced harmlessly from its armored scales, and men tumbled from the wall, along with the wreckage of their machines.

Clonogh frowned. Somehow, it seemed, Chatara Kral had induced a dragon to help her. But then the dragon, completing its sweep of the walls, turned its attention outward, trailing wreckage in its wake as it slashed through the Gelnian attack.

Puzzled, the mage watched from his high perch. The dragon veered here and there, smashing into concentrations of troops almost at random. And always, where it went—gliding low on great, flaring wings—it left a widening wake of fleeing men in its path. Spears and arrows arose from the human masses. Many bounced harmlessly off the dragon's armored scales. Others missed, to fall back among the humans below.

Around and around the attacking fields the huge beast flew, dipping and diving here and there while armed men ran screaming from it. Then with beating wings it rose above the walls and again descended upon Tarmish.

And now the grapple lines dangling from the walls, lines placed by the attackers, were alive with panicked soldiers trying to escape from the fortress. As the dragon descended into the central courtyard, the great gate of Tarmish swung open and fleeing defenders by the hundreds streamed outward, a shrieking stampede of men trying to get away from the fear among them. In the receding fields, armies blended—Gelnian and Tarmite fighters fleeing together in their panic.

For Clonogh it was beyond understanding. A dragon had come to Tarmish, and was raging among the combatants, but it seemed not to discriminate. It was attacking both sides with equal enthusiasm.

Clonogh could not identify the dragon. Several times, during the dragon wars, Clonogh had seen dragons. He had always identified them by their color. There had been the beasts in service of the dark lords—brilliantly-colored creatures of crimson or blue or green. And then there had been the others, those whose colors were the colors of fine metal—the silvers, the coppers, the golds. These, he remembered, had fought against the chromatic beasts.

But the dragon he saw now, wreaking havoc on Tarmish, striking attacker and defender with equal enthusiasm, was none of these. Its iridescent scales flashed in the high sunlight with definite hints of brilliant green but equally strong hues of rich umber and warm bronze.

It was a mystery, but it had nothing to do with him. He knew dragon magic had occurred, and that he had been strengthened by it, but he knew also that its purpose had been something else. He had just happened to be in the right place at the right time.

Now the far fields were alive with fleeing men, and Clonogh knew who they were. Mercenary soldiers, some wearing the colors of Tarmish and some of Gelnia, mingled in their retreat, and Clonogh smiled a cruel smile. Whatever the dragon's purpose here, both Lord Vulpin and Chatara Kral had just lost their hired armies.

His eyes roving the scenes around and below the tower, Clonogh saw Lord Vulpin raging along his southern rampart, followed now by only a handful of true Tarmites. And in the field beyond the gate, Chatara Kral stood in the midst of her desolated encampment, screaming orders at fleeing men who did not look back to respond. Only a few of her troops remained with her now, native Gelnians bound to the cause of the Tarmish campaign.

In the devastated footings of one of the great walls, where a jagged opening gaped above the city's underground, several furtive gully dwarves scurried from the shadows and darted for better cover. They disappeared into the dark hole, where drains led downward to the caverns. All but one. One of the gully dwarves held an ivory stick in its grimy fist—the Fang of Orm. And that one, darting for cover, encountered a Tarmite soldier. With a shriek the gully dwarf turned and fled, back into the base of the tower.

As suddenly as it had appeared, the raging dragon, which had now devastated and scattered the armies both inside and outside of Tarmish, was gone. As though it had never been there, it simply vanished, and once again Clonogh's magic-honed senses detected the ironlike taste of a dragon spell.

"Transformation," he muttered, recognizing the pattern of the magic, though he had no clue as to what the beast had become, or where it had gone. Dragon magic had restored him, magic drawn from the dragon's previous spell, but though his sorcery was now powerful again, he was still only human. The mind of a dragon was not the mind of a human, and the intricacies of its sorcery were beyond him.

Still, it was gone now from view, and whatever the beast's purpose had been, it did not seem to have any further effect on him. He stood unharmed on the skeletal remains of the tower, and Tarmish Castle lay in shambles around him, gaping and broken first by the missiles of contending armies, then by the wrath of a rampaging dragon.

The place was almost silent now. Here and there injured men cried out among the dead, and as the breeze shifted he could hear the strident, stunned voices of both Lord Vulpin and Chatara Kral, barking curses and orders at the scattered handfuls of Tarmite and Gelnian troops they still commanded.

The jagged hole where the gully dwarves had disappeared gaped dark and silent, like a beckoning cavern. Soldiers of Tarmish were hurrying toward it. On the south wall, several of Lord Vulpin's lieutenants noticed them and pointed.

Raising a bony fist, Clonogh muttered a small spell. On the south wall Lord Vulpin halted and turned, as though confused. For a moment he gazed around, this way and that, then his gaze fixed on the tower and he started toward it. Beyond the open gate, Chatara Kral also turned, hesitated, then strode toward the gaping portal and the tower beyond. Behind each regent, confused men milled about, some choosing to follow their leaders, others turning away.

With a savage grin, Clonogh paced the great tower, hearing the thud of little feet on the rising stairs. The Fang of Orm was on its way to him, in the hands of an innocent.

* * * * *

In dim recesses in the bowels of Tarmish, Graywing stared about him in bewildered disgust. The dragon that had been here not half an hour ago, seeming to fill the resonant caverns with its fearful presence, was nowhere to be found. He and Dartimien had searched for it, splitting up to scour the echoing, vaulted chambers in wide sweeps, poking and peering into every tunnel and shadowed niche.

There was no sign of the formidable beast anywhere. Now Graywing stood a few steps into the great chamber in which the castle's foundations towered like dark monoliths, and wrinkled his nose in disgust. There were gully dwarves everywhere he could see, doltish little creatures bumbling about here and there, more or less centering upon a major concentration of Aghar around the base of a huge pillar. Some sort of conference seemed to be going on there. A dozen or so gully dwarves were engaged in animated debate about something, while uncounted others looked on with dull curiosity.

A few yards back of the main swarm, he spotted Thayla Mesinda, trim and beautiful even here in these noisome surroundings. Small of stature though she was, she stood head and shoulders taller than most of the milling, blundering little creatures around her.

Scattering gully dwarves ahead of him, the warrior strode across the cavern toward the girl. As he approached her he held out a beckoning hand. "Come with me," he said. "I'll take you away from all this—" his voice broke abruptly into a grunt of surprise as a quick movement beside him warned him of attack. With a curse Graywing leaped straight up, drawing his feet up as a wide broadsword whistled past just below him, just where his shins had been.

Bron the Hero lost his balance as his mighty slash met nothing but thin air. Trying to keep his grip on the heavy weapon, he spun half around, tripped and

fell on his face. The broadsword clanged against the
stone of the cavern floor, and Bron's big iron shield
teetered for a moment on edge, then fell over on top
of him.

Cursing and furious, Graywing stepped over the
struggling gully dwarf, pinned the broadsword
beneath a soft-booted foot and leaned down. "Don't
ever do that again!" he ordered.

"Oops, sorry," Bron said, freeing himself from the
weight of the shield. "Didn' rec'nize you. Thought
mebbe you a enemy."

"Didn't recognize me?" Graywing snapped.
"You've seen me a dozen times!"

Bron got his feet under him, dusted himself off
with grimy hands and glanced up at the human. "So
what? Seen one Tall, seen 'em all." The little hero got
his shield upright and arranged its straps on his arm
and shoulder. He reached for his broadsword,
tugged on its grip, then noticed the human's foot
planted on the blade. "Pardon," he said. When the
foot didn't move, Bron heaved the heavy shield
around and smacked Graywing on the knee with it.
The human hissed, jumped back and hopped around
on one foot, cursing.

Bron retrieved his broadsword, squinted for a
moment as he tried to remember what he was supposed to be doing, then resumed his position in
front of Thayla. He was guarding her.

Thayla shook her head, her eyebrows arched in a
pretty frown as she watched Graywing shuffle
about, testing his sore knee. "You really shouldn't be
so rough with these little people," she scolded the
dour warrior. "They don't mean any harm."

"That little twit tried to cut off my feet!" the
plainsman growled.

"Bron? He's a hero," Thayla reminded the man. "That's what heroes do."

"Right," Bron agreed, "cut off folks' feet."

Graywing tried again, this time staying just out of range of the gully dwarf's weapon. "Let's get out of here, girl," he urged. "This place will be overrun by Tarmites any minute now . . . and that dragon is still around here someplace."

"No, it isn't," Thayla assured him. "Bron chased it away."

"He did not!"

"Did, too!" The voice almost directly below his chin startled Graywing. He looked straight down, into the stubborn, serious eyes of a little female gully dwarf who stood almost toe to toe with him. Her head was at about the level of his belt, her hands were little fists planted on her hips and she looked ready to take him on in either debate or combat, whichever he chose.

"Bron say dragon go 'way," Pert told him, "So dragon go 'way. Ever'body know that. Tall blind?"

Graywing took a deep breath and shook his head. The only thing dumber than a gully dwarf, he had heard, is the fool who tries to argue with one. If he wasn't careful, he realized, he was going to find himself doing just that.

"Get out of the way," he snapped, then stepped around Pert, who scurried to confront him again.

"Bron chase dragon away!" the little creature insisted. She glanced around. "Isn' that right, Bron?"

Bron peered over the top of the legendary Great Stew Bowl, looking puzzled. "Yes, dear."

"Pert's right," Thayla Mesinda said emphatically. "He did."

"Nobody just . . . just orders a green dragon

around," Graywing told the girl, his voice thin with exasperation. "Green dragons are—"

"It wasn't exactly green," Thayla pointed out. "It was more brown, or maybe like gold and wild honey."

"Bron's dragon!" Pert insisted. "Does what Bron says!"

"She's right," Thayla said, nodding. "It was a bronze dragon."

"Alright!" Graywing snapped. "Whatever you say! Now come with me, girl! We've got to get—"

From somewhere behind him came the ironic voice of Dartimien the Cat. "Will you all shut up over there? And stop aggravating those gully dwarves, barbarian! I'm trying to read."

The Cat was over by the main pillar, squinting in the dim light, running a finger down rows of glyphs on a metallic plate attached to the stone. Gully dwarves crowded around him, some of them clambering up his back, hauling themselves up by his shoulder straps for a better view. One chattering little oaf was actually sitting on the assassin's shoulders, peering over his head.

Graywing swore a muttered oath and headed that way. The distant sounds of battle, filtering in through cracks and grates, had risen in volume until it was a song of chaos. Then, abruptly, the world outside the cavernous cellars had gone silent. Any moment now, Graywing was sure, hordes of Gelnians, Tarmites, mercenary soldiers and who knew what else would be flooding into these recesses. And Dartimien was reading labels on posts.

Pushing through packed mobs of gully dwarves, the plainsman reached Dartimien and squinted at the bronze plaque. "What is it?"

"Sign," the gully dwarf on Dartimien's shoulders chattered happily. "Got runes on it. Say this place fulla crumbs an' shiny rocks."

"That's *fulcrum!*" Dartimien growled. "The fulcrum on the *shining stone!*"

"Yeah," the gully dwarf agreed. "Right."

The explanation was lost on most of the crowd of gully dwarves. Several dozen of them stared around, thoughtfully, then wandered off in search of crumbs and shiny rocks. Within moments some of them had found a vein of quartz leading upward, ridged with imbedments of gleaming pyrite. Forgetting everything else around them, these intrepid explorers dug out various tools and began climbing the cavern wall, mining pyrite as they went.

"Shiny rocks," some of them called. "Jus' like dragon said."

"That dragon kinda like Highbulp's dragon," a gully dwarf proclaimed, "Maybe same dragon?" Almost upsetting Graywing, he pushed forward between the tall man's legs. He was a portly little individual with a curly, iron-gray beard and puffy little eyes set close above a protruding nose. He wore a crown of rat's teeth on his unkempt head. "Yep, same dragon," he decided. "Same dragon as before, long time ago."

Beside Graywing, Pert bristled. "Bron's dragon," she insisted. "Not Highbulp's."

Ignoring all of them, Dartimien studied the runes on the metal plaque, then peered closely at the stone around it. Where the mildew was rubbed away, the stone glowed with a soft, pearl-white luster. "Interesting," the Cat mused. "I think we've found something of value here. Something about the high and the low—"

Fifty yards away, at the mouth of a dark, jagged hole in the cavern wall, torchlight flared and suddenly there were armed men there, dozens of them.

Dartimien straightened, daggers flashing in his hands. "Tarmites," he hissed. "They've found us."

"Ever'body run like crazy!" the Highbulp screeched. The crowd of gully dwarves roaming the cavern floor dissolved into a tumbling tangle of panicked little people as his subjects tried to respond, bouncing one another right and left in their haste. Several of them bounced off a wall and set off a chain reaction of tumbling bodies. The Highbulp was swept off his feet and buried in the turmoil. The lady Lidda dug him out, cuffing gully dwarves right and left. "Glitch a real nuisance," she observed. Gripping her husband's ear, she dragged him free and propelled him toward a wall. "Climb!" she ordered.

Shaken from his reverie, Scrib fell on the tottering old Grand Notioner, who cursed loudly, crawled free, got to his unsteady feet and flailed about with his mop handle staff, delivering swats and bruises with enthusiastic abandon. On the walls of the cavern, various gully dwarves looked downward at the melee. Some lost their holds and fell, joining the free-for-all below. Others, though, were absorbed in their tasks. They had found a vein of yellow pyrite above the tumbled portal, and were busily mining it.

All around the great column, the pandemonium spread. In the midst of it, Bron braced himself, his iron shield swaying this way and that. He had lost track of Thayla Mesinda, and without the human girl's presence to remind him, he was a bit confused as to what he was supposed to be doing. Then he saw a tumbling gully dwarf—one of his closest friends, though the name escaped him for a moment—rolling toward little Pert. Without hesitation he swatted the miscreant with the flat of his broadsword, then placed himself to protect little Pert. As a designated hero, he felt compelled to protect *somebody*, and Pert was a reasonable choice.

Graywing the barbarian stared around in open-mouthed disbelief. He had never seen such total, all-out confusion, all of it because the pompous little Highbulp—who now was among those on the wall, mining pyrites—had told them to run.

"There's no place to run to, you little idiots!" Graywing roared. "We'll have to fight!"

On the wall above, the Highbulp glanced around, almost losing his grip. "What?"

"I said, fight!"

"Okay," Glitch said. "Ever'body fight!"

All around, agitated Aghar froze, straightened and looked around them. "Okay," several of them said. "Whatever." Beside Graywing a husky gully dwarf swung a roundhouse punch that sent another gully dwarf tumbling. Several of them went down, bowled over by the ruckus. The riot became a melee as the entire tribe joined in, gully dwarves pummeling away at other gully dwarves, enthusiastic combatants piling onto those who fell.

Graywing stared around in disbelief. "Oh, for the gods' sake!" he breathed. Then, brandishing his sword, wading through rioting Aghar, he headed for the human intruders piling through the broken portal. Dartimien was beside him, bounding over clusters of gully dwarves. From a distance, somewhere behind the Tarmite warriors gaping around in the gloom, came the sounds of falling stone. Billows of dust issued from the jagged portal, partially obscuring the invaders. Dartimien's eyes narrowed, his darting glances scanning the humans in the dust. They were all footmen—tower guards and warders, low soldiers wearing the colors of home guardsmen. Nowhere among them were any officers' insignias.

Graywing filled his lungs and raised his sword, ready to fight, but suddenly Dartimien wheeled to face him. "Wait!" the Cat rasped. "We can use these dolts!"

Before Graywing could react, Dartimien turned away again, his hands empty of daggers, and strode toward the Tarmites. "Where is the rest of your detail?" he demanded, his tone as imperious as any field commander's.

The Tarmites huddled in confusion, their weapons lowered. "I don't know," one of them said. "Cap'n was right behind us a minute ago, but I don't see him now."

"He's still outside," another volunteered. "Lord Vulpin himself was . . . well, I think he sent us in here."

"Idiots!" Dartimien rasped. "Don't you see what has happened? The invaders have tricked you. That rockfall, they've sealed us up in these cellars. The attack is above, in the courtyards. Not here!"

"It is?" a burly Tarmite tilted his helmet to scratch his head. "Then what do we do now?"

"You can follow your orders!" Dartimien hissed. "You should be up in the main keep, defending against the enemy!"

"Y-yes, sir," the burly one said. "But how do we get back there?"

"The way you came, obviously. Now get in there and start digging!"

Obediently, most of the Tarmite warriors turned and headed back the way they had come, through the broken portal and up the tunnel. One or two glanced back, gawking at the scene in the catacombs. There seemed to be gully dwarves everywhere. "Wh-what about them, sir?" one asked, pointing.

"What about them?" Dartimien snapped. "They're only gully dwarves. Ignore them!"

"Yes, sir."

Within moments, more than a dozen yeomen of Castle Tarmish were at work in the tunnel, digging away fallen stone.

"That should keep them busy for a while," Dartimien confided to Graywing, who was shaking his head in disbelief.

"They took your commands," the plainsman said. "Why did they do that?"

"Don't you know about the Tarmites and the Gelnians?" Dartimien cocked an ironic brow. "The only difference between them is the colors they wear, yet they've been at war against each other, off and on, for hundreds of years. Not one in a hundred on either side has any idea what they fight about. They just take orders from whoever's in charge at the moment. It's always been like that."

"So they accepted you as being in charge? Why?"

"Because I acted like I was. Now I think we should see about getting out of this hole."

"How? The entrance is blocked."

"You really don't know anything about cities, do you, barbarian?" The Cat gestured toward a gloomy alcove a hundred yards away, in the recesses of the cavern. There, shadows among the shadows, a troop of female gully dwarves was descending from above, winding their way around a huge pillar. They carried loads of forage, found somewhere above.

"I suggest we use the stairs," Dartimien said levelly.

Chapter 21
The Hole Truth

Seething with malignant intent, Clonogh paced the wrecked tower. He had scores to settle, and now, thanks to the intervention of a dragon, he had the power to do so.

He might have gone out to face his enemies, but that was never Clonogh's way. Here in this tower, he felt aloof, above the turmoil beyond, and he liked the idea of his enemies coming to him—using their own efforts to go to their doom. So, a seething old spider in its chosen lair, he waited.

The skeletal structure of stone that had been the

great tower of Tarmish was a twisted ruin now, its precipitous stairway a shambles. But he knew the loft was secure. Where the stones had fallen away, where bombards had blasted outer walls to reveal the winding stairs within, and shattered the dark inner walls beyond them, white stone gleamed—a monolith of pure basalt that descended through the great structure, its foundations deep in the bedrock below. The trappings of mankind might fall away, but this stone was eternal.

Just beyond the sprung portal a wide-shouldered gully dwarf approached, scrambling upward through the ruins. Clonogh smiled faintly. The little creature was bringing him the Fang of Orm.

Shielding himself casually with invisibility, Clonogh waited by the doorway. The gully dwarf would be here in moments. And not far behind, climbing through the wreckage from different sides, were the spawn of a Dragon Highlord—Chatara Kral and Lord Vulpin.

The footsteps on the stairs hesitated, then a tattered Aghar crept out into the ravaged room, peering this way and that with nervous, beady little eyes. The creature was sturdy for a gully dwarf, squat and broad-shouldered. He was well over three feet tall, larger then most of his kind, and there were streaks and tangles of gray in his unkempt hair. Clonogh studied him for a moment, unimpressed. One gully dwarf was pretty much like another, despite slight differences. What did interest the mage was the thing the gully dwarf carried in his grimy hands— the Fang of Orm.

With a muttered spell, Clonogh dropped the cloak of invisibility and stood blocking the doorway. "That talisman is mine," he said. "Give it to me."

Clout whirled and gawked at the man, blinking in terror. "Wh-what?"

"That." Clonogh pointed. "It's mine!"

"This thing?" Clout raised the Fang, peering at it as though he had never seen it before.

"Yes," Clonogh said. "It's mine."

Clout stared at the man a moment longer, then backed away, frightened but stubborn. He had grown to cherish the implement he carried. "This thing my bashin' tool," he said. "Not yours."

"Give it to me!" Clonogh snarled, lunging forward. "That is no 'bashing tool,' you little twit!"

Clout dodged aside, ducked into a broken cabinet and peered out. "Is, too," he quavered. "Good for bashin' rats. Talls don' bash rats."

"I'll turn you into a rat!" Clonogh said. "My powers are restored. I command magic now!"

"Do?" Clout squinted, not understanding a word of it. The old Tall seemed to be as crazy as a loon, even crazier than old what's-'is-name, the Highbulp. The gully dwarf's sullen stubbornness dissolved, replaced by confusion. "How come?" he asked, hoping for a clue to what the human was talking about.

"There was a dragon here," Clonogh said, easing toward the broken cabinet. "It cast a spell, and I was within its range. It . . . it resonated me. I am finally complete!"

"Sorry 'bout that," Clout said, baffled.

"Why in the names of the gods am I trying to explain anything to a gully dwarf?" Clonogh asked himself, sneering. Another step, and he would be able to trap the gully dwarf at the cabinet. If he could just keep the creature distracted for a moment more . . . "It certainly did," he said. "I am no longer as I was."

"Poor Tall!" The gully dwarf's voice within the cabinet was full of real sympathy. "Wish you were."

Clonogh's shriek of anguish echoed from the broken tower walls as he felt his newfound powers, all his wonderful, dragon-induced powers, slip away. In an instant the dragon magic was gone. He couldn't for the life of him remember how to phrase the spells that had contained it. With a wail, he collapsed on the stone floor, and from the stairwell came the tread of hard boots, climbing toward him. He didn't know which was coming first, Lord Vulpin or Chatara Kral, but whichever it was, the other would be close behind.

"Please," he wheezed in an ancient voice, rheumy eyes trying to focus on the dull, confused face of the gully dwarf, "Please, reverse that wish."

"Do what?" Clout sidled from the cabinet, staring at the suddenly-collapsed human on the floor.

"Wish!" Clonogh pleaded. "You pathetic little twit! Why must you be so dense? Please, before my enemies find me like this. Make a wish!"

Clout scratched his head, deep in thought. "Wish? Okay. Bet ladies makin' stew 'bout now. Wish I had some stew."

* * * * *

In a realm far away as distances are measured, but very near as they are not, the great one-fanged serpent called Orm raised its evil head, slitted nostrils twitching, forked tongue tasting the air as resonances long awaited touched its senses. There! Just there, only a strike away for one whose plane was not bounded by the sensory dimensions, the creature's lost fang called—twice! Gigantic muscles tensed. But once again, the resonance was just too brief, just too uncertain for a clear target. The Fang had been used, its magic awakened, but its user's concentration had lapsed almost before the magic had occurred.

Hissing in frustration, Orm coiled and writhed, clinging to the tenuous sense of target, desperately seeking just one more "sending." The next time he would be ready. At the next emanation, no matter how slight, he would strike.

* * * * *

In the catacombs beneath Tarmish it was noticed, though only fleetingly, that there was a sudden shortage of Talls. Scrib the Ponderer became aware of their absence when he looked around from his study of runes and didn't see any humans. It was evident that they had all gone away, just as the dragon had gone away, and to the gully dwarf the departures were equally mysterious.

But then, who knew what humans, or dragons, either, for that matter, were likely to do next?

Anyway, Scrib had more important things to think about. The squiggles on the plaque were more than just random symbols, he realized. Both a dragon and a human had told him so. The symbols actually *meant* something.

"If you don't want to remember things," somebody had said sometime, "then you write them down."

Squiggles were writing, and writing was remembering. Somehow, to Scrib, that seemed to be an important notion. He wished he knew how to write it down.

Bron the Hero was aware, also, that where there had been humans, now there were none. But he had little time to think about it. Little Pert, having diverted the services of the hero from the human girl to herself, was busy consolidating her victory. It seemed to Bron that everywhere he turned, Pert was there, gazing up at him with wide, loving eyes and giving him orders. Her manner toward him reminded him vaguely of his mother's manner toward his father, and Bron found himself responding to each suggestion and request with a resigned, "Yes, dear."

He had a respite when the Lady Lidda and several other females accosted him to relieve him of his shield. They had a fire going, and needed the iron bowl to make stew. When they trooped away, carrying his shield among them, little Pert looked after them for a moment, then turned back to Bron. She patted him fondly on his lightly-bearded cheek, and took his broadsword from his hand. "This good for stir stew," she said, and followed the other ladies, trailing the heavy sword behind her.

"Yes, dear," Bron muttered.

"That'n got you wrapped up real good," a voice said, beside him. He glanced around. Scrib stood there, nodding sympathetically.

"Guess so," Bron said. "Keep meanin' to tell her scat, but then I forget."

"Write it down," Scrib suggested, sagely.

Old Gandy, the Grand Notioner, noticed that the Talls had gone away, and he sighed with relief, leaning on his mop handle staff. Many times in his long career, he had been in the company of humans for one reason or another. He didn't remember much about any of those times, but of one thing he was certain, no good ever came of associating with the tall people. They were best forgotten, so Gandy promptly forgot them.

There were always more interesting things than humans, anyway. Even here, in this place that was as unlikely and mysterious as most places were, there were things to think about. The bustling, clinging, wrangling people of his tribe were mostly up a wall now, clambering here and there on the vertiginous surface of the vast cavern's upper reaches. Every few seconds two or three of them would lose their holds and drop to the floor, but they scrambled right back up. The Highbulp had said to search for shiny rocks, and it was the habit of most gully dwarves to do what their Highbulp told them to do.

High above, almost at the curve where the cavern veered inward toward the great central pillar, they had uncovered a veritable treasure of shiny pyrite imbedded in the stone of the cavern wall, and now they were chipping away at it. Below them the floor was alive with falling, bouncing stones, deluges of gravel and occasional dislocated miners, and the Highbulp stood in the midst of the cascade, shouting orders and dodging debris.

"Highbulp a numbskull," Gandy muttered.

Nearby, several of the ladies had a concoction of rats, weeds, mushrooms and bits of pollywog beginning to steam in the legendary Great Stew Bowl, which had been Bron's noble shield until they confiscated it for better use.

At the fire, the Lady Lidda glanced around. "What?"

"Said, 'Highbulp a numbskull,' "Gandy repeated.

"Sure is," Lidda agreed.

Gandy pointed with his mop handle. A short distance away, it was raining debris. Old Glitch stood in the downpour, ducking this way and that, oblivious to everything except the gleam of pyrite far above. "Hasn't got sense enough come in out of th' rocks," the Grand Notioner explained.

Lidda glanced around. "Glitch!" she shouted. "Get out of way!"

If the Highbulp heard her, he ignored her. Gravel clattered around him, accompanied by flailing, bouncing Aghar, but he kept his eyes on the work above. "More that way!" he shouted to the clinging miners. "Lot more left right there!"

At the stew bowl, the Lady Lidda shook her head in disgust. "Bron!" she shouted. "Go get Highbulp!"

"What?" Bron blinked.

Pert looked up from stirring the stew. The broadsword was bigger than she was, but with the help of several other ladies she was managing. "Lady Lidda wants Highbulp!" she ordered. "Bron go get him!"

"Yes, dear," Bron said. Single-mindedly he waded into the confusion of the drop zone below the overhead pyrite mines.

Gandy watched him go, and shook his ancient head. "Like daddy, like kid," he muttered. "Couple real twits. Both of 'em nuisances an' numbskulls. Born for be Highbulps."

As the sturdy Bron dragged his struggling, complaining father toward them, towing the old Highbulp by his ankle, Gandy studied the pair with rheumy old eyes. Glitch's matted beard, once curly and wiry, was streaked with gray now, and his bald dome shone through his crown. It seemed a long time since he had shown any force of leadership. He still whined and complained when he didn't get his way, but the old quality of Highbulpery—the ability to get everybody to do whatever he wanted simply by making a nuisance of himself—was less evident than in the past.

Bron, on the other hand, seemed to have no trouble getting people's attention. Right now, for instance, he was a designated hero—whatever that meant— and very recently he seemed to have had himself a dragon. Of course, nobody had any idea how a Highbulp might be selected, but Gandy decided it was time to think about such things.

"Time for change," the Grand Notioner decided. He hobbled over to where the ladies were cooking stew. "What Lady Lidda think?" he asked.

Lidda glanced around at him. "Not much," she confided. "Too busy for think."

Crouching beside the cooking shield, Gandy dipped a grimy hand into its simmering contents to test it. Things wriggled between his fingers. Some of the stew's contents weren't quite dead yet. "Cook a little longer," he suggested. "How 'bout Glitch quit bein' Highbulp?"

"Good idea," Lidda nodded. "Get a little rest."

"Glitch gettin' tired?"

"I gettin' tired," Lidda said. "No easy job, tendin' to Highbulp."

At her side, the Lady Bruze chirped, "'Bout time that twit Glitch retire. Let somebody else have chance to be big cheese. Let Clout be Highbulp."

"Go sit on tack, Lady Bruze," the Lady Lidda suggested. "Clout good Chief Basher. Make terrible Highbulp, though."

"Would not!" Bruze snapped.

"Would too," Lidda countered. "Where Clout now?"

"Dunno," the Chief Basher's wife admitted. "Gone off someplace."

"Fine," Lidda said. "Highbulp can't go off someplace alla time. Gotta stay with clan. Like Glitch does."

"Highbulp doesn' stay with clan," someone nearby corrected her. "Clan stays with Highbulp."

"So there!" Bruze gloated. "Clout oughtta be Highbulp."

Behind them, Bron deposited his father unceremoniously beside the fire and glanced at the pot. "Stew 'bout ready?" he asked. "I'm hungry."

Glitch the Most, Highbulp by persuasion and Lord Protector of This Place and More Other Places Than Anybody Could Count, sat up and twisted around to rub his sore rump. "Some kin' way to treat Highbulp," he whined. "What Lady Lidda want now?"

"Don' remember," Lidda admitted.

Behind them, the cavern reverberated as a huge chunk of broken stone crashed to the floor, shattering into a thousand pieces. Where it hit was where Glitch had been standing just moments before. Panicked gully dwarves, carrying armloads of sifted pyrite away from the fall zone, scurried this way and that. High on the wall, a chorus of Aghar voices said, "Oops!"

"Oh, yeah," Lidda remembered. "Want Glitch stay out of way when rocks fall."

"Oughtta write that down," Scrib suggested, to nobody in particular.

Lidda ignored him. Thoughtfully, she gazed at her husband, and came to a decision. "Time for you give up bein' Highbulp, Glitch," she said. "Let somebody else do it."

Glitch clambered to his feet, gawking at his wife. "Give up bein' Highbulp? Mean I should jus' abdica . . . termi . . . res . . . quit?"

"Sure," the Lady Lidda answered. "Why not?"

"I Glitch th' Most!" Glitch blustered. "Highbulp, noble leader. Main pain! Biggest cheese aroun'. Been Highbulp long time! Always been Highbulp! Why quit?"

"Not much fun anymore?" Lidda suggested.

Daunted by the logic of this, Glitch subsided a bit, muttering to himself. "Quit an' do what?" he asked, finally.

Lidda only shrugged, but Gandy pointed his mop handle staff at the growing pile of gleaming pyrites beneath the wall dig. "How 'bout new career?" he suggested. "Clan got big, new mine here. Need somebody in charge of shiny rocks."

"Pretty big job," Glitch admitted. "Not jus' ever'-body know 'bout shiny rocks." He thought it over for a moment, then removed his crown of rat's teeth and dropped it on the floor. "Okay, somebody else be Highbulp. I quit. Hey, everybody! Bring shiny rocks over here!"

Grumbling at the aches in his old bones, the Grand Notioner picked up the dilapidated crown and thrust it at Bron. "Here," he said, "You be High-bulp now."

Bron didn't even look around. He was busy. Pert had him stirring the stew. "Nope," he said. "Don't want to."

"Gotta have a Highbulp," Gandy insisted.

"Get somebody else," Bron said.

With a determined sigh, Gandy hobbled away a few steps and thumped his mop handle on the stone floor until the clamor around him subsided. This was not going the way the Grand Notioner had planned, but it was too late to turn back now. "Glitch not Highbulp anymore," he announced to all who were listening. "Need a volunteer."

"For what?" several of his clansmen wondered.

"For be Highbulp," Gandy explained. "Crown up for grabs. Who want be Highbulp?"

Only silence and blank stares answered him. Then from high on the wall, a voice said, "Let Bron be Highbulp. Bron got nothin' better to do."

"Bron a hero!" Pert protested.

"Don't need hero." Gandy said. "Need Highbulp. But Bron says no."

"Don't wanna be Highbulp!" Bron insisted, still stirring stew. "Dumb job, bein' Highbulp."

"Any other nomina . . . sugges . . . any takers?" Gandy called, turning this way and that, holding up the crown. By threes and fives, the gully dwarves of Clan Bulp turned away, expressing their disinterest.

"*Somebody* gotta be Highbulp," the Grand Notioner insisted.

"You do it, then," a gully dwarf snapped, carrying an armload of pyrite to Glitch's pile.

"Make Bron or Clout do it," several said.

With an eloquent shrug, Gandy returned to the fireside. "Bron Highbulp now," he proclaimed. Standing on tiptoe, he tried to set the old crown on Bron's head. "Majority rule."

Bron glared at him, avoiding the crown. "How many majori . . . maj . . . whatever?" he demanded.

"Two." Gandy said, sagely.

"No way," Bron said. "Let Clout do it."

"Clout not here."

"Crown here. Jus' say, 'Clout Highbulp now.' "

"Okay." The Grand Notioner gave up. "Clout Highbulp now. Anybody see him, tell him so."

With that task completed, the Grand Notioner turned his attention to getting some stew. He retrieved an old wooden bowl from its hiding place in his garments, stooped . . . and stopped. Bron was still stirring with his broadsword, muttering to himself about the injustice of it all, but he was stirring nothing. Where the stew had been, simmering in the legendary Great Stew Bowl, now there was nothing. Even the great iron pot was gone. The whole mess had simply vanished, as though it had never been there.

*　*　*　*　*

At first, Lord Vulpin did not recognize the ancient figure sprawled beside the battered telescope cabinet in what was left of the Tower of Tarmish. Then the rheumy old eyes, staring at him with livid hatred, told him who this relic was. "Clonogh," the Lord of Tarmish purred. "So your tarnished magic has reduced you to this. Where is the Fang of Orm that you were to deliver to me?"

The old mage glared at him, despising him but helpless to harm him. Vulpin glanced around, wrinkling his nose. A foul stench seemed to pervade the atmosphere here, and he heard tiny, muffled lapping noises that seemed nearby. The din of battle below—the remaining forces of Gelnia and Tarmish were hand to hand and blade to shield now in the courtyard beneath the tower—almost drowned out all other sound. Then he turned crimson eyes on the cowering Clonogh again, and raised his black visor. A cruel grin split his beard. "The Fang or your life, mage. The choice is yours."

"Kill me," Clonogh hissed. A wavering, bony finger pointed at Vulpin's blood-stained sword. "I want nothing more than death."

"It is no matter," Vulpin sneered. "The Fang is

259

here. I saw the creature that brought it. But no clean death is yours, master mage." From his tunic he withdrew a little, glassy sphere, holding it casually between finger and thumb of a gauntleted hand. "Your soul, old man," he purred. "I said I would return it one day. So here it is."

"The Fang is no good to you without a wish-maker," Clonogh spat, struggling to arise. "An innocent. Where will such as you find an innocent, now that your captive girl is gone?"

"Gone?" Vulpin grinned, barked a command and a huge, armored brute stepped out of the stairwell into daylight. One of Vulpin's cave-vandal guards carried a struggling girl under his arm as casually as a smaller man might carry a puppy. The girl was Thayla Mesinda. "I found her just below," Vulpin said. "Apparently she and some others had been hiding in the cellars beneath this place. She will speak the wish I want, Clonogh, the wish that will rid me of all annoyances." With a sneer, Vulpin stepped to the precipitous edge of the broken tower and raised the glassy bauble in his fingers. "You have earned your reward, Clonogh," he said. "The return of your soul. Here it is. If you want it, go get it."

With a chuckle, Vulpin tossed the glass sphere outward.

"My soul!" Clonogh shrieked. With the last of his strength he darted past Vulpin and dived outward, trying to catch the falling sphere. It was falling free, at the limit of his reach. With his last strength he reached for the little sphere, and with his last breath, as he plummeted toward the cobbled courtyard, Clonogh voiced a spell. It was his last, and now the ravages of it no longer mattered. He put into it every shred of his energies, every trace of his hatred, and the arcane words still echoed above the tumult of battle as the old magician's fingers closed around his falling "soul" and his withered body shattered upon the stones of the court. "You will never leave this place," the echoes seemed to say.

A thin, dark cloud might have floated for a moment above the gore of the splattered corpse, then swirled and wound around the standing tower, darkening the stones. It might have, or it might have been no more than a trick of light and shadows.

Inside the telescope cabinet, Clout was sipping stew from a huge vat of the stuff that had suddenly, for no reason he could understand, appeared there beside him. The gully dwarf was aware of a great deal of commotion just outside the cabinet. There were Talls out there, arguing and shouting. But it meant nothing to Clout. He had wished that he had some stew. Now he had stew, a whole pot-full of fresh, hot stew, and the pot itself seemed to be none other than the legendary Great Stew Bowl of the Bulps.

Another person, even some other gully dwarves, might have found all this puzzling. But Clout had never been one to wonder about things beyond his understanding, and thus he rarely ever wondered about anything at all. The stew he had wished for was here, and he was hungry. Lacking any other utensil, he dipped in with both hands, then stuck his bearded face into the mess to lap at the juices.

He had just come up for air, belching happily, when the great, helmet-framed face of a fire-eyed human filled the broken panel beside him and the man's voice said, "Ah, there it is." A large, armor-clad arm reached into Clout's hiding place, swatted the gully dwarf casually aside, and gauntleted fingers closed around his bashing tool.

"Here, now!" Clout shrieked as the white stick was pulled away from him. With a lunge and leap that almost cleared the stew pot, but not quite, the Chief Basher of Clan Bulp caught his receding bashing tool and hung on. Half-submerged in noisome stew, he grasped the stick with both hands and clung to it. "My bashin' tool!" he wailed at the top of his lungs. "How come ever'body tryin' steal my bashin' tool?"

Chapter 22
Highbulps Lost and Found

"I thought you were watching her!" Graywing's feral eyes blazed with fury. He towered over Dartimien the Cat, hovering in rage to confront the smaller man nose-to-nose. "I turn my back for a moment, only for a moment, and you lose her!"

"Back off or you'll lose that yammering tongue, barbarian!" the Cat snarled, not giving an inch of ground. "Don't blame me if you can't keep track of your women. I was busy looking for a way out of this place!"

The stairs Dartimien had found, leading upward

from the great catacombs beneath Tarmish, had brought them into a labyrinth of interlaced tunnels—sewers and storm drains for the city above. It was a maze of buried pathways, some wide and some narrow, most dark and winding, many rambling aimlessly, and all ripe with the accumulated refuse of generations of Tarmish history.

A gaggle of gully dwarves had followed the three humans up from the catacombs, it seemed the dim little creatures were everywhere, and these scampered here and there, exploring. Normally, the dim-witted little people were terrified of humans. The gully dwarves were, in fact, terrified of nearly everything, at first sight. But they were as adaptable as they were dense. Once having become accustomed to someone or something, anyone or anything, and accepting its presence, they merely assumed that it had always been there and was simply a part of the mysterious world in which they lived. Gully dwarves had been known to tolerate the presence of humans, goblins, turkeys, an ogre or two and even, now and then, a dragon, once they became accustomed to its presence.

For their part, humans generally paid no more attention to gully dwarves than they would to any other vermin. They were, after all, only gully dwarves—a nuisance, but seldom worth worrying about.

The tunnels wound and intersected, lighted only by occasional small grates, iron-barred and opening into the courtyards below the tower. There in the daylight, beyond the stone-bound slits, armed men marched and scurried, some of them searching for others, some locked in combat with those they had found. Gelnians and Tarmites, the warriors of the Vale of Sunder seemed oblivious to all but their ancient feud. Here and there, the seeps from above were red with fresh-spilled blood. And beneath it all, the sewers wound here and there in reeking gloom.

In such surroundings Graywing the Plainsman—skilled tracker and pathfinder of the wild lands—was hopelessly confused. His was a world of open skies and long winds. The cluster and stench of cities left him disoriented. So the city-born Dartimien, to whom sewers and rancid alleys were second nature, had taken it on himself to chart a path that might lead to an exit.

But at an intersection of several tunnels he had paused to read the markings on a wall (accompanied by an interested gully dwarf or two) trusting to the sound of the plainsman's boots to lead him to the others. He had followed the sound, and found Graywing. But the plainsman was alone. There was no sign of Thayla Mesinda. They realized simultaneously that the girl was missing, when each discovered that she wasn't with the other. The two warriors faced each other angrily in the dim light of a sewer channel, while here and there frightened gully dwarves scurried for cover.

"I should put my blade through you, alley cat," Graywing blustered.

"Shake that fist in my face again and you'll pull back a bloody stump," Dartimien purred, razorlike daggers appearing in his hands.

"First you're hovering around her like a starved hound at a feast, then the minute I turn my back you lose her!"

"Who was hovering? Me?" Dartimien's tone was scathing. "From the minute you first saw that girl, you haven't had your wits about you! I never saw anything so pathetic!"

"I told you to look after her!"

"You ordered me to leave her alone!"

Among the nearby shadows, small voices whispered among themselves. "Why Talls hollerin' on each other? Gonna kill each other?" " Who knows?" "Who cares?"

Growling like feral beasts, the two men glared at each other, then lowered their gazes. "This isn't doing us any good," Graywing said. "Where could she have gone?"

"Obviously not where we did," the Cat admitted. "Back where the tunnels met, when you came this way, was she with you?"

"Of course she was! She . . . well, I thought she was, anyway. She was chirping about seeing light down one of the corridors, but . . ."

"But you weren't listening," Dartimien sighed, turning away. "You never listen!"

"I was so listening! She has a lovely voice! But I assumed she was talking to some of these Aghar."

Dartimien sneered. "You were listening to her voice, and paying no attention to her words? Well, she's gone now, and that's that. Too bad, but those things happen. I think there's a main outfall ahead a few hundred yards. We may have to bend some bars, you ought to be useful there, at least, but it's worth a look."

"We're going back," Graywing said.

"Don't be ridiculous! That girl could be anywhere by now. She's probably been caught and killed." Bits of grit cascaded from the roof of the tunnel, and the paving above thundered with the sound of many running feet. Distantly, there was the clash and clatter of a full-scale battle being waged. "We have to get out of here. Come on, now. Let's find that main grate."

"I'm going back," Graywing repeated, drawing his sword. "Thayla needs me." Without another glance he strode past Dartimien and headed back down the tunnel.

"Fool," Dartimien snarled. "Alright, so she's pretty, but she's just a woman. The world is full of women. You'll just get yourself killed . . . ." He let the words trail off. Graywing was already out of sight, around a bend. Dartimien shook his head. "Gods," he muttered. "Why should I have to bend bars by myself? That's brute work. That big oaf is better at such things than I am." Cursing under his breath, he set off after Graywing.

Behind him, a gaggle of gully dwarves tagged along, keeping to the shadowed places. They weren't the least bit interested in tall people's doings, but it was in their nature to follow whoever happened to lead. Right now the only people doing any leading seemed to be these incomprehensible Talls.

Where tunnels intersected, Dartimien found Graywing crouched, studying patterns in the mud. "She was here," the plainsman said, not turning. "I knew she was right behind me. But when I went this way"—he gestured back the way they had come—"she went off to the right. Up that rising tunnel over there."

"Stupid," Dartimien hissed. "That's only a storm drain. It leads right up to the inner courtyard, not fifty yards from where we found the opening down into the catacombs."

"How would she know where it leads?" Graywing snapped. "She followed it because there's daylight ahead there somewhere. Look. You can see it from here."

"I can also hear the clash of weapons from here,

and smell the stench of fresh-spilled blood."

Ignoring him, Graywing rose to his feet and headed up the tunnel.

"That barbarian is crazy as a loon," the Cat muttered. "You'd think he'd never seen a woman before."

"Sap's runnin'," a small voice beside him said.

Dartimien scowled at the grimy little creature. "Butt out," he snapped. "I don't need an explanation of the facts of life, and certainly not from a gully dwarf." With an oath he strode away, following Graywing.

"What Tall say?" Pad asked, cocking a brow at the confused Blip.

"Said he don' want facks 'splained," Blip said. "Was jus' tryin' tell him Sap ran off."

"Where Sap go?"

"Prob'ly downstairs," Blip answered. "Prob'ly tellin' ever'body where Clout is."

"Where Clout?"

"Upstairs," Blip said. "Sap heard him holler."

With nothing better to do, the remaining gaggle of gully dwarves headed up the tunnel, where the humans had gone.

At the top of the tunnel, Graywing peered out into the main courtyard of Tarmish from the shadows of a broken grate. Beyond, armed men slashed and hammered at one another, their cries blending with the ring of steel on iron. Thayla Mesinda had definitely come this way. There were distinct marks where her small slippers had climbed the last few feet of incline, and a small handprint in the grime of the tunnel wall where she had pushed through the gaping portal.

He was bracing himself for a charge into the open when Dartimien came up to him. The smaller man looked past him and grunted in distaste. "I guess you're planning to run right out there and join in," he said.

"Those aren't real soldiers," Graywing growled. "Just Tarmites and Gelnians, fighting one another. They always do that. They always have."

"So which side do you plan to be on?"

Graywing ignored the question. "I don't see any mercenaries out there. Do you?"

"No, maybe they all left. Civil wars don't pay very well. But there are some real hoodlums around somewhere. There were icemen in Chatara Kral's camp. Those brutes are here if the Gelnians are. They don't ever walk away from a fight."

"Vulpin has some personal guards, too," Graywing added. "I saw them when we first arrived. They looked like cave vandals. Real elite killers. But I don't see them now."

"They're wherever Vulpin is," the Cat said. "Look. Graywing, I hate to dash you with cold reality like this, but neither of us will profit from this mess. Whatever you were promised for bringing that magician here, you'll never collect it. And I most certainly am no longer in Chatara Kral's employ. The best thing either of us can do is turn around, find that outfall port, and get away from this place while we still have our skins."

"You go, then, if you want to." Graywing barely glanced at the city man. "Thayla needs protection, and I mean to protect her."

"From everyone but yourself, I suppose. How chivalrous of you. Anyway, you don't even know where she is."

"I'll find her," the plainsman growled. With a lunge and a Cobar war cry, he launched himself through the broken grate and into the thick of the fighting beyond.

"Fool," Dartimien sighed. His feral eyes narrowed as he watched the plains warrior cutting his way through the midst of battle. The barbarian's sword was a bright blur, dancing around him as though it had a life of its own. Its blade flashed from bright steel to bright blood, singing its song of chaos as it clove through the packed combatants. Graywing's flaxen hair and beard whipped in the wind as he dodged this way and that, making for the base of the tower. Beyond, in the shadows of the tall, tattered structure, figures appeared at a breach in the wall, paused for a moment, then filed out of sight, into the base of the tower itself.

"Chatara Kral," Dartimien muttered. There had been no doubt of identity. The Gelnian regent's brilliant armor was like no other. And with her were four of her personal guards, hulking icemen with brass-bound shields and great axes.

For a moment, in the intervening courtyard, the path behind Graywing was clear, swept clean by the ferocity of his charge. Then he seemed to be swallowed up in the crowd as howling Tarmites and Gelnians closed in around him.

"The gods must love fools," Dartimien hissed, filling his hands with daggers. "Otherwise there wouldn't be so many of them." With a snarl as fierce as any cat's, he vaulted through the broken grate and into the fray.

* * * * *

Soft, slanting sunlight washed the wooded hillsides west of the Vale of Sunder, filtering through the umbrella of leaves to paint myriad, flickering patterns on the forest slopes beneath. Soft breezes in treetops made the patterns dance, a subtle, intricate kaleidoscope of tiny motion obscuring the huge, graceful movements of the creature beneath the high boughs.

In her first life Verden Leafglow had shunned the daylight. A creature of stealth and deceit, she had preferred the dark hours to the bright. But now she found that the sunlight was a comfortable warmth, and the rightness of it reminded her of how much she had changed in recent times. She was not the same dragon she had been, either in that past life or in the early portions of this one. Rippling scales that had once been emerald green now were a rich brown in hue, iridescent across the warm spectra with overtones of scintillant gold.

Little by little, the god Reorx had worked his magic upon her, always by her own choice it seemed but never with any clear options in that choice.

In her dreams and her deepest soul the visage of Reorx spoke to her. *Free will*, it said. *The poisons of evil remain, and the antidote lies not in the frozen serenity of blind good. The true enemy of evil is free will. They must resolve their conflicts in their own way, and you must wait.*

Your task is not the disorder of human minds, Verden Leafglow. Your task is greater. There is an evil beyond evil, an ancient grotesquery left over from other reckless games, long ago. That is your mission, Verden Leafglow. You will know when the time is at hand. You will have the chance to prove yourself.

Prove myself to whom? Verden's question raged in her mind, for a god to hear if he cared to. I have nothing to prove!

Prove yourself to yourself, the dream-response came,

quiet and sure. *You chose to cast off your subservience, Verden. You rejected evil.*

Evil rejected me! I only accepted that.

And craved vengeance, the dream-voice pointed out. *As you still do. Crown your vengeance with wisdom, dragon. The true punishment of evil is its failure to succeed. You made a choice and a pledge, Verden. You chose free will, and rejected evil.*

I pledged it only to myself!

Then you owe it to yourself, the voice said, seeming amused.

Verden shook herself, chafing at the torment of the uninvited voice which goaded and guided her. Impatiently she stirred her great body on the forested hillside. But even as she spread her languid, lustrous bronze wings to catch the patterns of the forest sunlight, she growled deep within her mighty chest.

I could just blast them all, she thought to herself, angrily. Those humans—those petty, soft things—I could kill them all without effort. Her huge fangs glinted at the thought, and her talons twitched. Deadly vapors trickled like foul smoke from her nostrils, and a powerful, devastating dragon spell formed itself in her mind.

But in her dreams a voice like distant thunder, silent beyond her own ears, spoke. *Your magic is of this world, Verden Leafglow, just as you yourself are of this world. The thing you must defeat is not. Prepare yourself, Verden Leafglow. Your test is at hand.*

Deep inside she knew that whatever was going to happen, whatever task the god had set her to do, it would come very soon. It had already begun. Spreading gold-brown wings, her rear talons thrusting with huge, powerful grace, the dragon launched herself once more toward the battered fortress of Tarmish.

* * * * * *

In the deepest caverns beneath Tarmish, the combined clans of Bulp were settling in. Foragers had found a seep that provided an adequate water supply, and there were miles of crevices, tunnels and vermin-infested sumps to be explored, not to mention the most productive pyrite mine any of them could recall having seen.

Nobody knew why the Aghar were so enchanted with pyrites. The sulphur-colored iron nuggets, found here and there in old limestone formations, were useless as far as any other race of people knew. The metal melted poorly, tolerated little stress and had few of the qualities of good iron. But it was yellow, it was shiny and to the gully dwarves it was a fine treasure.

While various members of the clans foraged for food, all of which went into a new batch of stew that some of the females were brewing in makeshift pots over a central fire, others continued to clamber here and there on the west wall, gouging out chunks of pyrite-laden stone to be delivered to the former Highbulp Glitch, who was happily embarked on his new career as Keeper of Shiny Rocks and Other Good Stuff.

Everybody in the place knew where Glitch was. He was where the shiny rocks were being assembled. But when Sap descended from places above, looking for him, he couldn't find him.

Even the Lady Lidda, pulled away from supervising the stew by Sap's complaints, was a bit mystified. Glitch should have been right there with the shiny rocks. That was where she had last seen him. But now there was no sign of him.

Within a few minutes, every gully dwarf in the immediate vicinity was busily searching for the ex-Highbulp, peering into every corner, crevice, crack and shadow in the area. As minutes passed, some of them wandered off, forgetting what they had been doing.

But others kept up the search at the Lady Lidda's insistence. Having her husband retire from being Highbulp was one thing. Having him simply disappear was another, and she was becoming very concerned until she noticed that the largest pile of fresh pyrite was quivering. She stepped close to it, scratching her head in puzzlement as its top shifted slightly and a few bits of stone rattled down its slopes.

Then, distinctly, she heard a snore. It was a snore she recognized, and it came from the pile of shiny rocks.

"Bron!" she called. "Get over here!"

When Bron was at her side, she pointed at the pile of stones. "Dig," she said.

"Okay," Bron said. Using his broadsword like a spade, he began to dig, flinging pyrite pebbles this way and that. He had reduced the pile by a third when the remaining top of it shivered, parted and a disheveled head poked through from beneath.

"What goin' on here?" Glitch demanded.

"Ol' Dad!" Bron pointed at the head, then squatted for a better look. "What you doin' in there, Dad?"

"Dunno," Glitch admitted. "Sleepin'. I guess."

Hearing the patriarch's voice, Sap hurried over from across the cavern. "There Highbulp," he pointed.

"That not Highbulp," the Lady Lidda corrected him. "That jus' Glitch."

"Glitch not Highbulp?"

"Used to be Highbulp." Glitch struggled free from

the piled pyrites and stood atop them. "Quit, though. Too much responsi . . . resp . . . thinkin'. Dumb job. Let somebody else do it."

"Oh." Sap thought this over, then asked, "Then who I tell Highbulp stuff to?"

"Got 'nother Highbulp now," Lidda said. "Go tell him."

"Okay," Sap said. He turned away, then turned back. "Who is Highbulp?" he asked.

Several of them scratched their heads, trying to remember, Then Bron snapped his fingers. "Ol' what's-'is-name. Uh, Clout. Clout Highbulp now."

Sap frowned, truly perplexed. "Then how I tell Highbulp 'bout Clout, if Highbulp is Clout?"

"Might write it down," Scrib offered, but the others ignored him.

"Dunno," Bron said. "That a real problem. Lotsa luck." Shouldering his broadsword, the designated Hero wandered off in the direction of the stew.

"What 'bout Clout?" Lidda asked.

"What?"

"What Sap wanna tell Highbulp?"

"Bout Clout," Sap repeated.

"What 'bout Clout?"

"Nothin' much. Jus' know where he is, case anybody want him."

"Where?"

"Upstairs. Way up high. Heard him."

"Why Highbulp not in This Place?" a passing gully dwarf wondered. "This place not This Place 'thout Highbulp here."

"This not This Place?" another said. "Then where This Place?"

"Someplace else, I guess," Sap reasoned. "Maybe upstairs, where Highbulp is?"

A dozen yards away, thunder erupted and dust rolled as a great gout of loosened stone fell from the vaulted ceiling. Among the rockfall were various screeching miners. All around the shattering blast, gully dwarves scampered for safety. Several of them ran right through the new cook fire, spilling the stew and kicking coals in all directions.

Near the grand column Scrib turned, and ducked back as shards of rock whistled past him.

Out of the roiling dust, disheveled gully dwarves emerged, Glitch among them. "'Nough minin'!" the ex-Highbulp grumbled. "No fun anymore."

"Stew all gone," a gully dwarf lady announced. "Fire, too."

"This place a mess," several chorused. "Not fit to live in right now."

"So what we do now?"

"Better find Highbulp," the Lady Lidda said. "Highbulp decides stuff like 'what now.'"

Old Gandy, the Grand Notioner, hobbled up, leaning on his mop handle staff. "Guess everybody better pack up," he sighed. "Highbulp not here, we better go where Highbulp is."

"Clout only been Highbulp since today," Scrib the Scholar complained, unhappy at having to leave his squiggles. "Jus' one day, an' already gettin' be a twit. Maybe oughtta have different Highbulp?"

Gandy shrugged philosophically. "One Highbulp jus' like 'nother. All real nuisance. Anyway, gettin' hard to keep track of who Highbulp is. Too many Highbulps lately."

"Always hard to keep track of who Highbulp is," someone observed. "Who cares, anyway?"

"Prob'ly oughtta write it down," Scrib said, thoughtfully. All around him, gully dwarves were preparing to migrate.

"Kinda bad upstairs," Sap warned. Talls havin' a war or somethin'."

"No pro'lem," Pert said, proudly. "Bron take care of us. Bron a hero."

Bron blinked, considering the enormity of it all. He didn't want to be a hero anymore. But there didn't seem to be any choice in the matter. Unhappily, he shouldered his broadsword and headed for the "stairway" to the world above.

"Yes, dear," he muttered.

The Lady Lidda looked after her son, her head tilted thoughtfully. Little Pert was showing real skill at the care and tending of numbskulls, and it occurred to Lidda that Pert might make a fine consort for a Highbulp. The only problem was, Bron wasn't Highbulp. Clout was. But Bron had all the makings of a good one. At Pert's direction, he was leading the tribe.

Gandy was right, Lidda decided. There were too many Highbulps right now.

Chapter 23
Into the Dark Tower

Lord Vulpin encountered unexpected resistance in withdrawing the Fang of Orm from the broken cabinet. He pulled the thing halfway out, then blinked and caught his balance as the thing recoiled back into the shadows with unexpected strength. Somebody inside there, someone unseen, was trying to pull the ivory talisman out of his hand.

With a muttered oath, the lord of Tarmish braced himself, firmed his grip and heaved. In an instant the Fang was his, clenched in his steel-gloved fingers. But swinging from the end of it was a babbling, struggling, ugly little person half his height, a raggedly-clothed creature that vaguely resembled a diminutive human but distinctly was not.

"Gully dwarf!" the warlord rumbled. With a vicious shake he dislodged the little creature from his prize. The gully dwarf went tumbling into a corner and Vulpin lashed out with a steel-shod foot, barely missing the creature. The gully dwarf skittered aside, shrieked and dashed back into the sanctuary of the broken cabinet.

"Vermin," Vulpin muttered, then dismissed the imbecilic little creature from his thoughts. Gully dwarves weren't worth thinking about, beyond a mental note to have exterminators scour the premises when the present task was completed. He held the Fang of Orm high, gazing at it, his eyes glowing with a triumphant light.

"Mine," he said. "The Wishmaker is mine, and the world is about to be."

"Mine!" the broken cabinet argued. "My bashin' tool!"

Ignoring the objections from the furniture, Vulpin strode to the shattered wall above the inner courts. Below, a melee of armed men swept this way and that. Tarmites and Gelnians raged and strove, howling their bloodlust. From above it was impossible to tell one force from another. They all looked the same. Here and there, on the battlefield, the fallen lay in pools of gore. But these were relatively few. Vulpin's helmed face twitched sardonically. For all their ancient hatreds, the combatants were not very capable fighters. The battle raged, but it produced more noise than blood.

There were exceptions, though. A mismatched pair of warriors, neither Gelnian nor Tarmite—one looked like an urban alley-dweller, the other a tall, rangy plainsman—were making their way through the fray, slashing and countering, scattering combatants like wind-blown leaves. Vulpin recognized the plainsman, and he heard the cry of his prisoner as the girl saw those below. "Graywing!" she called, her cry a plea.

"Graywing," Vulpin sneered. A Cobar, with that code of honor that the plainsmen cherished. The other man below he did not know, but he knew the type. Thief or assassin, the smaller man was lithe as a cat, quick and deadly. A dagger-wielder. Vulpin peered downward, where the two were headed. At the base of the tower, a pair of axe-wielding icemen held both Gelnians and Tarmites at bay. Those would be seasoned mercenaries, Vulpin realized, part of Chatara Kral's personal guard. Which meant that Chatara Kral was here, in the tower.

"Your timing is perfect, little sister," he rumbled. "Come up. Come up now and face your destruction." To his guard he snapped, "Give me the girl."

Thayla Mesinda was shoved forward roughly, and Vulpin closed steel-sheathed fingers on her arm. "You have been well-treated, girl," he said. "You have been fed, made comfortable and protected. Now—"

"You kept me prisoner!" Thayla snapped, then gasped as his iron fingers tightened cruelly on her arm.

"I have kept you safe and pure, for a purpose," Vulpin said. "Now it is time to pay your debt. I require only one thing of you. You must make a wish."

"I wish you'd let me alone!" Thayla shouted at him.

"A wish," Vulpin growled. "But it must be my wish, and no other." With a sudden movement he released her arm and his steel fingers closed around her throat. "I will tell you what to wish. You will wish exactly as I tell you. If you alter my wish, even in the slightest way, in that instant I will snap your neck. Do you understand?"

She struggled and fought, but to no avail. The man was incredibly strong. Her flailing little fists, her soft slippers and her clawing nails met only metal armor. She saw the light dimming, like a tunnel closing in around her. She could not breathe.

Dimly, beyond the armored lord, Thayla glimpsed movement. A gully dwarf darted furtively from the broken telescope cabinet and peered over the outer wall, waving.

"Hey, ever'body!" the little creature called. "Could use some help up here!"

Vulpin's fingers relaxed slightly and Thayla gasped for breath. Her throat throbbed and ached.

"Do you understand?" Vulpin demanded.

Defeated and barely conscious, the girl gulped air into her burning lungs. She nodded, trying to speak. "Yes," she whispered.

Still holding her by the neck, Vulpin raised the Fang of Orm before her eyes. "Do you know what this is?"

"No," she breathed, unable to use her voice.

"This is the Wishmaker," Vulpin said. "When I tell you, you will hold this in your hand, and you will speak a wish. You will wish exactly what I say. No more and no less."

"Yes," she whispered. "I will wish as you say."

Violent sounds erupted from the stairway. Steel rang against steel and voices clamored. Among them was a woman's voice, deep and angry.

"Chatara Kral comes," Vulpin smirked. He gestured to his cave-assassin guards. "Stop them."

As one the guards turned, drew their weapons and raced through the stairway portal.

"Now I will tell you what to wish," Vulpin told the barely-conscious girl. "Listen closely, if you want to keep breathing."

* * * * *

Graywing headed for the battered tower, his sword slashing this way and that, barely visible as it wove a bright pattern around him. Thrust and parry, cut and recover, disarm, slash and stab, the plainsman's blade was a crimson-and-steel kaleidoscope, opening a path through the throng of howling warriors surging about the lower court.

At his back, covering his every move, was the Cat—dark wrath with daggers for fang and claw.

The two barely slowed as they crossed the courtyard, right through the thick of battle, making for the base of the tower. From high above, Graywing heard the scream of a girl, and redoubled his efforts. Like a great dire wolf with a panther at its side, the pair fairly flew toward the tower's base.

They were within fifty feet of the structure's inner gate when the massed combatants parted ahead and they had a clear view of the shadowed opening. It was the same gate they had exited earlier, but now it was occupied. Two huge, glowering icemen barred the entrance. Their great axes dripped gore, and a dozen fallen Tarmites lay about them, hacked to death.

Dartimien grimaced as the plainsman at his side

roared a battle cry and charged.

"Oh, gods," the Cat hissed. "The barbarian's in love."

* * * * *

From the narrow grate leading into the courtyard, the scene outside was horrendous. There were Talls everywhere, running and dodging, striving against one another, slashing away with swords, shields, mauls, axes, clubs and scythes. Dead Talls lay among the live ones, and weapons were scattered all over.

"What Talls doin'?" Sap wondered, peering out wide-eyed.

"Fightin', looks like," Scrib suggested, looking over Sap's shoulder.

"Wonder why?"

"Who knows 'bout Talls? Prob'ly ticked off 'bout somethin'," old Gandy said. "Where Clout?"

Sap scratched his head, trying to remember. Then he snapped his fingers. "Up there," he pointed, indicating the top of the tower.

"Clout really dumb," Gandy shook his head. "Coulda picked better place than that to be."

"Don' matter," Bron reminded him. "Clout Highbulp now. Highbulp can be anywhere he wants to." He peered out at the melee beyond the grate. There were an awful lot of Talls out there, doing an awful lot of fighting. And they were between the gully dwarves and the route to the top of the spire, where the new Highbulp was. "Prob'ly could use a notion 'bout now," he suggested to Gandy.

Gandy leaned on his mop handle staff, deep in thought. "Maybe better get 'nother Highbulp," he said, finally. "That one not worth gettin' to."

But Scrib was there, crowding others aside to gape through the opening. "Fling-thing," he said, thoughtfully.

"What?"

"Fling-thing!" The doodler pointed off to one side, at the broken remains of a trebuchet near the west wall. "Talls use fling-things, throw big rocks an' stuff. Ever'body gets outta way when big rocks come."

"Maybe good notion," Bron said. "Anybody know how use fling-thing?"

"Dunno," a gully dwarf beside him said with a shrug.

With sudden resolution, he and another slipped through the grate, ducked into the shadows of stone rubble near the wall and scampered toward the trebuchet.

"Where Tunk an' Blip go?" Lidda asked.

"See 'bout fling-thing," Bron pointed. "Scrib got a notion. Can't get to Clout, then throw rocks instead."

"Okay," Lidda said. She turned to a gaggle of ladies crowded behind her. "Gonna throw rocks at Clout," she told them.

The Lady Bruze frowned. "Can't throw rocks at Clout! Clout Highbulp now!"

"Nobody tol' him so, though," little Pert reasoned. "So maybe okay throw rocks."

"Bad idea!" Bruze snapped. "Pert hush!"

"Go sit on tack, Lady Bruze," Pert suggested.

Blip and Tunk were back, then, just outside the grate. Behind them they dragged a long, slender pole of pliant willow wood. "Fling-thing broke," Tunk reported. "Devasta . . . smither . . . all busted up. Got piece of it, though."

Ignoring the combat going on just beyond, several

DRAGONLANCE Lost Histories

gully dwarves squirmed through the grate and studied the pole. The thing was nearly twenty feet long, shaped like a sapling with all its branches trimmed off. The remains of leather lashings hung from its ends.

"How this thing work?" several wondered out loud.

Gandy paced the length of the pole, studying it. "Maybe plant it," he decided. "Then bend it over for throw rocks."

"Plant it where?" Bron puzzled.

"Right there," Gandy pointed at a mound of debris. "Where rocks are."

"Okay," Bron said. With others helping, he lugged the pole to the top of the mound, and used his broadsword to force a gap between stones there. A half dozen gully dwarves raised the pole upright. It swayed this way and that.

"Other end up," Scrib said. "Plant big end, not little end."

"Okay."

They turned the pole and thrust its butt into the hole Bron had made. It fit tightly, reluctantly, but with six or seven pairs of hands working on it, it finally settled in with a satisfying thunk.

Bron picked up a large stone, it was almost as big as he was, then paused, frowning at the tall shaft. "How fasten rock for throw?"

Scrib puzzled over the problem for a moment, then turned and grasped old Gandy by an arm and a leg. Unceremoniously, he flipped the Grand Notioner upside down and peeled off his robe. "Use this," he said, holding the empty robe aloft. "Make sack. Rock sack for fling-thing."

Gandy, naked now except for a tattered rag around

his loins, got to his feet, muttering angrily.

With the robe and some bits of thong, Tunk started up the staff. It shivered and swayed, throwing him off. "Need a hand here," he said.

Having nothing better to do, seven or eight gully dwarves began climbing the upright pole. Others, momentarily losing interest, wandered about the fringes of the battlefield, picking up whatever caught their eyes—a few knives and short swords, an axe of two, a leather boot . . .

Under the weight of ascending Aghar, the willow staff swayed and began to bend. By the time most of them were halfway up, the pole was bent in a tight arc and its tip was only a few feet from the ground.

Bron grabbed the vibrating tip, clinging with one hand, while the swaying pole swung him this way and that. "High enough!" he barked. "Tie it on!"

Obediently, the gang on the pole clung where they were, and Gandy's robe was passed up to them. With thongs, they secured its sleeves to the pole, then a brigade of helpers handed up a stone. Those on the staff wrestled the stone into place and dropped it into the open top of the fluttering robe. It fell through, and out the bottom, taking one or two gully dwarves with it.

"Oops," Tunk said.

"Need more thong, tie up end of sack," Blip suggested. "Anybody got more thong?"

As one, those crowding the top of the bent pole bailed off, and those dangling from its underside let go, all of them searching for bits of thong.

The pole, released, whistled upright. Bron, still clinging to its very end, found himself flying—tumbling through the air, over the heads of the men locked in mortal combat below, and the great portal of the tower loomed to meet him.

Somewhere behind him, Scrib stared, wide-eyed. "Fling-thing work pretty good," he said.

"That not rock!" Pert shrilled. "That Bron!"

"Pretty good shot, though," several of the gully dwarves observed.

Scrib found his chalk and got busy, scrawling doodles on his slate. He wasn't sure what he was doing, but he had come to the realization that when something momentous, or at least unusual and interesting, like Bron flying through the air, occurred, squiggles should be drawn to commemorate it.

Making up squiggles as he went along, Scrib wrote it down.

Gandy leaned on his mop handle staff, gazing upward sadly. The breeze was cold on his naked old hide. High above him, his robe whipped and fluttered like a dirty blue flag, and the Grand Notioner didn't have the slightest notion how to get it back.

Encouraged by their success, Tunk and Blip rounded up several of their reluctant peers and began climbing the fling-pole again. This time when they reached Gandy's robe, about the time it neared the ground, they tied off the bottom of it with cord and filled it with fifty pounds of gravel. Then they all piled off and the pole snapped upright. The load of rock took the momentum and continued it, arcing toward the base of the tower, where fierce fighting was going on.

The problem was that the load of gravel, once confined to Gandy's robe, stayed there. When it took flight, propelled by the released pole, it took both robe and pole with it.

"Nice shot," Scrib said, adding more doodles to his slate. "Can't do it again, though."

"Quit foolin' 'round!" the Lady Bruze demanded. "Le's go find Clout!"

"Clout a twit," several around her pointed out.

"Highbulp, though," the Lady Lidda said. "Okay, ever'body go upstairs."

"Can't get in there." Tunk pointed at the wide portal in the tower's base. The opening was filled with humans in combat.

"Then climb wall," Lidda said. "Ever'body come on!"

* * * * *

When Graywing and Dartimien reached the tower they were fighting for their lives. Both Gelnians and Tarmites—interrupted in their attempts to slaughter each other—had turned on the intruders. Now like a pack of raging beasts, the combatants surrounded and harassed the "outsiders."

Graywing parried a thrusting pike, kicked aside a Gelnian warrior and disarmed a Tarmite right behind him. Beside him Dartimien was a frenzied flurry of lithe motion, stabbing here, slashing there, now and then releasing a dagger to do its deadly work.

"These people are getting mean," the plainsman panted, whirling to drive back several attackers.

"It's what we get for butting in," the Cat snarled. "This is their private war, and I don't think we're welcome."

"Make for the tower gate," Graywing ordered, indicating the portal which was now behind him. "We'll take cover in there."

Dartimien sneered. "We'll have to get in, first. Look."

Pivoting, Graywing glanced at their destination, now only a few feet away. In the doorway were icemen—huge, glowering brutes brandishing axes the size of singletrees. "Gods," he muttered.

But they were committed now. There was no turning back. Clearing a space around them, their blades driving the attackers back, the Cobar and the Cat found themselves face to face with Chatara Kral's best mercenaries.

"You!" one of the giants rumbled, recognizing Dartimien. "I owe you this, little man." He grinned, raised his axe . . . and froze as a thrown dagger blossomed in his throat.

"Only three knives left," Dartimien muttered, as the iceman pitched forward, blood spurting from beneath his beard. "I'd better start recovering them."

"Count your toys later," Graywing growled. His blade rang against another descending axe, barely deflecting it. The shock of impact numbed his arm, and the iceman towering over him growled and struck again. Graywing dodged aside, evading the great blade by inches. He tried to thrust with his sword, but the giant parried it easily with a huge, banded arm.

The axe rose again, and suddenly the iceman stumbled back. His face was covered with disheveled gully dwarf, clinging to his head.

"Oops," Bron said. "Sorry 'bout that."

Seeing his opportunity. Graywing ran his sword through the iceman's brisket, then leaped over him as he fell. "Get in here!" he yelled at Dartimien.

"Okay," the unexpected gully dwarf said.

Beyond the shadowed opening were stone steps, leading upward. Graywing sprinted for them, with Dartimien right behind. For a moment it seemed they were alone in the dark base of the tower. The Tarmites and Gelnians outside had noticed one another again.

Graywing sped upward, taking the steps three at a time, then stopped so suddenly that Dartimien collided with him from behind. They dodged aside, clinging to the wall, as the limp body of still another iceman tumbled past. A broken spear shaft protruded from the big primitive's back. Even in the dim light they could see the black markings on its shaft.

"Cave vandals," the Cat hissed. "Vulpin's pet assassins."

Above were the whispers of soft boots on stone, and descending shadows. Dark cloaks swirled and the shadows were men—tall, silent, dark men with painted faces and painted weapons, descending from somewhere above.

As they saw the assassins, the assassins saw them. The one in the lead didn't so much as hesitate. Bright steel glinted in shadow and flashed downward, a thrown dart with triad points. The device clanged off the wall where Dartimien had been an instant before, and the lead assassin pulled another from his belt. But before he could throw it, Graywing reached him, a howling fury of lethal Cobar with his razor-edged sword singing its song of death. The lead assassin never knew what hit him.

A second dark cloak shrilled and pitched from the stairs into darkness below, clutching at the hilt of Dartimien's thrown dagger which stood in his breast.

Then a third assassin screamed, staggered and seemed to shrink abruptly. Graywing blinked in surprise. Neither he nor the foe had noticed the little gully dwarf with the big broadsword, until its blade slashed across the caveman's knees. It was the same gully dwarf who had sailed out of nowhere moments before, right into the face of an iceman.

"Wow," Bron said. "Pretty good bash. Real hero stuff."

"Where did you come from?" Dartimien hissed.

Bron looked puzzled. "Dunno," he confided. "Guess I was jus' born. Ol' Glitch my dad, so Lady Lidda prob'ly my mom."

"I don't want your lineage!" Dartimien snapped. "How did you get to this tower?"

"Oh, that," Bron said. "Fling-thing flang . . . flu . . . toss me over here."

Below them, a faded blue robe full of gravel crashed through the doorway, rattling and scraping as it dragged a long, flexible pole across the stone paving.

"That fling-thing," Bron pointed. "Guess ever'-body through with it."

Another cave assassin appeared on the stairs above, and from beyond came the abrupt sounds of fierce combat. Dartimien recognized the rumbling oaths of at least two more icemen and the soft, shuffling footsteps of cave assassins. The last, best forces of Lord Vulpin and Chatara Kral had met, somewhere above.

"Thayla's up there," Graywing growled. With a bound, the plainsman dodged the falling, tumbling corpse of a beheaded caveman and charged up the stairway.

"You're crazy!" Dartimien shouted after him, but Graywing was already gone. "Gods," the Cat muttered. Relieving a dead cave assassin of a pair of serviceable daggers, he sprinted upward, grumbling.

Chapter 24
Wishmaker, Wishtaker

Chatara Kral, rumored daughter of the mightiest of Dragon Highlords, was a formidable warrior in her own right. Though striking of face and form, the daughter of Verminaard despised and shunned the gentle teachings offered in her childhood by tutors and tenders. She hated them, just as she hated her arrogant brother Vulpin. Since childhood she had trained in the deadly arts, preparing for just this time—when she would face her despised brother and claim the legacy that should be hers alone, a legacy promised by her father when he pledged the dark ways in exchange for power.

From the day in Chatara Kral's childhood when her father had dedicated his service to Takhisis, goddess of evil, Chatara Kral had known her destiny. She would rule! By any means necessary, she would have everything and anything she wanted, when she wanted it. All around her would be her subjects, and none would dispute her dominance and continue to live.

Pure, unencumbered power would be her inheritance. Her father had bargained with a goddess for such rewards, but something had gone amiss. Takhisis had abandoned her quest and her followers.

But still Chatara Kral blazed with ambition. If she could not inherit absolute power, she would take it for herself. She would have the world, or as much of it as she cared to take, and all its riches. And she did not intend to share.

Chatara Kral had always known that one day her brother Vulpin would be an obstacle. His dreams were like hers, but in the world they both envisioned there could be only one absolute ruler.

Thus Vulpin—now the Lord Vulpin of Tarmish as she was now regent of Gelnia—must be eliminated. With him out of the way, Chatara Kral would be invincible. The Vale of Sunder would be her base. From here, her armies of conquest would march.

Such was her legacy from that shadowy, cruel figure who had sired her. And she knew beyond doubt—none other than Dred the Necromancer, communer with the dead, had told her—that nothing in this world could stop her from claiming it.

She was invincible, and she was without scruple. Thus when she and the last of her elite guard—brutish, stoic icemen from the frozen south—found themselves trapped in the Tower of Tarmish, Chatara Kral did not hesitate. Behind her and ahead of her were cave assassins, the favored instruments of Lord Vulpin. When these met her phalanx of axe-wielders, Chatara Kral committed her icemen to a battle to the death.

She would lose most of them, she knew. She might even lose all of them. It made no difference. She could always entice more followers. Casually she betrayed them, and the chaos that ensued in the murky tower gave her what she wanted. As her faithful savages bled and died for her on the winding stairs, demolishing Vulpin's assassins even as they fell, Chatara Kral slipped past and headed for the top.

From the shattered portal opening onto Lord Vulpin's aerie, she saw her goal—Vulpin himself, holding an ivory stick in one hand and a cringing, frightened girl in the other.

The Wishmaker! So Vulpin really had it, and had found someone to activate it!

With a snarl like a serpent's hiss, Chatara Kral started toward her brother. Two cave assassins came from shadows to confront her, guarding their lord, and she knew that they were the last. Chatara Kral's gleaming sword glinted in the light. The primitive cave vandals were among the most feared fighters in Ansalon, but for Chatara Kral they would be the work of a moment. Then Vulpin would be alone.

Vulpin saw his sister emerge from the portal, and was not surprised. He had known she would come. But now his haste became frenzied. The girl, Thayla Mesinda, was so terrified that she could hardly speak. Yet the words she must voice, the spoken wish that worked the magic of the Wishmaker, must be exact.

"Listen to me, girl," Vulpin snapped, impatiently. "You must memorize this! The talisman is a spell-maker. Your wish will shape the spell. You will wish three things! Do you understand?"

"Three . . . three things," Thayla whispered.

"Three things. The first is that Chatara Kral must die."

"Chata . . . Chatara . . ."

"Chatara Kral!" Vulpin spat the name.

"Chatara Kral," Thayla repeated it. "I will wish for Chatara Kral to die."

Vulpin's last two assassins were blocking Chatara Kral's path, their weapons threatening. Somewhere near, Vulpin could hear a scraping sound, like that of metal on stone. He glanced around. The irritated little gully dwarf was out of its cabinet. Stooping and panting, it labored, dragging a wide, iron bowl behind it.

"You will wish that I, Lord Vulpin, never be driven from this place," Vulpin ordered the girl.

"I will . . . will wish that Lord Vulpin never leave this place," Thayla managed.

"And you will wish that I, Lord Vulpin, shall prevail!"

"I will wish that Lord Vulpin pre-pre—"

"Prevail!" Vulpin hissed.

"Prevail," Thayla whispered, struggling with the word. The big man's fingers on her throat were an agony, but she was helpless to escape.

"Those are your wishes," Vulpin said.

Across the stone floor a cave assassin screamed and doubled over, impaled on Chatara Kral's flashing blade. The remaining assassin dodged aside and attacked. Vulpin raised the Fang of Orm and a tentative voice behind him announced, "Got lotta stew here. Anybody want some?"

"Get out of here!" Vulpin shouted, glancing around. With both hands occupied, he aimed a kick at the annoying gully dwarf. Clout dodged aside, and the man's booted foot collided with the legendary Great Stew Bowl, throwing sprays and dollops of noisome concoction in all directions.

In Vulpin's cruel grasp, Thayla squirmed and kicked. "Clout, get away!" she urged. Then the fingers tightened again and she hung silent, half-conscious and struggling for breath.

"The wish!" Vulpin ordered. "Remember the wish!"

"I . . . remember," she gasped.

He loosed his hold slightly, set her on her feet and thrust the Fang of Orm into her hands, his angry eyes watching the last assassin fall. Chatara Kral stepped over the body and smiled a cruel, victorious smile. Raising her sword again, she stepped toward Vulpin.

"Wish, girl!" Vulpin hissed. "Wish, now!"

Thayla grasped the Fang of Orm. "I wish . . . " she said, and the daylight seemed to darken around them. Great, dark clouds sprang into being overhead, swirling and coiling like a massive storm aloft. "I wish that Chatara Kral die," Thayla gasped. "I wish that the Lord Vulpin never leave this place."

"Good," Vulpin whispered. "Very good. Go on."

Overhead, the dark clouds rolled, forming themselves into a wide ring with darkness at its center—a darkness that was beyond darkness.

"I wish," Thayla said, gasping, "that the Lord Vulpin pre-pre . . ."

"Means wind up on top," a helpful little voice nearby said.

"That Lord Vulpin wind up on top," Thayla said, obediently.

On the near horizon a dark shadow streaked toward the tower. The shadow grew, revealing wide, graceful wings, a long, sweeping tail and extended talons. "Now," a voice like distant thunder rumbled. It was the dragon's own voice, speaking to itself. "Now is the time, Verden Leafglow!"

For a long moment, the humans atop the tower stood frozen, gawking at what was happening in the sky above. Out of the blackness within the ring of clouds, a gigantic head appeared, the sloping, glaring head of a great serpent. A mouth the size of a maize field opened wide, and black vapors drifted about the gleaming, curved luster of a single fang.

"Run like crazy!" Clout gurgled. In panic he upended the legendary Great Stew Bowl and ducked as it fell upside down. It clanged to the stones, with Clout hidden beneath it. Its surface was no longer dull, aged iron. It blazed now, like mirrors in sunlight, and the radiant, complex visage on its surface seemed to hang above it.

"No!" Chatara Kral screamed her anger. "This is a work of magic! But you will not see its end, Vulpin!" She launched herself at her brother, her blade singing.

Vulpin broke out of his trance at the last instant. Thrusting Thayla Mesinda aside, he blocked his sister's lethal cut with a steel gauntlet. Her momentum carried them both back a step, as they grappled and fell. They struggled on the stone floor, Vulpin delivering mighty blows with a steel-clad fist, Chatara Kral kicking and biting, pushing aside his visor as nails like tiger claws sought his eyes.

Thayla Mesinda slumped nearby, half-conscious, her hand still holding the Fang of Orm. Then there were strong arms around her. She was swept up in big, gentle hands and a voice said: "Drop that thing! It's evil!"

As the Fang of Orm slipped from her fingers she looked up into concerned, sky-blue eyes. "Gray-wing," she breathed. She blinked and her eyes went wide with new terror. Beyond his begrimed, bearded face, an enormous serpent descended from the swirling sky. Mouth wide, single fang dripping evil vapors, Orm struck.

The great head descended with incredible speed, and just beyond it a dragon wheeled downward, wings folded, plummeting like a falcon in stoop.

As the viper's head reached the tower, Verden Leafglow hit the thing from behind, driving it downward. Her tons of falling fury added to the serpent's momentum, driving the great muzzle with its extended fang as a hammer drives a nail.

Neither Lord Vulpin nor Chatara Kral ever saw the giant fang that impaled them both. Needle-sharp ivory drove through Vulpin's mass, downward through the armored breast of the woman struggling beneath him, through paving tiles and floor structure, to imbed itself solidly in the white stone beneath—the cap of that mighty pedestal on which the entire fortress rested.

Verden Leafglow was shaken by the impact of her strike. Hitting the great viper's skull had been like hitting a mountain. But she shook herself, flapped mighty wings, circled aloft and stooped to strike again, driving the giant head downward, the great fang deeper into its stone prison.

With a hiss that shook the landscape, Orm lunged and struggled, trying to free himself. This could not be happening again! But his fang would not budge.

He roared and tugged, rearing upward, shaking from side to side, and suddenly he was loose. Free! Yet even as he realized that, he saw the gory stump of his last fang still standing above the tumbled bodies of his prey.

His shrill of anguish made hillsides dance in the distance. He raised his serpent's head and saw a dragon before him, a tan-brown, metallic-hued dragon veering this way and that in the air, taunting him. "Go away, worm," the dragon said. "You do not belong in this world . . . or in any other."

With a final hiss, Orm withdrew. Toothless and defeated, the great viper recoiled, diminishing into the clouds from which he had come. When he was gone, the ring of storm clouds collapsed upon itself, following him into that nothingness between universes. It was a nothingness infinitely large and infinitely small, a mere suggestion of distance but now so far away that Orm could never again return.

Clout peeked out from beneath his shield, peering around with puzzled little eyes. "Wow," he said. "Musta been some kinda storm." Then he saw faces he recognized. All along the broken wall, gully dwarves appeared, clambering over the sundered rails to look around in confusion. "Hey ever'body!" Clout greeted them. "What ever'body doin' here?"

"Lookin' for Highbulp," Gandy said, searching the area for scraps of cloth to wrap around himself. "Don't see him," Clout said.

"I do," Scrib pointed. "You him. Clout th' new Highbulp. Congrat . . . alla best . . . hey, there, Highbulp."

"No way!" Clout yelped. He clambered out from under the Great Stew Bowl. "Not me! I don't be Highbulp. Get somebody else!"

The Lady Bruze was beside him, then. She inspected him for breakage, decided he was unharmed, and grabbed him by the ear. "Clout is Highbulp!" she ordered. "Behave self!"

Clout let it sink in, then shook his head violently, dislodging his wife's grasp on his ear. "No way, dear," he said. "Won't do it. Clout not dumb 'nough for be Highbulp. Get somebody else!"

"Who else?" Scrib asked, looking around.

At that moment Bron appeared at the stairway portal, loaded down with loot. He had swords, daggers, helmets, water jugs, several sandals, a broken spear and a large, scuffed boot. He had been foraging in the stairwell.

"Get him!" Clout pointed. "Make Bron be Highbulp. He'll do!"

Scrib peered at the happy Bron, trying to remember whether this ground had been covered before. "How 'bout it, Bron?" he asked. "You be Highbulp?"

"No!"

"He will," Pert interrupted. "Might as well. Nothin' better to do."

"Don' wanna be Highb—" Bron tried to protest.

"Shut up, you twit," Pert suggested. "Jus' shut up an' be Highbulp!"

"Yes, dear," Bron muttered.

"Think I oughtta write this down," Scrib mused.

Clinging to Graywing's hand, Thayla Mesinda crept forward and looked down at the sprawled, tangled remains of the two who would have ruled the world. They lay together in death, impaled on a great, gory fang.

"Chatara Kral is dead," the girl whispered.

"Sure is," Graywing nodded in agreement. "Vulpin, too."

"He never left this place," she said. "And he pre . . . he came out on top."

Graywing gazed around, listening. Then he recognized the sound that was bothering him. It was silence. The fierce fighting in the courtyards below had gone still. Still holding Thayla's hand, he stepped to the rampart and looked down. Below, clusters of exhausted Gelnians and Tarmites stood here and there, their weapons lowered. And among them walked Dartimien the Cat, gesturing and waving, turning this way and that to hold the attention of all of them.

The city man's voice did not carry to the top of the tower, but Graywing recognized the posture and the gestures.

"Cats always land on their feet," the plainsman told himself. "It looks like the Vale of Sunder is about to have itself a new leader."

Epilogue

Sheer exhaustion and clever words ended the civil war in the Vale of Sunder—the exhaustion of those who had spent their last energies in combat, and the quick, persuasive tongue of Dartimien the Cat.

The wandering mercenaries who had been the backbone of both armies were gone, and most would not return. Mercenaries fight for gain, and there was nothing to be gained where the makers of conflict were dead. Those few who might have returned on the chance of looting, changed their minds when they glimpsed a flying dragon in the distant sky above Tarmish. The dragon danced among storm clouds, plummeting again and again to strike at the wrecked tower.

Whatever was happening back there, no sane mercenary wanted any part of it.

For a time after all was quiet, Verden Leafglow patrolled the Vale of Sunder on mighty wings, fascinated by what she had encountered there. She might even have wished for further communion with the god Reorx, who had spoken to her so casually when he chose. But, godlike, Reorx had finished with her. She had served a purpose and was no longer needed. So she heard no more from the deity. It was the way of gods.

One thing she did retain, though, and with time she would come to regard it as a high prize. She was free. For the first time in her life, in two separate lifetimes, Verden Leafglow was bound by no pledge, encumbered by no obligation. Her life was her own, to live as she would, and neither a god nor any creature had claim upon her anymore.

Scarcely a hint of green remained in the coloration of her body now. Her great wings had warmed and darkened in hue to a flowing gold-brown color, deepening almost to maroon along the trailing vanes and rich umber in the folds between flexors. Her back and tail, scales and crests, were an iridescent kaleidoscope of colors—shifting light—bright rainbow hues flirting among somber browns and pale tans, laced with metallic glints of copper and gold. Her underbelly was a rich, warm brown and her eyes, once emerald, now shone like mountain crests bathed in summer sun.

Free! No longer bound by oath, pledge or even color to any enforced ethic, Verden Leafglow was free to be what she chose to be, to do as she chose to do, and she wondered if this, in itself, might be a parting gift from Reorx.

She soared above the mean, scarred bastions of Tarmish and contemplated with casual interest the doings of the small creatures below. Humans and not-quite-humans alike, they were creatures of kinds other than her kind. Yet for an age, it seemed, her life, her *lives*, had been bound to them.

She had detested them. She had despised them. Yet now she felt no real malice toward them. They were as trapped within their small existences as she had been within hers. Just as she had been bound to gods, they—the little creatures below—had bound themselves by choice or chance to leaders and causes, and they had inherited the grief that came of bondage.

Most of them would do it again. They knew no other way.

Yet they were sentient creatures, and could change. Maybe one day she would see whether any of them had. The humans, some of them, might. But those others down there, burrowing beneath the bastions and scurrying among the shadows, Verden doubted that they ever would. A gully dwarf would always be a gully dwarf.

Forever Aghar, she thought, and there was a touch of wry amusement in the notion. The lowest of the low, most despised of all the demi-human races of Krynn, the gully dwarves had only two things in their favor—inadvertence and a stubborn resistance to change that bordered on being an elemental force.

Twits, she thought. Somewhere deep within her she made a sacred promise to herself. As long as she lived, she would never again associate with gully dwarves.

Nobody, not even a mighty dragon, the greatest of all creatures, could be a match for such absolute simplicity.

* * * * *

Sheer exhaustion had ended the bloodletting between the people of Gelnia and those of Tarmish. Confusion and a sudden shortage of leadership kept it from flaring up again. With both Lord Vulpin and Chatara Kral dead, their followers were at a loss as to what to do next.

It was exactly the kind of situation Dartimien the Cat was born for, and he wasted no time in establishing himself. While sweat still stood on the brows of the warriors and their blades still dripped fresh blood, he went among them, pointing out the error of their ways.

"Men of Tarmish!" he exhorted, "Look about you at the fallen! Your own kinsmen lie at your feet, along with the kin of Gelnian men, and the blood that mingles there on the stones is all the same color. Your comrades and your enemies have joined forces in death. Friend and foe alike, they are gone from you forever. Now who will share a draught with you on a cold evening? And who will fill your granaries? Who will roast your meat, and bake your bread, and who will tend the fields from which these things arise?

"Men of Gelnia!" he continued, "see your comrades where they lie, and see who shares with them this final cold bed! Look about you at what remains of great Tarmish! Only ruin and wreckage. Among your dead lie Tarmite dead. Now who will pay the price of your harvests? Who will craft the plows for your fields and the shoes for you children's feet? Whose walls will give you refuge when there are invaders?"

So skilled was Dartimien's persuasion that most of them—Gelnian and Tarmite alike—listened to his words and slowly, hesitantly, put away their weapons.

*　*　*　*　*

But not all. Gratt Bolen, a huge Tarmish street-bull with bulging shoulders and hardly any forehead, took exception to the outsider's interference, as did Melis Shalee of Gelnia. No amount of persuasion would bend such as these, so Dartimien relied on other skills.

Both the challengers eventually recovered, Melis Shalee from a broken shoulder and Gratt Bolen from multiple dagger wounds. Both became captains in the First Sunderian Legion, but that was later.

At Dartimien's direction, the Tarmites resurrected their doddering old Grand Megak from the dungeons of Tarmish castle, and the Gelnians brought from his hiding place the infant Prince Quarls. These two were displayed with great honor before the gates of Tarmish, and co-rulership of the Vale of Sunder was bestowed upon them, with Dartimien as crown regent.

The Gelnians went back to their fields and villages, and the Tarmites to the rebuilding of their city. Then the plainsman Graywing asked Dartimien, "How long do you honestly expect such harmony to last in this place?"

"Maybe a few months," the Cat grinned. "But in that time we should see some real progress."

Dartimien himself—exercising his new, self-proclaimed authorities—performed the wedding ceremony of Graywing and Thayla Mesinda, and only those at the altar heard his muttered comment when the bonding was complete. "What a waste," he said, "that such a beauty should settle for an unredeemed barbarian when she might have had me."

* * * * *

Through it all the Combined Clans of Bulp, unperturbed and oblivious, went about their day-to-day business in the catacombs beneath Tarmish.

Glitch the Most, once Highbulp and now Grand Chief of Mines and Stuff Like That, had become disenchanted with the search for pyrite. Four times now he had found himself buried under mountains of the shiny nuggets, simply because he happened to fall asleep at the collecting point during times of peak discovery. The experience was beginning to wear on him. So Glitch was receptive when Scrib the Doodler proposed a new project.

"Signs on shiny rock not much fun anymore," Scrib complained. "Those all other folks' squiggles, say other folks' stuff. We oughtta make squiggles of our own."

"What for?" Glitch grumped.

"For say stuff 'bout us," Scrib suggested. "Talls an' swatters allus make squiggles, for pres . . . commem . . . keep track of glorious stuff they did. Aghar oughtta do that, too."

"Why?" Glitch wondered aloud.

"For keep track," Scrib said, struggling with the concept. "Make squiggles so someday ever'body know what stuff we did. We do some pretty great stuff. Oughtta write it down."

"What kin' great stuff?" Glitch peered at him.

"What did we do . . . did?"

Nearby the Lady Lidda was stirring stew and listening. "Not much," she muttered,

"Great stuff," Scrib said. "Like time when Highbulp had own personal dragon."

"Bron's dragon?" Glitch frowned. "So what? Bron tell dragon scat, dragon scat. Big deal. Glitch had dragon once. Big green dragon. Glitch's dragon. Maybe even two dragons. Who knows? Slew red dragon once, too. Glitch did that. Single-handy."

"Hmph!" Lidda said.

"If make squiggles to chronic . . . record . . . keep track, then everybody know 'bout all that, even after tomorrow," Scrib pursued.

"Ever'body know all 'bout glorious Glitch th' Mos'?"

"Legendary great Highbulp," Scrib assured him. "Big cheese. Main pain. Highbulp of all Highbulps."

"Real twit, too," the Lady Lidda muttered, glancing fondly at her husband.

"'Bout time great Glitch got some recog . . . recog . . . what's word?"

"'Preciat . . . notori . . . respect," Glitch agreed. "That it, respect! Glitch prob'ly bes' Highbulp ever was!"

"Right," Scrib said. "So le's do squiggles."

"Right," Glitch said, nodding enthusiastically. "Le's do squiggles! Uh, where we do squiggles?"

"Dunno," Scrib answered. Make a monume . . . edif . . . squiggle place, I guess."

"Right!" Glitch got to his feet and cupped his hands. "All miners!" he shouted. "Front an' center!"

Instant pandemonium erupted in the area. Gully dwarves of the mining persuasion converged from all corners, all trying to be in the same place at the same time. The resulting collision sent gully dwarves tumbling in all directions.

"No more shiny rocks!" Glitch told them. "Got 'nough shiny rocks. Now gonna build a squig . . . edif . . . monument to glory of Glitch!"

"Why?" several wondered. But Glitch ignored them. Within moments he had several dozen puzzled gully dwarves organized into precise ranks of three to five and marching purposefully toward the tunnel which led to the world outside. Scrib followed along happily, doodling notes and plans on his piece of slate, and even old Gandy went tottering after them, clad in a cast-off grain sack and leaning on his mop handle staff.

At the fireside, Lidda looked after them, shrugged and returned to her concoction of stew. She stirred it contentedly, pausing now and then to swat some ingredient that still moved of its own volition.

The Highbulp Bron and his consort, the Lady Pert, wandered up from someplace, staring after the squadron of reassigned miners. "What goin' on?" Bron asked.

"Gonna squiggle Glitch," Lidda said.

"Okay. Uh, why?"

"Glitch been glorious Highbulp," Scrib explained. "Oughtta write down stuff like that."

"How 'bout squiggle Bron?" Pert suggested. "Bron kinda glorious, too, for a twit."

"Sure," old Gandy added. "Been lotsa Highbulps. More'n two. Oughtta squiggle all of 'em."

"Okay," Scrib said. The more the squigglier, he supposed. Maybe Gandy or somebody would remember about other, past Highbulps and their glorious careers. If not, they could just make it up as they went along.

* * * * *

It took the better part of four days for the miners of Bulp to build a grand monument on the parade grounds outside the main gates of Castle Tarmish, and more than a week for Scrib to carve upon its surface the epic history of the Aghar of Clan Bulp.

He chronicled every great event anybody could think of, and every legend and tale from the history of his race. In painstaking hieroglyphic he recounted the legend of the mine that flowed wine, told of the time when his people had been adopted by an ogre, elaborated upon the resurrection of the world's greatest fling-thing in ancient times, chronicled the tale of the great dragon who had led his race to the Promised Place, and of the dragon that had hatched from the Highbulp's throne. Every nugget of fact and legend of the Aghar race—from the imprisonment of notables by Tall slavers to the finding of the legendary Great Stew Bowl, Scrib documented with loving care.

And when he was done he stood back, staring in awe at the monumental thing he had done. Here, captured in chiseled squiggles, was the entire epic story of a great people—the definitive history of the Aghar of Krynn, immortalized for all time. Somehow, Scrib felt that a great destiny had been fulfilled and he had been its instrument. He was awed and humbled at the enormity of his accomplishment.

"Aghar forever now," he breathed. "Forever Aghar."

* * * * *

That was on a Tuesday afternoon, by Tall reckoning. The following morning, a Wednesday, Captain

Gratt Bolen led a work party out of Tarmish to secure and repair the peripheries of the stronghold. The first thing he noticed was a weird, grotesque little monolith standing in the parade ground. It looked as though someone had collected every shard and fragment of broken stone in the area into a tall, ungainly pile, then plastered over the whole thing with mud. And every inch of the dried mud was covered with scratches, gouges and chisel marks.

Gratt Bolen walked entirely around the thing, shaking his head and growling. Even to his coarse sensibilities, the odd, ugly little monument was an eyesore.

"Get some men to clean up this mess," he ordered. "This is a parade ground, not a garbage dump."

Thus was the grand history of the combined clans of Bulp lost forever. But by that time the Aghar of Bulp were some distance away, moving generally westward. They didn't know where they were going, nor did it matter. They were simply moving.

The new Highbulp, Bron the First, had decided it was time to vacate the premises when a horde of Talls armed with scoops, pails and brooms invaded the catacombs.

Cringing in the shadows, the gully dwarves watched for a time as the Talls went to work, tidying up the entire area for human use.

"This place not fit to live in anymore," Bron decided. "This place all infested with Talls. This place not This Place anymore. Time to move."

The Lady Pert nodded in agreement and gazed at her husband with approving eyes. Bron was sounding and acting more like a true Highbulp every day. He even walked with an arrogant swagger sometimes, when he thought about it. Given time, the consort decided happily, her husband could turn into a real twit.

Bron had no idea where the new This Place would be, but he felt he would recognize it when he saw it. After all, there had always been a This Place. Therefore, there always would be a This Place.

This Place was wherever the Highbulp said This Place was. And wherever This Place was, there the gully dwarves would be—bumptious and innocent, grotesque and oddly appealing, operating on simple inertia and inadvertence, as changeless as any elemental force could be on the world of Krynn.

If you enjoyed reading *The Gully Dwarves*, be sure to read these other books in the DRAGONLANCE® Lost Histories Series.

In *Land of the Minotaurs*, exiled champion Kaz must discover the terrible secret of the empire before he and his entire race suffer disastrous consequences. The minotaurs envision themselves as the future masters of the world, but their own arrogance may prove to be their downfall.

(ISBN 0-7869-0472-0)

The Kagonesti tells the story of the wild elves of Krynn who call the woodlands their home. As centuries pass and Dragonwars rage, the tribe of Kaganos has to battle encroaching humans and the minions of the Dark Queen who are aided by a potent legacy guided by revered pathfinders. Soon they are faced with the deadliest challenge of all—one that marks a choice between annihilation and survival.

(ISBN 0-7869-0091-1)

Originally beautiful, proud and intelligent, ogres were cursed by their own mistakes and transformed into one of Krynn's most ugly, despised, and villainous species. *The Irda* recounts the history of a small group of ogres that took a different path, learning to accept goodness and fight for freedom. They escaped their race's fate to build a utopian civilization of their own on an island paradise in the Dragon Isles.

(ISBN 0-7869-0138-1)

No soul has encountered the fabled Dargonesti or visited the city of pearl marble that rises from the sea floor—and lived to tell about it. But in *The Dargonesti* an elven princess of Qualinost attempts to do just

that. She and her companions meet the race of sea
elves, experience a fantastical underwater world,
face a foe counted among the legends of Krynn, and
accept an impossible mission that will bring them
back to the land they call home. (ISBN 0-7869-0182-9)